I0767908

The Things I Do For Her

Tara Ryan

Copyright © 2022 by Tara Ryan

All rights reserved.

No portion of this book may be reproduced in any form without written permission from the publisher or author, except as permitted by U.S. copyright law.

For Amy, who may have left my life but never left my heart.

Chapter One

"Junie, stop primping. You look great." Ally propels me out of the bathroom toward the front door.

The mirror in the entryway reveals a spot of brown on the back of my shirt. Exactly how does one manage to get chocolate on the *back* of her shirt? At least I hope it's chocolate. "Hold on a sec, Ally. I've got to change."

Ally follows me into the bedroom and collapses on the bed in a heap of sighs. "A sec? You've been trying on outfits for hours." This from the girl who set the record for trying on the most prom dresses junior year. I think we went to every special occasion shop in the state. "We're gonna miss everything!"

Of course, my best friend is excited about attending our ten-year reunion. She was extremely popular and looks exactly the same as she did in high school. If we hadn't been friends since the first grade, I doubt she would have paid a lick of attention to me back then. I was the head-down, suck-up-to-the-teacher type who blended into the crowd. Come to think of it, not much has changed since high school.

As I try on my umpteenth outfit, Ally becomes more discontented. "We should have left hours ago. If I miss seeing how fat Stephanie Lewis got, you're gonna pay."

"Why don't you just go without me?" I slide a crinkly rayon shirt over my head. Hopefully it will disguise my decidedly lumpy middle.

"*You* are not fat." It's freaky how she can read my mind. "And you know I can't go without you."

"Well, are you planning on whining the entire two hours we're in the car?" The drive back to our hometown will be bad enough without her huffing and puffing in the seat beside me.

"I will if we don't leave right now." She precedes me out of the bedroom, her tiny hips swaying to a beat I can't hear. I mope behind her, dreading the event that will highlight the ten pounds I have gained, or the fact that I am still completely unfashionable, or that I'm stuck so deep in a rut I need a ladder to climb out. Most likely, the reunion will be buzzing with fond memories of the well-loved Ally—and as usual, I'll be her plain friend just tagging along.

The hotel ballroom was probably considered elegant when we were actually in high school. Now, the carpet is threadbare, the chandeliers are sorely out of style and the brocade on the chairs has seen a thousand asses too many. To make matters worse, the reunion committee has splashed our school colors all around the room. Somehow green and gold don't scream "sophisticated."

Tammie Marsh is reigning over the entrance table, exclaiming like a cheerleader on PCP. She looks basically the same, except now her hair color can be found on aisle three at Walgreens.

I approach the table as a small crowd retreats from it. Tammie looks up, clipboard in hand, smile plastered on her face. "Welcome! And you are?"

Shocking that she doesn't remember me. "June Hinderson."

Tammie sucks in a deep breath and her face folds in on itself. "Oh my goodness. You're Ally's friend."

Yup, this is how I'm known to the class of 2012. Ally's friend.

Somber now, Tammie hands me a nametag and I slap it on my chest. This is going to be a blast. Might as well get it over with.

I wander through the crowd of twenty-somethings, most already bleary from the open bar. Maybe a drink will take the edge off, make the party more fun. I can always crash at Mom's house. Scratch that. A night with my mother would not be a step up from a night with 378 of my furthest friends.

Instead, I head for the tables on the left side of the room where many of the faculty members have gathered. These are the people I miss.

Before I can reach the safety of my former teachers, I am accosted by the Kilmore twins. "Marcy, Marta, how are you?"

Ally leans toward me and mutters, "Oh great, the 'Dork-le-mint Twins.'"

I shoot her a look meant to shut her up, but Ally has never been very good at censoring herself. Turning back to the two women with cherry-red hair, I notice a look of confusion flit across their faces. Nothing I'm not used to.

Marta recovers first. "June, it's so good to see you. Remember when we had that great sleepover and watched all nine Friday the 13th movies?"

Ally laughs out loud. "Oh my god, Junie. Did you actually go to that party? That is so lame."

Marcy grabs her sister by the arm. "Marta. You're embarrassing me." Turning back to me, Marcy replaces her look of wrath with a smile. "June, I remember that you wanted to open that dog business. Is that what you're doing now?"

Does taking my terrier mix for a walk eight times a day count? "Not exactly. Right now, I'm working at Kink—" Ally knocks against my hip so hard I nearly fall over.

"What harm is there in telling them that you opened your daycare? High school reunions aren't about the truth. They're about what *could* be." Ally is getting all philosophical and she hasn't hit the bar. I am definitely in trouble.

"I'm sorry. Will you excuse me for a minute?" Ducking away from the bewildered twins, I lead Ally into a corner behind a Ficus. "I can't lie, Ally."

She peers between the leaves, scoping out the room. "Why not? You live in a different city. How are these people going to know the difference? While you're at it, you might as well invent a boyfriend."

Wow. Is my life really so pathetic that I need to make up a new one at my high school reunion? Honestly? Yes. I turn back to Ally, but she's gone. I'm on my own. Time to create a new life for myself.

When I step back into the room, I head for the buffet. There are plenty of people there I can try out my new life on.

Chase Hugh, a linebacker who has only increased his padding over the last ten years, is hovering over the pigs-in-a-blanket. I approach him and swipe a crescent roll-wrapped dog from beneath his nose. "Hey Chase, what's up?"

I'm not sure which surprises him more—the fact that I'm speaking to him, or that I've stolen one of his weenies. "Um, hi, um," he squints at my nametag, "June."

The man doesn't have a clue who I am. Even though I spent a significant portion of my junior year tutoring him in math. "What are you up to, Chase? Did you get drafted for the NFL like you hoped?"

Chase is squirming in his size 42s, his eyes darting around the buffet table for something to shove in his mouth. "Um, not exactly. I, um, had an injury. Forced me to rethink my career options. I sell used cars now. What about you?" He settles on a bacon-wrapped scallop and stares over my shoulder while he chews.

Seems like good old Chase is just the sap to try my new life out on. "I recently opened my own business. It's been wildly successful, which doesn't leave much time for my boyfriend, but he's pretty busy with football season coming up."

"Football? He a sportscaster or something?" The hulking man beside me thrusts another scallop in his mouth, but I definitely have his attention.

I pluck a celery stick from a platter. "Nah, he just plays for the Panthers." I swing around and walk away, but not before I hear him choke on his lard-wrapped crustacean.

"Junie, I am so impressed. I didn't know you had it in you." Ally's back just in time to share in my glory. I have to admit it feels good to be seen as successful. Too bad it's all a lie.

"You are such a bad influence on me. I don't know why I keep you around." I can't help but grin at her.

Ally circles my shoulders with her arm and steers me toward a cluster of giggling women. "Can't get rid of me."

Lord knows I've tried.

As we approach the women, I realize it's the Quad Clique. Girls like me walked out of their way to avoid this group in high school. Chase was easy, but I'm not sure I can keep up my poker face with these classmates.

Ally whispers in my ear before pushing me into the middle of the crowd. "Successful business, famous boyfriend."

"What the?" One of the Jennifers pushes me away from her. "Are you drunk or something?"

"Sorry, I tripped." Standing in the middle of this group is like a bad dream from my teenage years. The only difference is that I'm clothed in this version.

Brittani peers over her margarita at my nametag. "June? I don't remember a J..." Her voice trails off as realization hits. "Oh, you were Ally's friend."

Just then the final Clique member approaches the group.

"Stephanie!!" Squeals abound and for a moment I'm forgotten.

"I knew it." Ally's behind me, smirking and nodding her head. "Like a blimp."

Her arch nemesis can't be more than a size 6, but Ally seems vindicated. True, you couldn't be in the Quad Clique if you were over a size 4, but still.

I try to sneak away amongst the excitement, but Kylie pulls me back in. She always was the nicest one. "June, wait. You've got to tell us what you're up to."

Ally's gesturing at me to stand up straight and get on with it, but I'm having doubts about the whole fake life story thing. "I, uh, I…"

The other Jennifer cuts me off before I have to make a decision. "Can you imagine what Ally would be up to now? I mean, if she were *alive*." The last word comes out like it's a state secret.

Several of the women gasp, shocked that she dared to bring up the taboo subject, others cover their mouths as if to suppress a sob. What if I told them exactly what Ally is doing right now? Would it freak them out that she's walking around behind them with her arms held out imitating the Michelin man and pointing at Stephanie?

More likely they'd be jealous that she'd chosen me to hang out with for the last ten years. Hang out with, haunt, same thing, right?

I know then that I'm in charge of my destiny. I might be the only one who can see Ally, but I'm only crazy if I continue to thwart my own dreams. "Do you want to know what I'm up to, Kylie?" I don't wait for a response. "I'm getting ready to open a doggie daycare."

Chapter Two

I'm standing in the lobby at the bank and Ally is trying to push me into a cute executive waiting for the elevator. Of course, he can't see her, so it looks like I've been drinking at nine o'clock in the morning.

Since I'm not cooperating, Ally takes matters into her own hands and knocks the pile of papers I'm holding to the ground. Because what are friends for, if not to make you look like a fool in front of potentially eligible men?

Cute executive guy bends down to help me pick up my papers and Ally is behind him checking out his ass. Two thumbs up, must be pretty good, although Ally's standards are usually limited to nice body, not too smart.

"Do you work in the building? I've never seen you before."

My attention is drawn back to the man mere inches from my face. "Oh no. I have a meeting on the fourth floor." Which I will be late for, thanks to my ~~dear~~ dead friend.

Cute executive man has a great smile. "I work on the fourth floor. Are you applying for a loan?"

Papers gathered; we rise at the same time. "Yes, a small business loan. I'm going to open a doggie daycare."

"Well, if it were up to me, the answer would be yes." He chuckles a fake sort of laugh. "But, alas, I'm in the mortgage department."

The elevator dings and the doors slide open. We step inside, Ally positioning herself between us. "Junie, he is totally hot for you. Go for it."

I swat at her but keep my mouth shut. A familiar, confused look flashes across the loan officer's face. Another ding and the doors slide open once more. We step out of the car.

"Yes, well, good luck. And if you find yourself needing a mortgage, be sure to let me know." He holds out a business card, flashes another smile and is gone.

"Way to blow it, Junie."

Hands perched on hips; I glare at my friend. "He was just trying to drum up business."

"If you'd played your cards right, you could have had hot elevator sex."

"Ally!" Her goal seems to be getting me laid. Our goals often clash.

"I'm sorry, ma'am, we don't have an Ally here. Do you have an appointment?" The receptionist is leaning over her desk, most likely searching for the person I'm talking to. I'm convinced that most people think I'm nuts.

"I'm sorry, I, uh, thought I saw someone I knew." People hardly ever believe that one, but I'm running out of excuses. "I do have an appointment, though—with Ms. Marshall."

"Of course, just have a seat and she'll be right out."

Hopefully she won't tell Ms. Marshall about my questionable mental status.

Ally's managed to keep quiet through my entire meeting with Ms. Marshall and I've been approved for the loan. It's nerve wracking to carry around a check with this many zeros. My personal bank is just down the street, so we head in that direction.

"We have to celebrate! Macy's here we come." Ally spins around the statue of a mother throwing her child into the air. "Heck, with all that money, we can go to Nordstrom."

The streets of uptown Charlotte are teeming with people on this busy week-day morning, so I dig into my purse for the earbuds I have started wearing. They stopped working after Ally knocked them into the toilet, but hopefully it makes me look a little less crazy when I'm talking to a person no one else can see. "Ally, that money is for the daycare. Not for shopping." Sure, she's been seventeen for a decade, but even she should be able to understand this.

Traffic breaks, and I jog across the street, not waiting for permission from the flashing man on the sign. I have so much to do.

"You have *celebrating* to do. At least get a drink, or something."

"It's ten o'clock in the morning." Celebrating does sound like fun, but I'm quitting my job today, so the more rational side of me (i.e., *my* brain, not Ally's) knows I need to get this business up and running.

Ally steps into my path, her lower lip in full pout.

Stopping suddenly on a busy urban sidewalk is never a good idea, but I hate the idea of walking *through* my friend. Ew. Instead, I step to the side, knocking into a frail woman who looks as if she's escaped from hospice. Bumping into the almost dead is still a happier alternative. "Sorry." I help her regain her balance, and continue on my way.

"You are too serious, June. I swear you are going to die a sad, boring death at an early age. Cause of death: no fun."

"Trust me, Ally. As long as you're around, I never have to worry about my life being boring." Entering my second bank of the day, I step into line behind the velvet rope.

Ally's scoping out the prospects nearby. She's always on the lookout for someone to embarrass me in front of. In an area set up with refreshments, she stops next to a broad-shouldered man in a blue polo shirt. "Look, Junie. It's your fake boyfriend."

The man turns slightly and I can see the Panthers logo on his shirt. I shake my head in a sharp "no" and gesture for her to come stand by me. Which of course makes it look like I'm gesturing at the football player.

I turn away, praying that he didn't see me. "Ally, if you weren't already dead—"

"I'm sorry. I didn't realize you were on the phone." From the teller's pinched face, I'm guessing she isn't all that sorry. But she's momentarily saved me from public humiliation.

Gratefully, I step up to the counter and tap my earbud (to "end my call"). Glancing back over my shoulder, I see the football player noshing on the free bagels near the fireplace. Crisis averted. I refocus my attention on the teller. "I need to open a new business account."

The look of disdain transforms to one of boredom. "New accounts are handled over there." She points in the general direction of no fewer than six office doors.

"Which office?"

She lets out a sigh of what can only be exasperation at my complete helplessness and slides off of her stool. "I'll show you."

While waiting for her to come out from behind the long counter, I reconsider my choice of banks. Is this an example of the customer service I can expect?

Entering the third office on the left, I realize that the only reason she's bothered to slink out of her chair is the extremely cute account manager occupying the space. After a sugary sweet introduction, the teller leaves me alone with William Charles Clayton III, according to the plaque on his desk.

"Please call me Will."

Hopefully I mumble my name, because in my head I'm thinking that I hope he isn't stuck on the idea of having a William Charles Clayton IV. I prefer unique, non-traditional names.

"You meet a hot man and you immediately think about having his children? Junie, there is something wrong with you. All you should be thinking about is whether or not you shaved this morning."

Obviously, sitting in Will's office, with him looking all Ivy League and, well, normal, I can't respond to Ally.

"So, what can I do for you today, June?"

Good. I did tell him my name. "I need to set up a commercial checking account."

Will flashes a brilliant smile. Either his parents popped for a good orthodontist or he has really good genes. I'm hoping it's the latter.

"That I can help you with. Is this a new business venture?"

I'm not sure if the stirring in my belly is excitement about my dream of owning my own business finally coming true or a visceral reaction to the charming, helpful man across from me. "Yes, I was just approved for a small business loan. I'm opening a doggie daycare.""Junie, the master of the flirt. Way to reel him in."

I shoot Ally a look suggesting that she butt out. It's doubtful.

"That sounds lovely."

"Ah, that's too bad. I thought we had a live one. No straight man uses the word lovely."

Maintaining my I-swear-I'm-not-crazy image is getting more difficult.

"It's a shame really, 'cuz he has huge feet." Ally's voice floats up from beneath the desk.

I lift my hand to my ear. "Excuse me one second, Will. I need to take this call." Tapping the headset, I step outside the office door. "Ally? Get out here!"

Will gives me an uneasy smile through the glass wall.

My teeth clench behind my grimace.

Ally finally shows up in the hallway. "Junie, you're so tense. We need to loosen you up. I keep saying—"

"You have got to stop invading people's private space like that. And I can't think with you in my head all the time."

I feel sorry for the two men walking past me just then. The confused looks always make me feel guilty. I've gotten over the embarrassment—well, mostly.

Ally's bottom lip is protruding and I know the quiver isn't far behind. I switch tactics. "This is really important, Ally. It's about the daycare. Please just sit quietly. I promise when we leave, I'll find a guy to talk to. Just for you." I feel like I'm bartering with a toddler. Too bad I can't offer her a piece of candy.

But it works and Ally nods her head in agreement.

Unfortunately, it appears that Will has heard my entire conversation, and for the rest of the meeting looks a tad nervous. I don't blame him. I'd be scared of me too.

Chapter Three

At the grocery store on the way home I manage to flirt with not one, but two guys. Somehow, I always need something off the top shelf. Being short has its advantages. Ally harasses me about my inability to secure a phone number but appears appeased.

Arriving home, I carefully balance the bags as I make my way up the two flights of steps to my apartment. This is one of the many times that Ally being alive would really help out. Funny how she can heave a water balloon off my balcony at the unsuspecting lawn maintenance guy, but she can't carry the bag containing my yogurt for the week. The strip of grass below my apartment hasn't been mowed for over a month.

I've cleared the steps and am rounding the corner to my apartment when I run smack into a very tall, very sweaty guy. I peel my cheek off his chest and bend my head back to meet his gaze.

The corners of his hazel eyes are crinkled into a smile and a chipped tooth is peeking from between his lips. "Sorry, ma'am. I didn't see ya there." His strong Texan accent sounds out of place in my suburban apartment complex.

I clutch the handles of my bags, willing them not to break. "It's okay. I should have been watching where I was going."

Ally's perched on the railing nearby as if she's watching the latest episode of *Friends*. "Is his chest hard? I bet it's real hard."

I roll my eyes and move to step around the burly man.

Instead of moving on, he extends a hand. "I'm Jesse. I'm movin' in. 'Partment 14C."

Obviously, I can't shake his hand. My six pack of IBC is threatening to erupt from the bottom of the flimsy grocery bag. I look down at my hands, hoping he'll get the picture.

Ally continues to be helpful with her running commentary. "Well, lookie there, Junie. You've got yourself a studly new neighbor. Not too shabby."

Jesse lets out a deep, rolling chuckle. Although he would probably call it rollin'. "You must think I was raised in a barn." He grabs the bags out of my hands before I can protest. "Born in the barn, but raised in the house, I swear." This is accompanied by a wink.

I'm not sure what to make of my new neighbor, but he certainly is more helpful than my dead friend. I lead him to my door and fumble with the key a bit.

"What you so nervous about, Junie? The big, hot man standing behind you checking out your ass?"

I drop the keys. Fully conscious of Jesse's view, I swing my backside toward the door and crouch down to retrieve them. I attempt a laugh to cover my embarrassment, but it comes out more like a snort.

Jesse just smiles.

As I push the door open my eyes flash on the inside of my apartment, which isn't fit for habitation, let alone a viewing by said studly man. Midge, my scrappy terrier/hound mix comes barreling around the corner—straight at the stranger standing in the doorway. As the unfolding catastrophe flashes before my eyes, I grab the bags from Jesse, block Midge with my left leg and slam the door shut.

And that's when the root beer breaks free from its plastic prison and leaves Midge, the living room couch and me soaked and sticky.

I'm thinking it'd be easier to move than to clean up the mess. Midge is happily licking root beer from my legs where I am splayed on the floor. I can't bear to deal with it. Of course, my ever-helpful friend is nowhere to be found, not that it would matter. She will only touch things when it suits her. And Ally has never been one to embrace cleaning.

Making messes, however, she is brilliant at.

In grade school, she would lean across the aisle and doodle on my desk with her Sharpie. In high school, she backed my Honda Civic into the dumpster outside the cafeteria. Just yesterday she destroyed one of my feather pillows because she missed seeing snow, hence the current state of my apartment.

There's a knock at my door.

No, please, God, no. Let him go away.

It's not likely that he will think I'm not here. Unless I leap off the balcony...

"You alright in there, miss?"

I'm not a rude person, or messy for that matter. Sometimes I worry that Ally has taken over my life.

"I'm fine, thanks. I appreciate your help, really."

I see his shadow appear in the window to the right of the door. Luckily Midge can't reach the cheap plastic blinds on that window, so they are still intact. She eyes the shadowy figure and emits a low growl, but the sugary sweetness on my legs wins out over her job as guard dog.

"Okay, then. 14C if you need anythin'. Anythin' t'all." I hear his footsteps travel away from my door and down the stairs.

Moving looks better all the time.

Chapter Four

Rubbing the keys between my fingers, I feel a tingle of excitement rush up my spine. Sure, it took a huge chunk of the money I just got from the loan department, but first, last and a security deposit later, and the vacant storefront is mine. Space in this picturesque small town rents quickly, so when I found the listing, I jumped at it. Sight unseen.

Well, I saw the front of the building. The matching picture windows, the ancient front door, the graceful sidewalk lined with old-fashioned lamp posts and wooden benches—it was like a scene from a movie.

Now, standing here, moments away from unlocking the door to my future, I'm a tad nervous about what lies behind that newspaper covering the glass. I was told the space included its original details: hardwood floors, tin ceiling, elaborate molding. There's even an exposed brick wall along the back.

I insert my key into the lock, wiggle it back and forth, remove it, turn it over, stick it back in, wiggle it some more and nothing happens. I am unsuccessful on the next two tries as well. Fumbling in my bag, I pull out my phone and the lease I've just signed and call the agent.

"It's an old door. You'll need to give it a shove."

Apparently, I have to break into a space that legally belongs to me.

Not willing to let anything get me down on this exciting day, I reinsert the key and lean my whole weight into the door.

The dank and dusty air inside nearly chokes me. The newspaper-covered windows allow only the faintest bit of light into the space. But even through the darkness I can see piles and piles of what I can only assume is trash. I reach up and tear a strip of the paper off, allowing a stream of light into the room. Looking down at the broom and dustpan in my hand, I realize that a bulldozer would be more appropriate.

As I tear the remaining newspaper down from the windows, I begin to make a mental list of the things I'll need. Trash bags, although a dumpster would be more efficient; a ladder, to reach the spider webs which appear to span the entire width of the room; clothes that I feel comfortable burning after I'm done.

I planned on one full day for clean-up. It will likely take me closer to a week.

I've already scheduled the fencing to be delivered and installed in two days. That is so not going to happen.

Returning almost an hour later, I feel better prepared to tackle the mess before me. I've changed into a pair of long overalls from high school that Ally made me swear I would never again wear. I'm sure she'll show up for the burning.

I've wrapped a bandana around my brown locks, hoping to shield my recent highlight splurge from all the dust.

And I've got industrial-strength trash bags. Seventy-two of them.

Donning a pair of canvas work gloves, I start picking through the debris. Fast food wrappers, pieces of cardboard, dust bunnies bigger than my dog, some things that are completely unidentifiable. My oddest discovery is a battered copy of Ayn Rand's *The Fountainhead*. The previous tenants may have been slobs, but they were literate slobs.

I'm snapping open my third garbage bag when Ally appears. At least I think it's her—hard to tell through all the dust.

"Ugh. Junie. This is disgusting."

I hadn't noticed. "Thank you for your insight."

She balances atop one of the larger piles of trash. "There's no way you're going to be open next week. You'll be lucky to be open next month."

Ally rarely spins a positive light on things.

"And it's so blah in here. At least turn on some music." She scrunches her face in concentration. "Madonna. The early stuff. Good cleaning music." And she's gone.

That's my dead best friend for you. Pops in and out as it suits her, shedding a ray of light wherever she goes. But the music is a good idea. When I take a break for lunch, I'll have to run home and grab a speaker. This process is going to take a while, some music might make the time go by faster.

By 12:30, my car won't hold another bag of trash and my hamstrings are screaming, "Do not bend over anymore!"

I decide to break for lunch.

Driving back to my apartment, I glimpse my reflection in the rearview mirror. Grime lines my face; hair is sticking out of the bandana at odd angles and now appears to be a slate-gray color. It seems silly to shower halfway through the process, but I am going to have to wash my face.

Pulling up to the dumpster in my complex, I glance around to see if anyone is nearby. Namely anyone who might point out that we have a five bag a month limit and I have eleven bags in my car this trip alone. But technically, it's not *my* trash.

I'm pulling into a space in front of my building when I see the hunk from yesterday coming down the stairs. I can't let him see me looking like this, or smelling like this. Ew.

He's coming closer, so I shrink down in my seat, trying to cram myself in the limited space between the steering column and the pedals. I think I've effectively hidden, but I can't see out now, so I don't have any way to know when he's gone.

My muscles were aching before I tied myself into this knot.

I hear a car start and pull out of a space near mine. Yes!

Untangling myself, I push the door open and half fall/half step onto the blacktop. When I right myself and turn around, Jesse is sitting at the foot of the steps directly in front of me. Why, Lord, why?

He's obviously engrossed in a conversation on his phone, but that doesn't keep him from grinning at me with an expression that clearly says, "Caught ya!"

Straightening myself to my full 5'4" height, I slam the car door, walk right up to him, step past his wide shoulders and proceed up the stairs. Once at the top, I peek back down to find his eyes still on me, goofy, chipped-tooth grin still on his face.

I don't even want to think about how wide my ass looks in these overalls.

Half an hour later, face washed, hair firmly secured under a new bandana, and my belly full of leftovers from the night before, I peek out my front door to make sure that the coast is clear. Sure, I look a little more presentable now, but nonetheless, the next time I see Jesse I'd like to look a lot better than presentable.

The steps are clear and I don't see him in the general vicinity, so I grab my Bluetooth speaker, a roll of paper towels and a jug of water. Now that my ass has recently garnered all this attention, I figure I better focus on eating less fat and drinking more water. And I suppose I should throw some exercise in there.

When I pull back up in front of the space that will soon house my future, I realize how grimy the windows are. Maybe I should've left the newspaper up.

Resolved to get this place into shape as quickly as possible, I get back to work, this time grooving to "Material Girl."

As I'm bagging up the remains of what I can only guess was a store for alternative lifestyles (I've found several half-burned sticks of incense, three roaches—the illegal kind, not the bug kind, and a foam rubber stress ball shaped like a Buddha), I hear a pounding noise that doesn't quite follow the beat of "Holiday."

Looking up, I don't see anyone out on the sidewalk, so I turn down the music and try to ascertain where the noise originated. Once Madonna quiets down, I can hear music coming from the space adjacent to mine. The thudding seems to follow along to the rhythm of the melody.

Stepping out onto the sidewalk, I notice for the first time who my neighbors are. On the right is one of those fancy stationary stores that sells monogrammed note cards and on the left is a yoga and aerobics studio, which explains the competing music and accompanying clamor. Peering through the window, I see about a dozen sweaty women jumping and clapping to what sounds like techno music. At least I don't have to worry about this neighbor complaining about dogs barking. And I guess it will be convenient if I want to, say, work out sometime.

Returning to my storefront, I gaze at the remaining piles of trash. It may take me all night, but I'm determined to stay until every last hamburger wrapper is secured in black plastic.

I drag into my apartment at 9 pm, dirty, hungry and feeling like I've just competed on *Wrestlemania*. Not that I watch that crap.

My urgent needs compete for attention, but the dirty, achy me wins out over the hungry me, and I head for the shower. The hot water washes away filth and sweat that have combined to make some sort of paste. The heat soothes my aching muscles. I stay in until the water runs cold. Which isn't very long, because the water heater in my crappy apartment only allows for a seven-minute shower.

Wrapped in a towel, I pad out to the kitchen, searching the cabinets and refrigerator for something appealing. I settle for a grilled cheese sandwich. I'm on a budget.

I've been ignoring my poor dog, who now walks over to the front door and pees just to spite me. Stuffing the last bite of sandwich into my mouth, I head into the bedroom and throw on the closest pair of shorts and a shirt.

Dropping an old towel on the puddle, which is only of the warning size, not the "I'm serious" size, I click Midge's leash on and we head out the door.

She's pulling me through the parking lot, toward her favorite spot, when I hear footsteps behind me. Mind you it's dark, and while Midge can be ferocious, she is only twenty-three pounds and I doubt she could do much damage. So, I'm a little nervous as the pounding gets closer. I quicken my pace toward the well-lit area near the dumpster, where Midge has marked out her own little potty patch.

Just as we step into the pool of light provided by overhead flood lamps, my new neighbor appears. Man, this guy is everywhere.

He's a little out of breath, which is surprising, because he appears to be in excellent shape—with those rippling muscles and toned legs—not that I'm looking.

"I was tryin' to catch up with you, but you move those little legs pretty fast." Again, the charming smile.

Don't stalkers and serial killers always have charming smiles?

He dumps a bag of trash into the dumpster. Okay, I feel better now.

"Sorry, I didn't see you. Midge really needed to go." I point down at my dog, who has been emptying her bladder this whole time.

"No problem. Wouldn't want you to think I'm a stalker or anythin'."

A nervous laugh escapes my lips. "No, of course not."

"It was right nice seein' you again." He tips an imaginary hat and steps back into the darkness.

I indulge another ten minutes of Midge's sniffing and exploring, mostly to give Jesse time to get back to his apartment. I'm not sure what it is about him, but he scares me a little. Is it his sheer size, or the sexual energy that emanates off of him? Not that I've noticed.

Chapter Five

Looking around the space, I feel a swell of pride. I did this. All by myself.

A little more than a week ago, the storefront was a wreck. I've removed a whopping thirty-four bags of trash, stripped the woodwork, painted the walls, and even fixed the leaking faucet in the bathroom. Tomorrow the new flooring will be installed (did I mention the gaping holes I found in the "original" hardwood floors once I removed all the debris?) and after that fencing to divide the playgroups. With luck, Hound'n Around will be open for business sometime next week. And I'm only eight days behind schedule.

My dad would have been so proud. All the years I followed him around the house with my little pink tool belt finally paid off. Times like this, I really miss him. Because when he died, he had the decency to stay that way.

Unless he's following Mom around bugging her, and she's too embarrassed to tell me.

"Junie, you should have painted the walls a brighter color. Like chartreuse." Ally waves her hands and strikes an indignant pose.

"I wasn't really going for the whole color-of-puke theme." The walls are a soft blue, except for the exposed brick wall at the back of the space. It feels peaceful. Something I definitely need in my life.

Checking the clock on the wall above the front counter, I realize I had better get a move on if I'm going to get my sign before the shop closes. "Come on, Ally. Let's go for a walk. We can pick up the sign for the front."

"That sounds boring. I'll see you later." And she's gone.

So that's the secret, I just need to be boring and she'll leave me alone. Funny, but up until this venture, my life has been pretty boring. Well, the part I had control over at least.

Take my first real job after college. Assistant to the assistant of human resources. They called me A2. For three painful years, my life consisted of getting coffee, filing and making copies. Right before I quit, they had added the task of scanning insurance forms into the computer. Wahoo.

Next, I snagged the much-sought-after job of all-night copy girl at the local Kinkos. Which consisted of me drinking coffee, playing computer solitaire and oh yeah, making copies.

This is what a business degree qualifies you for.

But it was those jobs that led me to ~~insanity~~ pursuing my dream. What's better than playing with dogs all day? They are so much cooler than people. And Midge only occasionally looks at me like I'm crazy.

So, I saved my $2-over-minimum wages, researched doggie daycares and dusted off my college textbooks to draw up a business plan. Tada! A mere six years, two horrible jobs, four increasingly bad apartments and three rejected loan applications later and I'm living my dream.

As I head out the front door, I'm tempted to skip, but being uncoordinated, I settle for a subtle twirl and a big grin. The guy sweeping the sidewalk across the street smiles (or laughs, it's hard to tell from this distance) and waves. I wave back. Nothing can steal my joy today.

Heading down the quaint street, I pass the hardware store, a children's boutique and a coffeehouse that turns into a bar at sundown. I've chosen Belmont as the location for my doggie daycare because a) real estate rates in Charlotte are ridiculous, b) it's only a ten-minute drive from my apartment via I-85, and c) it's the cutest freaking little town you'll ever see.

A scenic park—complete with a pond and real, live ducks—traces along Main Street for several blocks. I cross over the pond on the most adorable little foot bridge and stop to watch the ducks for a bit. It's like a fairytale land, complete with weeping willows and squirrels chattering in the trees.

I'm snapped out of my fantasy world when Midge dives off the bridge into the water. I watch in disbelief as the leash slips through my fingers and my monster-of-a-dog paddles determinedly toward the nearest mallard. She doesn't look too happy when it takes flight just as she reaches it.

Running off the bridge and around the side of the pond, I order Midge to "come." She crisscrosses the small pond chasing the ducks, which are quacking and fluttering their wings in distress. Finally, the last one flies away and Midge drags herself, sopping wet and covered in pond scum, out of the water. I guess I should have specified "come now."

Glancing around, I'm relieved to see I'm alone in the park. No one to witness my embarrassment. The scene certainly doesn't speak to my dog-handling skills.

Wiping debris and muck from Midge's leash, I drag her the remaining two blocks to the sign place. Joy a little muddy, but still holding.

When I return from the sign shop, a giant orange sticker is plastered on my front door. I attempt to remove it, but apparently the city's building inspectors use Gorilla Glue to affix their highly-unjustifiable and completely-incomprehensible notice of violations. What the heck is Building Code AXO-591b anyway?

I make a note to pick up a glass scraper at the hardware store. It's after five, so I also make a note to call the city offices on Monday. Joy scraped, but intact.

My newly installed answering machine is blinking its red message light at me. Funny, my number is officially four hours old, so it seems odd to be receiving calls so soon. Most likely it's my very first customer inquiring about my fabulous new facility, so I excitedly press play. Joy rebounding.

"Yes, Ms. Hinderson, this is Dr. Susan Walton from the North Carolina Department of Agriculture Veterinary Services Division." Boy, that's a mouthful, but she certainly says it with pride in her voice. "We received your application for licensure and have scheduled your inspection for three weeks from this Friday, at which time, should you pass inspection, you will be able to open for business. Please be sure to adhere to all of the guidelines in the updated Animal Welfare Act. Good day."

Updated? As in different from the regulations I slaved over a mere two weeks ago updated?

Wait a minute! Did she say three weeks? *Three weeks?* I punch the play button to listen to the recording again. Funny, but this time around I distinctly hear arrogance in her tone, not pride. Of course, it could just be that the black hole where my joy resided a few seconds ago is affecting my perception. I have to wait three more weeks before I can open?

Listening to the message once more, I now distinctly hear the growl in Dr. Susan Walton's voice. How rude.

As I click through to the NC Department of Agriculture's website, I hear *myself* beginning to growl. It appears as though the surly woman has rubbed off on me.

My growl erupts in a full-out roar when I see that the guidelines I painstakingly followed fourteen days ago have been radically changed. The word "updated" has been slashed across the page in red ink with exclamation points.

Generally, I handle stress well, but as I grab the new regulations off the printer, I can feel the blood rising to my head, filling my cheeks with a flush and pounding in my temples. In just under three weeks, the landlord will be pounding on my door, my utilities will be due and I will have zero customers. And oh yeah, according to the freaking Department of Veterinary Services, I have about a thousand dollars' worth of improvements yet to make. Joy? What joy?

In the car on the way home, I express my frustrations in a rambling tirade—and Ally isn't even around to listen—so apparently, I'm crazy independent of her. I'm still grumbling and growling as I ascend the steps to my apartment.

Wary of running into neighbors who already whisper about me, I stomp quickly toward my unit, managing to seethe quietly.

Sitting on my doorstep is a mason jar filled with an assortment of wildflowers that I recognize from the commons area behind the building. It's the thought that counts, right? But who would have thought about me?

As I pick up the jar, my question is answered when Jesse appears from around the corner. Was he waiting for me? I'm trying to decide whether to be flattered or terrified when he flashes his chipped tooth and tilts his cowboy hat down. If he wasn't well over six feet tall, he'd look like a little boy presenting flowers to his mama after he'd gotten into trouble.

But I should be the one extending an apology—not him. He's been nothing but sweet and helpful the past week, and I continue to treat him like a possible stalker. I feel the frustration of the last hour drain from my body. Has a guy ever brought me flowers?

"Brought, not bought." I was wondering where Ally had gotten to. "What a cheapskate. At least he could have gone and bought a rose or two."

I'd like to remind her that just the other day she called him studly, but I refrain in favor of preserving my sanity in front of Jesse—for a time at least. Smiling back at him, I raise the flowers to my nose. "Thank you, they're beautiful."

"You seem to be havin' a rough time of it." Shifting his feet, he looks down. That's when I notice that in place of the sweaty wife beater and sneakers he was wearing the first day I met him, he is now decked out in a neatly-pressed shirt, nice jeans and loafers. Loafers? Shouldn't he be wearing cowboy boots?

I'm distracted by the loafers, but I manage a response. "Yeah, about the way I've been acting. I want to apologize. You were only trying to help and I was rude."

"Naw, you were no such thing. I was bein' pushy. Pretty lady like yourself can't be lettin' strange men near her apartment."

Strange doesn't begin to describe this man. But he brought me flowers. And he is studly.

"And he was checking out your ass. If that didn't chase him away, then you'd better snag him fast." Leave it to Ally to cut to the chase.

"Well, I appreciate your help. And the flowers." I smile coyly at the well-built Texan wearing loafers. After all, he doesn't appear to be scared of the size of my ass.

He takes off his hat, revealing a full head of dark hair, only slightly marred by hat head, and grips it in both hands. "I didn't catch your name."

I giggle. Apparently, flowers reduce me to a teenage girl with a crush. "June."

"June. That's a right pretty name. Fittin' I suppose."

Is this guy for real? Do people actually talk like that in the new millennium? In Charlotte, North Carolina? "Where did you move from, Jesse?"

"Oklahoma." Ah, I wasn't too far off. "But I grew up in Texas." Or maybe I was right on the money.

"Did you move here for work?"

"Blah, blah, blah. Unless you plan on christening this concrete slab, I suggest you invite him inside." And Ally shatters my pleasant conversation with the nice man.

I've missed his answer, and it appears he's waiting for some sort of reply. Welcome to my world. The exit is just behind you. "Thanks again for the flowers, Jesse, you shouldn't have. I need to—," what the heck do I need to do? Watch a *Friends* marathon? Heat up my frozen dinner? Scrub the hardwood floors to remove the remainder of IBC from between the cracks? "—get Midge some dinner before she gnaws her leash in two."

"Sure thing. Nice to see you again, Miss June," Replacing his hat, he disappears around the corner.

"Way to score, Junie."

I don't have the energy to take her on tonight. Hopefully my scowl says it all.

Chapter Six

Another trip to the hardware store and my brand-spanking-new business checking account reads $42.09. It's taken me two of my three weeks, but everything should meet with the new standards. Until they change them again.

Today I am going to tackle the building inspector's list of petty adjustments and alterations. I'm balancing on a ladder replacing the battery in the smoke detector. Only lithium allowed. Through the glass transom above the door, I spot my neighbor across the street scrubbing the sidewalk in front of his store. Seriously, I have never seen anyone so fastidious about a clean sidewalk. His bookstore must not stay too busy.

He glances up to find me staring. Then falling. I really should mind my own business and not judge other people's.

The cushiony rubber flooring I had installed only covers the play areas for the dogs, so I am greeted by less-than-cushy commercial tile. Midge, who has stuck by me through this entire renovation, assists me by licking my face. Ally continues to be MIA. Funny, the only time I see her anymore is when she's embarrassing me in front of Jesse.

The door opens, slamming into my side. Apparently, I've landed in its way.

"Are you okay?"

Funny, he looks taller up close. Although it could be my dog's-eye view. "I think so."

Extending a thin, smooth hand he helps me to my feet. I thought for sure his hands would be calloused from all the sweeping. "You should sit down."

I allow him to lead me to a bench in my lobby area. Tracing the lump that is forming on my head, I try to act brave.

"That's quite a bump. Do you want me to call someone?" He sits beside me, concern etching his fine features. He looks delicate, refined, but not in a sissy way.

"No, I'm sure I'll be fine."

He rises. "At least let me get you some ice." He's out the door and across the street before I can protest.

My gaze follows him to the sign perched over the door of his shop. It's intrigued me for weeks, but I've been too busy to go over. Nelson Brantley's Rare and Essential Books. What makes a book essential? He can't have more than 800 square feet. How could one possibly fit all the essential books in the world into 800 square feet?

He's back before I can begin to ponder where he would fit the rare books if the essential books are taking up all the space.

He presses the ice pack against my head and tucks a stray hair behind my ear. Such an intimate gesture for someone I've known for all of three minutes.

"I'm Nelson." His gaze is penetrating mine, and combined with the pounding in my head from the fall, it's too much. I look away.

Midge, obviously shocked by the whole affair, has turned off her guarding instincts and is sniffing Nelson's shoes. Loafers again. What's up with all the men my age wearing sensible loafers? It seems so grown up. "I'm June." I allow myself to meet his gaze once more.

"Nice to finally meet you, June." He extends his left hand, as his right one is occupied with my lump, and we attempt an awkward handshake.

I'm trying to decide if the pain in my head is worse than the pain where the door slammed into my ribs when Nelson jams the ice pack against my head and shrieks. Not some primal manly shout, but a-woman-jumping-on-a-chair-to-escape-a-mouse shriek. The pain in my head is definitely winning now.

He completes the little drama by jumping up onto the bench and practically knocking me to the floor.

"Your dog bit me!" He's clutching his ankle and looks like he might pass out from the non-existent blood.

I can't really claim that this is the first time Midge has chomped down on an unsuspecting male companion. Between her and Ally, it's a miracle if I ever get asked out at all.

Scooping up the twenty-three pound ball of terrier (or terror, depending on your perspective), I deposit her in one of the play areas. Returning to ascertain the damage, I try not to hold it against Nelson that my head now hurts worse than before he "rescued" me. "I'm so sorry. Let me see."

As usual, Midge hasn't succeeded in breaking the skin. There's a faint impression of a tooth mark, but the area's barely even red.

Manly pride, or whatever it is that requires men to save face, kicks in and Nelson regains his composure. At least he climbs down off the bench. "It just shocked me is all." He's already backing toward the door.

I've managed to scare another one away. Well, Midge has.

Chapter Seven

"I really appreciate you helping me with this." I hold open the front door of Hound 'n Around as Jesse passes through, loaded down with the bulky armchair.

Ally might as well be glued to his back. "Look at his muscles rippling. It's enough to give a girl heart palpitations."

I'm glaring at my friend and Jesse is standing in the middle of the lobby, holding the chair as if it's one of those resin deck chairs, and not a sixty-pound monstrosity. "Where do ya want this?"

"Make him hold it a little longer."

"In the corner." I have perfected the art of ignoring Ally.

"Damn, he has great biceps. Make him move the desk."

Well, most of the time.

Jesse is scanning the room. "Wow, June Bug. This place is great."

Did I mention that Jesse has taken to calling me June Bug? There was a boy in the third grade that called me that and I punched him in the nose, but when Jesse says it, I melt a little.

"I can't believe you haven't done him yet."

"Ally!" The scream leaves my lips before I can stop it.

And there it is. The confused look. Poor guy.

"Who's Ally?"

It briefly crosses my mind that I could faint. But I'm far from Scarlett O'Hara and I don't think I can pull off a "spell."

The front door chimes. I send a silent "thank you" heavenward. Sweet distraction.

"Hey, June. I saw you come in. I was just checking to see how your bump was doing..." Nelson's voice trails off when he notices Jesse standing behind me.

As I step to the side, I can see the guys sizing one another up. It's quite a comparison actually. I can't think of two guys who are less alike.

"Oo, they're gonna fight over you! I just know it."

Logically, I know that Ally's prediction is highly unrealistic, but I toy with the notion for just a second. By the time I return to reality, they've introduced themselves. They're quite civil unfortunately.

"June Bug, shame on you for not tellin' me 'bout your accident. Next time you ask for my help before gettin' up on a ladder." Jesse sidles up to me and places his arm protectively around my waist.

Whoa. Jesse has his arm around my waist.

Ally's jaw is scraping the floor.

Nelson shrinks against the door.

Squeezing out of Jesse's grasp, I approach Nelson. "My head is fine, thanks to your help." I'm relieved he's not avoiding me after the Midge incident.

Nelson stands up straighter and Jesse looks affronted. I feel like I'm watching a mating battle between two male peacocks.

Ally begins to narrate. "Notice how the larger, more buff male looms over the scrawny, geeky one. Let's watch as the nerd retreats to his book-filled lair."

I'm happy to see Nelson hold his ground. Not that I'm taking sides or anything—I've just always rooted for the underdog.

A delivery truck pulls up in front of the bookstore. Nelson looks reluctant to leave.

"Thanks for checking on me." I flash what I hope is a reassuring smile.

Perfectly aligned white teeth flash back at me. I didn't notice the dimple yesterday. It must have been the blinding pain.

"It was nice to meet you, Jesse." Nelson nods in the larger man's direction. "I'll see you later, June." He squeezes my hand before hurrying across the street.

Jesse's shoulders deflate slightly. "Seems like a nice 'nough guy, I suppose." He peers through my large window. "Books, huh?"

Ally follows his gaze. "I can think of something a whole lot more essential than books."

There was a time when books were the basis of our friendship. Apparently dead people don't read much.

Jesse has left and Ally is throwing a tennis ball for Midge. Not that Midge is chasing it or anything. She actually looks annoyed by the ball ricocheting off the wall.

"I don't get what you see in that Nelson guy."

"I don't see anything in Nelson. We're just friends." Ally tires of the ball and starts doing hurdles over the shorter sections of fencing. "Okay, because I can't read your mind or anything."

Occasionally that fact slips my mind. What would it be like to have a normal friend that you could lie to? Not that I condone lying, but sometimes you need to get used to an idea before you go around announcing it to your friends.

Like I need to get used to the idea that I like Nelson.

"The bookstore geek." In case I wasn't sure who he was.

"Ally, you seem to have forgotten that we were geeks in high school."

This stops her from jumping around the room. "I was no geek. You maybe, but not me."

"Two words: band camp." I have her now.

"Brad never seemed to mind my horn skills."

"You didn't!" I've always been unclear about Ally's "romantic" status before the accident. I mean, the way she harps on sex, one assumes certain things, but I always thought she'd have told me.

She is now balanced on top of a section of fence like a tightrope walker. "A girl doesn't kiss and tell."

How unfair is it that she knows everything I'm thinking and I can't decipher 90% of what she says?

"Jesse is totally into you." Her feet are hanging out of my window as we speed down the highway toward home.

"He's just being nice."

Ally shakes her head from side to side. "Nope. He wants your body. I've seen him check out your boobs."

"I'm so sure. June Hinderson—sex goddess." Next to Ally, I've always felt huge, especially now that you can literally see through her.

"You don't give yourself enough credit, Junie. You've always been adorable. Brian Wright was mad about you in high school."

Until I fell into a wicked depression after Ally died. I admit I wasn't much fun to be around. And once she reappeared, I wasn't able to focus on a boyfriend. He broke up with me right before the prom. Said it was like I had died with her. Part of me had, I guess.

"Too bad he wasn't good enough for you." Sometimes it's not so bad that she can read my mind.

"Anyway, Jesse's not really my type."

"Do you have a problem with buff, beautifully-sculpted men?"

She has a point. He is extremely nice to look at. "I just don't think we have much in common."

"If you tried a little harder, you could have sex in common."

"Ally, why are you always trying to get me laid? What is the big obsession with sex?" I figure if she can read my mind, I might as well say what I'm thinking.

And she's gone. I guess that's one way to get out of an argument.

Chapter Eight

"You have to say yes." Even though she's technically blocking my path out the front door, she *is* dead, so the tactic doesn't prove too effective.

I run down the steps. "I can't do this right now, Ally. The inspection is today."

As I'm unlocking the car door, she flicks the keys out of my hand.

"Seriously Ally, this is important." I fumble around on the ground as she kicks the keys away.

When I bend down to look under the car, I'm startled to find her there. You wouldn't think she could surprise me anymore, but she's always coming up with new places to appear.

Just last week, I pulled back my shower curtain to find her lounging in my tub. No water or anything, just lounging.

"Your social life is important, too. You haven't been on a date this millennium."

I grab my keys before she can take them again. "That's a bit of an exaggeration."

"I've had more dates in the last ten years than you, and I've been dead the whole time." She's waiting for me in the passenger seat when I climb in the car.

"You can date in heaven?"

"Where do you think I go when I'm not here? To wash my hair?"

Trying to wrap my mind around the "rules" of the dead is too much for a Friday morning. A very important Friday morning. "I'll decide after the inspection."

"Just don't wait too long or you'll lose your chance. Jesse's a good-looking guy. If you don't want to go out with him, there are plenty of sane women who would love to." She twirls the volume dial on the radio and starts singing along with The Bangles.

Nelson rushes over to greet me as soon as I pull up to the curb. Which is not normal. Something's wrong. "June. I'm so glad you're here. Some lady from the Department of Agriculture was here about an hour ago."

"An hour ago?" I've never heard of a state employee doing anything before nine o'clock.

He hands me a business card. "Yes, she was here at eight o'clock on the dot and didn't seem too happy. You're supposed to call her."

Great. What a way to make a first impression. "I hope this doesn't set things back any further than they already are. As it is, I've been eating Ramen noodles for the past week."

"June, that's awful. Those things aren't fit for human consumption. I'm taking you out for a real dinner tonight after work."

He didn't ask, he declared. I like this assertive Nelson.

"Besides," his dimple appeared as he smiled, "we'll need to celebrate you passing inspection."

"Are you seriously going out with this weenie when you could be going out with a real man?" Ally's timing is impeccable as usual.

I shove open the front door and smile back at Nelson. "I need to call the inspector, but dinner sounds great."

Ally is rambling on about all of Jesse's positive attributes and Nelson's lack thereof as I close the door.

Picking up the phone, I dial the number on the card and implore Ally to hush.

I am connected to Dr. Walton's voicemail and frustrated, I leave a message. I swear I don't grovel. Too much.

"Junie, if you go out with that book-weenie, you are making the biggest mistake of your life!" Did I mention that Ally was in drama in high school? Who am I kidding? Ally's middle name is "Drama."

"Why do you care so much who I go out with? Normally you bug me to go out with *anyone*."

She's digging through a basket of squeaky toys, testing each one out. I guess it's a noise I'll have to get used to if I can ever actually open the business. "Well, usually you don't have multiple choices. I mean, two guys asking you out at the same time? That's not a normal problem *you'd* have to deal with. I'm just trying to help you make a wise decision."

Ouch. Nice friend, huh? But she's right. Damn. I hate that. I make a decision right then. "Who says I can't go out with both of them?"

"Nice Junie. Very nice. Keep your options open. Play the field. Shop around. I like it." She's nodding her head so hard I fear it will fly off.

"But if it's going to work with either of them, then *you* have to behave." I point my finger all stern-like.

This earns the-I'm-completely-innocent angel bit from Ally. "I would never intentionally try to get in the way, Junie."

I know my friend. And I see the glint in her eye. It could be the sun streaming through the large picture window, reflecting off the sequins on her shirt. But I know it's a glint of mischief. I've seen it too many times. She's got something up her three-quarter sleeve.

The night that Ally was killed, she was returning from a party with Brad, the drunk jerk. We'd gone shopping the day before to pick out just the right outfit. It was a college party, so Ally wanted to impress everyone with her "mature style."

The top was a clingy, shimmery thing with a low neckline and a short hem. I complained that paired with the too short sleeves, it was impractical for the cool weather. Because it showed off her recently acquired belly-button ring, I got vetoed. She matched it with a pair of dark, low-rise jeans that hugged every inch of her stick figure shape. Sure, Ally's skinny, but she's not curvy. Not that the guys seemed to mind.

I had no idea that the outfit I helped picked out would be worn for all of eternity.

You'd think there'd be a dress code in heaven.

As I'm heating up my stupid ramen noodles, and dreaming of where Nelson will take me for dinner, the phone rings. Weaving through the fencing, I race to catch it.

"Hello?" Gasping for breath, I can barely hear the dial tone buzzing in spite.

The caller id reveals a 919-number. Most likely the inspector returning my call.

I need to make a more efficient path from the back of the building to the front. Most likely something else that will cost me money. Money that I don't have.

Returning the call I've just missed, I leave another message for Dr. Walton. At least it was her cell phone. Maybe she's still close by.

I'm halfway to the back when the phone rings again. Am I training to run the hurdles?

"Hello?"

"Yes, is this Hound'n Around?"

Oh yeah, I should probably work on a greeting. Silly me, I'm focused on breathing. "Yes, it is. How may I help you?"

"I'm interested in doggie daycare. I have a four-month-old lab named Billie. I love her, but she's eating my couch while I'm at work."

Score! My first actual, potential client. Assuming I'm going to pass inspection eventually, I set up an appointment to meet with her the following week.

Scared to miss another call from the elusive Dr. Walton, I station myself at the desk the rest of the afternoon. I don't even retrieve my disgusting lunch from the microwave. Three orange Tic-Tacs and half a granola bar left from I'm-not-sure-when make up my lunch.

I hope Nelson was serious about dinner.

At 4:35, the phone finally rings, producing an actual conversation with Dr. Walton. She's on her way out of town and will be stopping by in approximately ten minutes. Now all I have to do is pass.

Dr. Susan Walton, the arrogant, growling woman from the message three weeks ago, is about 4'11", maybe 95 pounds, and is older than my grandma. A Chihuahua could knock her over. I lock Midge in one of the kennels.

I almost let the woman's appearance fool to me. Until she opens her mouth.

My grandma would have told her, "If you can't say something nice, don't say anything at all."

Dr. Walton would probably have knocked Grandma out.

My fencing isn't high enough. My flooring was a waste of money. The comfy chair in the lobby has to go. Then there are the things actually listed in the regulations.

After waxing poetic about the Animal Welfare Act for nearly an hour, the old bird slaps a piece of pink paper on my desk. Her writing takes up every spare inch, but my eyes only see the tiny box checked at the top of the paper. Approved.

Approved!

She says something about returning next month for a follow-up and is gone.

Approved!

Nelson must have seen my dance of joy through the window, because the bell dings and he appears.

Midge barks and Nelson goes over to let her out of the pen. Stooping down he scratches her between the ears and slips something under her nose. Over the last week, they have made some sort of peace. I have my suspicions it includes liver treats.

Whatever, I passed!

Chapter Nine

I have a ball at dinner with Nelson. Despite Ally's best efforts.

First, he chooses the perfect restaurant—not too fancy, but just enough pretention to impress me. The food is to die for. Or maybe anything tastes divine after a lunch of Tic-Tacs and a granola bar. And I'm pretty sure Nelson is a stunning conversationalist. At least the parts I hear are interesting.

The ambience of the place is only slightly marred by my best friend perched on a plant shelf behind my booth. She is listing all of the reasons why I shouldn't be on this date with Nelson and I should be on a date with Jesse. The possibility of having mind-blowing sex pops up about every fifth reason.

As I look across the table at the guy I'm currently out with, I wonder why she assumes the sex would be better with Jesse.

"Because Jesse's probably actually *had* sex before."

Nelson is talking about his recent trip to London and some of the first editions he was able to acquire.

"Instead of only *reading* about it in a book."

I let out a huff of air, which sends my bangs vaulting toward the ceiling.

The look on Nelson's face suggests he took my frustration at Ally personally.

"Sorry, I had a piece of fuzz in my hair." Yeah, that was convincing. "You were saying?"

He looks skeptical, but continues on about a rare, signed copy of *Oliver Twist*.

When Nelson talks about books, he takes on this scholarly look. You know, chewing on the earpiece of his glasses, furrowed brow, animated hands. Who doesn't harbor a few naughty professor fantasies?

His sandy-blond hair is straight and fine, and about every three minutes he flicks it out of his eyes.

"Get a haircut already." Ally obviously doesn't appreciate the cute gesture.

I, on the other hand, am completely enamored. Talking to Nelson reminds me of college. I loved getting into intellectual discussions about everything from string theory to serial killers. (Hey, I was a sociology major for, like, a semester.) The only friends I had in college were my study groups. Usually Ally deemed them "boring," so she wasn't there to get in the way of me just being June. Unfortunately, none of those relationships lasted past final exam review.

"So, what made you want to open a doggie daycare?"

Oh, now I need to participate in the conversation. Sorry, I don't do this much. "Well, I've always loved dogs, but growing up we couldn't have any because my dad was allergic. Actually, it was my best friend who got me hooked." I glance over my shoulder in time to see Ally cover a grin. "Her family used to raise cocker spaniels. Whenever they had a litter of puppies, I was at their house more than my own."

"Do they still breed dogs?"

At that, Ally's gone.

"No, after she died, her parents couldn't bear to keep breeding. She loved those dogs so much. I guess it was just too painful."

The familiar look of concern etches Nelson's face. "She died?"

I look around briefly, but I have a feeling Ally won't be back. She doesn't handle talk of her family well. "Yeah, she was killed in a car accident when we were seniors in high school."

"Oh, June, I'm so sorry." He reaches his hand across the table and covers mine. It feels nice to have contact with another person—the breathing kind. "You must miss her so much."

I suppress a laugh. "Sometimes."

Hoping to lighten the mood, I launch into a series of questions about his family and childhood. Soon he's regaling me with stories of his historian grandfather traveling the world and bringing back suitcases full of books for the curious Nelson.

For the next hour, it's just the two of us. I can't help but like it.

When Nelson pulls up in front of the bookstore, I get a twinge of anxiety. It may have something to do with possible-first-kiss jitters. Or it may just be because Ally is perched in the space between us.

Before the car stops, I jump out to the curb. "Thanks so much for dinner, Nelson. I had a wonderful time."

"What? You aren't even going to stick around for a kiss? Not that this wienie has the balls to actually do it." Ally is seated on the roof of the car, legs crossed, left foot planted on the hood.

Before I can think too much about it, I rush to the driver's side window, lean in and plant one on Nelson. On the lips. I think. It all happens pretty fast.

On my way across the street to my car, I glare at Ally. "Who has balls now?"

"Well, not the guy who just sat there and let you do all the work."

Will nothing make her happy?

Chapter Ten

Maybe if I ignore it, the pounding will stop.

Squinting at the glowing numbers on the clock, my suspicions are confirmed. It *is* the butt crack of dawn.

I plod to the front door, shielding my eyes from the blinding rays of sunlight streaming through the front windows.

Focusing with two eyes is hard enough, but making one eye look through the peephole is even more difficult. A tall blur has awakened me.

"Who is it?" This doesn't exactly come out as a polite inquiry. But seriously, who gets up before ten on a Saturday?

"June Bug? Did I wake you up?"

I should have known. Jesse is the tallest blur I know. "Um, no, I just haven't, um, gotten dressed yet." It's official. World's Worst Liar.

"I'm sorry, darlin'. I'll come back later. I just got your note last night, so I wanted to come over and—"

I wrench the door open without thinking about the state of me or the apartment of horrors. "What note?"

A look of—surprise? disgust?—crosses his face. Serves him right for waking the dead on a Saturday.

A significant portion of my hair has fallen out of the Scrunchie that held it in place and is now plastered—most likely by drool—to the side of my face. My Duran Duran t-shirt skims the top of my thighs and if I'm remembering correctly, I'm wearing a pair of hot pink undies two sizes too big that my cousin Kendra left here during her last visit. It was dark last night and I may have drunk a little too much after the awkward kiss with Nelson.

The right side of Jesse's mouth hitches up and is eventually followed by the left side. Soon he's grinning like the Cheshire cat. I don't even have the decency to be embarrassed. I must still be drunk.

He leans against the door frame, crossing his arms over a broad chest. "Rough night?"

I smooth my hair off my face. Well, that is my intention, but in reality, I *pry* my hair off my face. "No. My night was fine. In fact, it was great." Did I write him a note and don't remember it? I really shouldn't drink alone. And Ally does *not* count as a drinking buddy.

"I'd be willing to bet that tonight will be even better. What time should I pick you up?"

Well, aren't we just full of ourselves?

I'm searching my brain for some memory of writing this supposed note or agreeing to go out with Jesse. Not real effective, considering my head is currently full of rocks and other painful debris.

Sure, I decided yesterday to go out with him—was that just yesterday? But that was to spite Ally, mostly. Honestly, this man scares me a little. Mind you, it's a good scary. He's just so much *man*. But he's here, grinning at me, in spite of the way I look, and apparently still wants to take me out. Who am I to say no to that? "How's seven?"

"I'll be here with bells on, little lady." He chucks my chin and takes off down the stairs.

Did he just chuck my chin? Is this guy for real?

Maybe I'm still dreaming.

If I go back to bed, perhaps I can rewrite the ending.

By two o'clock, the wine has worn off and the reality of my situation has taken its place. I'm searching my closet for something suitable to wear.

Because I have a date with Jesse. A date. With Jesse.

Why does this freak me out so much? I went on a date last night, and other than the weird kiss-and-run, I handled it just fine.

Basically, it's that Nelson is comfortable. He's like the guys I've dated in the past (except that brief period of dating wanna-be-rock-stars). Nelson makes sense to me. He's smart and responsible and stable and sweet and—

"Boring." Ally peeks out from between an old bridesmaid dress and a winter coat.

"Nelson is not boring. He's intelligent." Let's just say that Ally never once dated a guy for good conversation.

Ally plucks a short, low-cut dress from the rack. I haven't worn it since middle school. Before I had anything that could fall out of the neckline. Why do I hold on to these clothes?

"Jesse is a real man."

Which is exactly what scares me. He's got this raw—I don't know—energy that emanates off his flesh like heat. I'm scared of getting burned.

"You're scared of what you might do."

Well, she hit that nail right on the head.

I pride myself on being in control, on being reasonable (except for the whole talking-to-my-dead-best-friend thing). With Jesse, I don't feel in control of my-self. And I'm not certain I can be reasonable in the face of all that manliness.

"Just let go, Junie. Be in the moment. Let Jesse rock your world."

"A) I'm not even sure Jesse wants to rock my world. B) I'm not sure if I want my world to *be* rocked. And C) I don't have anything to wear." Burying my head in the mound of clothes heaped on my bed I start to panic. If my mouth wasn't full of rayon/cotton blend, I'd probably be hyperventilating.

Ally grabs my hands and pulls me off the bed. "Snap out of it, Junie!" She braces her hands on my shoulders. Her words come out slow, as if addressing a toddler. Well, if this isn't a role reversal... "Jesse likes you. He *likes* you. Why else would he have asked you out like twelve times?"

I start to refute the number, but she cuts me off.

"I counted Junie. Twelve. He's a hunk and a nice guy to boot. Go out and have fun. Don't think so much. If you want to sleep with him, sleep with him. If you never want to see him again, fine. I mean, I won't understand it, but fine." She releases me and perches on my pile of discarded clothing.

This is new. I'm not used to her being so reasonable. What is this, opposite world? Hunky guy apparently likes me, Ally's being reasonable. Am I *still* drunk?

"Wear the black skirt and purple top." And she's gone.

Damn, I hate it when she's right.

Jesse has brought me flowers again. This time they obviously didn't come from the commons area out back. I take the bouquet of pale pink roses from him and go about arranging them in a vase.

He's crouched in the middle of my living room, charming the fur off of Midge. My typically tenacious terrier is stretched out on her back squirming with pleasure as Jesse rubs her belly.

After Ally selected my outfit for the evening, I had time left over to clean my apartment. With all the time I've spent cleaning at the daycare, the apartment has been a bit neglected. By the time Jesse arrived, I felt calm and somewhat put together.

Until I opened the door. Tonight, Jesse is dressed in dark jeans, a white, button-down shirt and a black sports coat. He looks yummy.

"He's managed to tame the wild beast." I look away from the fine specimen crouched in front of my couch to find Ally sitting on top of my entertainment center. She and Midge have never really gotten along. Something about dogs sensing paranormal phenomena.

I decide to take Midge's approval as a sign of good things to come.

Jesse looks up at me, grin revealing that chipped tooth I've become awfully fond of. "You ready, darlin'?"

Hopefully my smile doesn't look as strained as it feels. "Sure."

All of a sudden, Ally's beside me, arm around my shoulders. "Junie, relax. It will be great. Don't assume the worst."

The words are comforting, but when Ally's wrong, she's really, really wrong.

Dinner was great. I was able to relax and enjoy myself. And it turns out that Jesse is a really smart guy. He transferred here to head up a new division of his company and only moved into my crappy complex (my words, not his) until he found a house he liked. The most surprising thing I found out is that my burly Texan cowboy has never even ridden a horse. I'm from North Carolina, and I've ridden a horse. Anyway, I guess that explains the loafers.

Somehow, I've found myself back at his place, sitting on a couch in a mostly empty living room. Jesse is pouring us a glass of wine. I'm not real sure that I want my inhibitions weakened by alcohol right now. But how do you turn down a man offering you a glass of wine?

For a guy who has very little furniture, Jesse sure does have a lot of candles. They cover nearly every surface in the room. The counter in the kitchen, the rickety table his TV rests on, the window sills lining the front wall. There's even a candle on top of the refrigerator. It took him a full five minutes to light them all.

Within two minutes of him returning to the couch, I'm trying to figure out how I can throw something on one of those candles to start a fire.

Jesse's kissing my neck, and it feels really good. Too good. Remember how I like to remain in control? Ally doesn't even have the decency to distract me from enjoying myself.

I push lightly against his chest. Gosh, it is hard. She was right. Somehow my pushing him away turns into me caressing his well-defined pecs and thick, muscular arms.

Jesse responds by slipping his hands down to rest on my lower back. Who am I kidding? He's grabbing my ass. He shifts slightly and pulls me onto his lap. The reality pressing against my thigh startles me enough to remove my neck from his mouth. And my ass from his, um, lap.

As I'm fleeing through the door, I mutter something about forgetting to turn off my oven.

Chapter Eleven

What is that jabbing into my back? And what is that God-awful noise?

Coming into semi-consciousness, the details of the previous evening creep back into my mind. I'm curled up in my closet, wrapped from head to toe in my fluffy lilac comforter, where I fled to escape Ally's incessant tirade after I left Jesse's apartment. As if it's possible to escape her completely. At some point during the night, I managed to fall asleep, but apparently, I've rolled over onto the three-inch heel of my Steve Maddens. And now Ally is singing—entirely off-key—a warped version of "I Hate Myself for Loving You".

I guess it's time to get up.

Luckily, it's only nine-thirty, so I have time to make it to church. I figure I need all the prayer I can get right now.

I shower, get dressed and am eating breakfast when the knocking begins. Damn, I had to live on the second floor. No back door.

So, instead of going to church, I spend the next hour trying to be completely silent so Jesse will go away. He alternates between knocking and calling my cell phone. Which sucks, because he can probably hear it ringing. Well, he'll just have to think I've left it at home.

Ally's standing at the front door, trying to summon all of her "poltergeist" energy to take the chain off the door. I'm sure Jesse won't think it's at all weird if the door swings open on its own.

Why does he have to be so persistent? Most guys would feel rejected/angry/frustrated after a girl walks out on a make-out session. They'd have the decency to write said girl off as a tease/lunatic/hopeless virgin. What Jesse doesn't realize is that I'm all three. Run while you have the chance.

I creep across the living room and ease my phone out of my purse. Pressing the voicemail button, I listen to the four messages he has left.

"You there?"

"June, I just wanna make sure you're okay."

"You left so suddenly last night, June Bug. I hope I didn't offend you, darlin'."

"I'm such an idiot, Junie. Please tell me I haven't gone an' messed everything up. Call me. Please."

Junie. He called me Junie.

"Because that's what those of us who love you call you." Ally sits on the floor beside me and wraps her arms around me. I can almost feel her hugging me.

Jesse gives up around noon and I'm able to leave the complex without seeing him. I'm not sure where I'm headed, but after about twenty miles, I realize I'm going home.

Mom only lives about two hours away, but I don't find many reasons to go there. Ever since Dad died, things are a bit awkward between us. He had acted as a mediator between my mother and I most of my life.

For my seventh birthday I wanted to get my ears pierced, because, well, Ally had. Mom refused. No way was she letting me "scar myself". Well, that night, Dad took me out for ice cream and instead of mint chocolate chip, I got pink rhinestone studs.

As a preteen Dad drove me to my first boy/girl party and told my mom he was taking me to a special youth event at church.

And when Ally died, no one could comfort me like him.

My junior year of college, Dad was diagnosed with a malignant brain tumor. The doctors warned us that his personality might change and not to take the things he said personally. My dad's sweet nature was stronger than that tumor. He never turned nasty or bitter.

Since his death, Mom and I have fallen into a don't ask/don't tell relationship. I call home once a month and visit when I have to, but basically, we talk about the weather and what she's making for the potluck.

Today, I need the comfort of home. Even if my dad isn't there.

My tires crunch on the driveway, which is littered with blossoms from the nearby crepe myrtles. The arbor leading to the back yard, which has sported chipped paint for as long as I can remember, is painted a bright, fresh white. Stepping into the yard, I notice other anomalies. The broken railing on the deck has been repaired and a new pair of rockers sit in the shade of the elm tree. Something is very wrong.

As I peer through the sliding glass door, I find that something attached to my mother's face.

I can see they've recently finished lunch—a half-eaten pot roast sits in the middle of the dining room table, congealing in its own juices. I notice other changes in the adjoining kitchen, like a new ceiling fan and freshly painted cabinets. But the biggest change is definitely the short, balding man with his arm around my mother's waist.

"Whoa! Go Ma!"

I glare at Ally, who is clearly not helping.

"June, goodness. What are you doing here?" My mother's hands are fluttering around like a fish flopping around on the dock. She must realize they are out of control, because she grips the sides of her apron.

My glare travels past my mother to Frodo. Okay, that's not fair. His eyes aren't blue. And there's the obvious lack of hair. "What am *I* doing here?"

Mini Me (yeah, that's way more appropriate) steps forward, extending his hand. "June. It's so nice to finally meet you. Helen talks about you all the time."

My mother, *Helen*, refuses to meet my eyes. She begins clearing the table.

"I wish I could say the same was true about you." I begrudgingly extend my hand. My parents didn't raise me to be rude. Of course, they also didn't raise me to keep huge secrets from them.

A look passes between them and Mom finally looks at me. "Honey, I'm sure I've told you about Harry. He's been helping me around the house." This statement garners a surprised look from the un-hairy Harry.

Ally jumps up and down, clapping. "I'll bet he's been helping her in the bedroom."

Not a thought I need in my head. I duck down the hall and into the bathroom. After I've emptied my stomach of last night's dinner (I may never be able to eat shrimp again) and the pop-tart I had for breakfast, Mom knocks on the door.

"Honey," I hear the intake of breath that signals my mom's frustration. "Please be reasonable. You did show up unannounced."

Of course. This is all my fault. I was just trying to escape my life for a few hours. I bury my face in the freshly laundered towels. It seems like I'm spending an awful lot of time hiding from people lately. I open the door and march resolutely past my mother and up the stairs. Slamming my bedroom door, I flop onto the bed. If I'm going to hide out, I'd best get comfortable.

The smell of hazelnut lulls me from dreams of Jesse and Nelson. I can't even escape my problems in my sleep.

"Yeah, having two great guys to choose from is a real problem." Ally has preceded my mom into the room.

Did she just acknowledge that Nelson's a great guy? I sit up in bed and gratefully accept the mug of coffee from my mom.

She perches on the end of the bed. "I figured you'd need caffeine to make it home tonight."

I haven't slept over since Dad died. It doesn't sound like such a bad idea right now, but I do have a business to run. "Thanks."

"There's lasagna downstairs if you want some." She tucks a strand of platinum gray hair behind her ear.

Is that what my hair will look like when I get older? I smooth my own messy locks with one hand while I sip the scalding brew. "So, are you guys, like, dating?" The coffee burns my tongue and I lower it to the bedside table.

When she finally looks up at me, my mom looks every one of her sixty-two years. "Yes, sweetie."

I try to absorb this information like a rational adult.

"I bet your mom's getting more than you are." Ally, on the other hand, continues to think like a teenager.

"How long?" I can barely get the words out, images of Dad flashing before my eyes.

She scoots closer to me and takes my hands. "June, I miss your father so much. No one could ever replace him. But it's been eight years, and I'm lonely."

She doesn't point out that her daughter only visits during major crises and holidays.

"Harry's a good man, June. He's helped out so much around here and he really cares for me. His wife died a few years ago. I hope you can be happy for me." She places my hands gently in my lap and smoothes out the covers around me.

Before she can rise, and I can think too much about it, I throw my arms around her and bury my head in her familiar scent. I'm not sure how long we sit there, holding onto each other for dear life, but by the time I leave the house, it's already dark.

Chapter Twelve

Somehow, when I wake up in my own bed the next morning, life seems better. I'm not sure how that happened, but I'd guess it has something to do with Mom's lasagna.

Besides, it's a great day. Hound'n Around is officially open for business.

Knowing I will be inundated with a flood of eager customers, I stop by a local coffee shop to charge up with a double shot and a cinnamon roll. I'm trying to balance my food, keep Midge from running into the street and fumbling to answer my ringing cell phone when Nelson sprints across the road.

Memories of the awkward kiss come flooding back. Before I can get embarrassed about that, memories of the not-awkward, extremely-pleasant kissing with Jesse replace them. I imagine my cheeks are approximately the shade of my candy-apple red coupe.

"June. Let me help you." Nelson grabs Midge's leash, slipping her a covert treat.

Yeah, I saw that, mister. I finally manage to find my cell phone. Jesse's number is flashing on the screen. Apparently, this man does not understand the concept of being ignored. I dump the phone back into my bag.

The sun is easing over the buildings of downtown Belmont, waking the sleepy little town. It promises another hot day.

That's when I realize that it's seven-fifteen and Nelson's bookstore doesn't open until ten. "Good morning, Nelson." I try to keep the smile out of my voice. I must have managed to land that kiss fairly close to his lips, because he doesn't seem to be holding any ill will against me.

Midge dances up and down on the sidewalk as I dig for my keys. Didn't I just have them?

"She seems excited about the new friends she'll make today."

My laugh comes out more like a snort. "More likely she's wondering who she can terrorize."

"Or terrierize." Nelson's dimple makes an appearance, brightening my morning. I love that he's corny. And that I don't feel the least bit scared I'll lose control around him.

Ally is waiting inside, lounging on the bench in the lobby. "I think losing a little control is fun. And good for you."

I have a business to open, a dog ready for the breakfast she missed in our hurry to leave home this morning, and a cute bookstore owner leaning against my desk. I'm pretty sure that leaves no time for arguing with my dead best friend.

I dump Midge's food in a bowl and settle at my desk to eat my own breakfast. Nelson is talking about a book fair he attended over the weekend and asking if I did anything exciting. It's a shame that my mouth is crammed full of cinnamon roll at the time.

But I'm forced to quickly swallow the massive bite when my phone rings. My business line. The deluge of new customers has begun. "Good morning! Hound'n Around, this is June, how may I help you?"

"June, darlin', you've gotta talk to me."

Can't say I expected it to be Jesse. So much for my deluge of new customers. "Yes, I can help you with that." I force my lips into some semblance of a smile for Nelson's sake.

He smiles back at me encouragingly, even gives me a thumbs up.

Jesse is rambling on about how he'll do anything to make it better. "You gotta forgive me, Junie."

There it is again. Junie. What gives him the right to call me that? A few minutes of necking on the couch? "I'm sorry, but this isn't the best time. I have a customer waiting." I cover the mouthpiece and mouth the word "solicitor" to Nelson. He nods in understanding. "Maybe you could call me at a later time?"

"Gosh, I'm an idiot. You're at work, of course. Sorry, darlin'. I'll call you later."

"Thank you." I hang up the phone, and notice that my hand is shaking. The problem is that I haven't exactly filled the guys in on my decision to be a liberated girl of the new millennium and the whole playing-the-field plan. And I've never been very good at covert operations.

Growing up, Ally had this annoying little brother. I guess all little brothers are annoying, but Seymour took the art of annoyance to a whole new level.

Basically, he wanted to be everywhere we were, doing everything we were doing. Even if it involved trying on our mom's bras over our sweaters.

So, we were constantly on a mission to avoid/lose/get rid of Seymour. And I was usually the one that screwed it up. (In my defense, I'm an only child, so I never had to hone my ditching-a-sibling skills.)

One winter day, an unexpected burst of snow paralyzed the city. (Luckily, it only took an inch or two to accomplish this.) I hiked over to Ally's house to go sledding, but no way did we want Mr. Annoying to tag along. So, we devised a plan to meet at the hill at the end of the street. That way I wouldn't have to come to Ally's house, and Seymour wouldn't ask to come along.

Normally, I'd walk down my street, across Henning Creek Rd, and then up Ally's street to her house. But, because of the snow, I wanted to avoid having to walk up the hill. The very hill we were planning on sledding down all day. (Okay, I admit, I wasn't too bright as a kid. Sometime during my high school years, I must have sprouted a new patch of brain cells. Funny, because most of my friends were smoking theirs away.) So, to avoid climbing the icy hill, I went up my street, across Old Henning Creek Rd and down Ally's street. Right past her house. Right past Seymour's face plastered to the front window.

Not my brightest moment. And definitely the day I realized a career in international espionage was probably out.

So, now I'm totally trying to play off the phone call as one of those obnoxious telemarketers, with as little actual lying as possible.

"Those people will hound you any hour of the day."

Nelson grins and laughs. "Hound."

Okay, I didn't intentionally make the pun, but I'm going to roll with it for distraction purposes. Insert fake laugh. "See, I can make a funny too." Oh God, I can hear this in my head and I sound like one of those cardigan-sweater-clad substitute teachers on the afterschool special. Do they still have those? Afterschool specials, not substitute teachers.

"You two are pathetic. It's sad, because you deserve each other." Ally is sitting smack dab in the middle of my desk somewhat blocking my view of Nelson. (It really disturbs me to look through her.) "Which sucks, because I want you to have the hunky guy." Her voice has reached a pitch that only dogs can hear, which might explain Midge's sudden efforts to attack the side of my desk.

Nelson jumps out of his chair, most likely terrified that Midge will try to maul him again. "What's gotten into her?" His voice is shaking just a bit.

I grab Midge by the collar and pull her into my lap. To calm her, I pop a bite of cinnamon roll into her mouth. She's a sucker for people food. Insert second fake laugh of the morning. Man, it's only seven thirty-five. "That was weird, huh?"

He's looking across the street at his shop, and moving toward the door. I feel a bookstore emergency coming on. "You know, I've got so much to do before I open today. I should..." His voice trails off as he looks longingly at a terrier-free space across the street.

"Yeah, I've got loads to do too. But thanks for helping out this morning." My forced cheerfulness sounds like fingernails on a chalkboard to my ears, so I can't imagine what it sounds like to him.

Before Midge can finish chewing her unexpected treat, Nelson is out the door and across the street.

With Nelson across the street from my work, and Jesse down the hall where I live, it seems there will be little peace for my waking hours. I need to meet a guy who lives across town.

Scratch that. I do *not* need to meet any more men.

Chapter Thirteen

My first day of business is not exactly how I pictured it.

As far as the deluge of customers goes, the only reservation I had got pushed back to Wednesday, the phone rang a total of three times (two of those were *actual* solicitors), and the only human interaction I had after Nelson left was the guy who stopped in to see what kinds of dogs I had for sale.

Suffice it to say, I'm bored.

Ally has been MIA since her parting shot at Nelson's nerdiness and even Jesse has stopped calling every hour. So, I'm playing computer solitaire. Funny, but this was nowhere in my business plan.

Even Midge appears to be bored. She has strewn squeaky toys from one end of the space to the other and is lying on the bench in the lobby peering out at the empty street.

What I didn't realize about Belmont is that 90% of the businesses are closed on Mondays. Foot traffic is basically non-existent, and I can count the number of cars that have gone by on one hand. Oh God, I've been counting the number of cars that go by. I think I might cry.

Suddenly I feel an overwhelming need to procure a rare or essential book. Who am I kidding? I need contact with the outside world. Besides, Nelson is probably bored too. I haven't seen anyone enter his shop today. And I've had plenty of time to check.

I'm locking the front door when car number six pulls up in front of my building.

My body responds in a physical way at the sight of Jesse. I hate that he does that to me.

"Hey darlin'! I was hopin' you'd have time for lunch." He holds up a bag of Chinese food. The smells of nuts and spice tickle my empty stomach. I've been avoiding my ramen noodles.

Realizing that I've sucked my gut in, I let out a breath releasing the flab. I will not focus on impressing Jesse. Even so, he doesn't need to know where I had been going. "That's sweet, I was just going to run out and grab something." Unlocking the door, I realize I'm getting better at the lying thing. I'm not sure if I should be proud of that or disgusted with myself.

Jesse follows me inside and I notice that both Midge and Ally are very excited about the new arrival. (Yup, Ally's back. She doesn't miss a moment with Jesse.)

If Ally could roll over at Jesse's feet and have him rub her belly, I have no doubt she'd punt Midge across the room and take her place. My friend is actually preening. Apparently, she's forgotten that not only can Jesse not see her, but he doesn't know she exists.

"That's because you haven't bothered to talk about me. It's as if you don't miss me at all."

How can I miss her when she never leaves?

"So, it's been a busy day?" Jesse is nice enough to phrase this as a question, but he's a smart guy and he probably notices that Midge is the only canine in sight.

I shrug my shoulders and wiggle my hands to indicate that it's been so-so. Maybe lying with my gestures will be more believable than my words.

After a glance around the empty room (save the squeaky toys), Jesse grins and places the bag of food on my desk. "Well, then I'd say you have time for lunch."

No arguing there, mainly because my stomach is a cavernous pit of emptiness. And the fact that I can't lie about an imaginary client when Jesse is in the room. "This was so sweet of you." I dig through the bag for a pair of chopsticks. "I'm sorry if it seems like I've been avoiding you since Saturday." Okay, so that's absolutely what I was doing, but he doesn't need to know that. "I've just been so busy getting ready for today and then I went to see my mom in Asheville yesterday."

He raises his eyebrows in a questioning look, but his mouth is full of cashew chicken.

"It was a last-minute thing." I so do not want to get into that. Just the thought of the whole thing with Harry makes a Kung-Pow shrimp catch in my throat. I focus on Jesse's hands holding the pair of chopsticks. Their sheer size dwarfs the wooden utensils, reducing them to toothpick status. Yet despite the size difference, he's adept at spearing nuts, chicken and even rice.

Having never mastered the art of the sticks, I stab each shrimp with the point of whichever chopstick is closest and avoid the rice altogether.

Three shrimp later, I realize that my efforts at distraction were in vain. Staring at his hands only serves to remind me of the way those hands felt on my back, on my neck, on my face. I'm not sure how long I sit not moving, not eating and certainly not reliving those moments on Saturday night. But when I snap out of it, Jesse is sitting back in his chair, empty carton pushed to the side and chipped tooth peeking out of his parted lips.

For the second time that day I feel my face burn with the heat of embarrassment. Damn these men and their ability to turn up my heat so easily.

His grin grows even wider.

I gesture toward my white and red container. "Spicy stuff."

His head bobs up and down, indicating he believes me, but his eyes tell a different story. Either he has a good read on me, or I'm as transparent as the scotch tape on my desk. Neither bodes well for me.

"So, are you having a busy day at work?" I stuff another shrimp in my mouth, praying that he won't realize what a stupid question it is. How busy can he be if he had time to drive to Belmont to bring me lunch?

"Naw, not too bad." He's kicked his feet up on the edge of my desk and looks a tad too comfy.

I'm trapped. I can't very well fake an emergency with him sitting right here. I will the phone to ring. Why can't Ally be helpful, like say, a poltergeist?

"No way. I'm not getting in the way of this. You need to talk to him about why you were a weenie and ran out on a perfectly nice make-out session." She's been surprisingly quiet since Jesse arrived, taking on the role of a silent observer. Trust me. This is not her normal mode.

I'm not sure how long the silence has stretched between Jesse and me. But he looks content to hang out until I crack. I hate that I'm one of those people who feels the need to fill up awkward silences.

"You know, when I was alive, I always filled up awkward silences with kissing."

Just when I thought my face had returned to its normal shade.

All of a sudden, I feel a ping on my shoulder. A quarter rolls down and rests on top of my left breast. Eyes narrowed; I look across the desk.

Jesse's expression hovers somewhere between mischief and regret. "For your thoughts."

Plucking the coin off my chest, I fling it back at him. "It's a penny."

"No, it's a quarter." He grabs it before it can whiz over his right shoulder. (I have horrible aim.) "Inflation."

Dammit. He's hot and he's witty.

"She's thinking that you're hot and witty." Ally screams, trying to break the sound barrier between herself and the man who doesn't know she exists.

I laugh in spite of myself. He thinks I'm laughing at him. I roll with it. "Okay, give me the quarter back then."

He gently places it in my outstretched hand.

It's a Wyoming quarter. The image of a cowboy on a bucking horse bolsters my confidence to open up to my loafer-wearing, non-horseback riding Texan. Tracing the design with my thumb, I look up at Jesse and try something new. Being honest about my feelings. Out loud.

My legs are shaking so hard, I fear he can feel the motion through the desk. "I was thinking about the other night."

His expression grows serious and he lowers his legs from the desk.

"Dinner was great and afterwards was great, but then—"

The phone rings. Of course. Now that I'm actually dealing with my life. Where are the distractions when I want to avoid things?

Jesse can't hide his disappointment that I've been cut off. He jumps out of his chair and paces to the other side of the room.

By the third ring, I'm calm enough to answer it. "Hound'n Around, this is June."

The man on the phone wants to set up an appointment for daycare. You'd think I'd be thrilled. I mean, I am, but why couldn't he have called when all I had to do was count cars? By the time I finish answering his questions, a woman and her Pomeranian have entered the building and Midge is barking her little brains out trying to get through the fence and to the froufrou dog.

As I'm talking to my second new customer in under ten minutes (yay!), Jesse cleans up our lunch mess and waits near the door, glancing at his watch.

I'm trying to hurry through my "please bring your dog here and give me money" spiel, but the woman has more questions than the SAT. And she keeps glancing nervously at the rabid ball of fur in the kennel behind my desk.

"Midge is so excited to meet your little guy. But it takes time to introduce new dogs, so we'll have to wait until Oscar (de la Renta, I'm not kidding) comes on Thursday."

Appointment set, I finally manage to (politely) shoo the socialite and her puff of fur out the door.

Jesse takes one final glance at his watch and sighs. "Darnit, Junie, I gotta go. There's gonna be a bunch of people in my office in about ten minutes and not much will get done if I'm not there." Not a trace of anger lines his voice, only regret.

"I'm so sorry. I swear this place has been dead all day."

"Don't apologize. It's a good thing." He pulls me into his arms.

I could hide from the world inside his embrace. "Thanks for lunch." I crane my head back and look up at him.

Smiling, he plants a kiss on my forehead. "No problem."

We untangle our bodies and he opens the door. His broad shoulders fill the doorway and I hate how good he looks in his casual suit. No tie, top button on his striped shirt open. Why have I been avoiding him all weekend?

"Dammed if I know. Doesn't make a lick of sense to me." Ally looks set to follow Jesse back to work. I wonder if that's where she's been disappearing to lately. Wonder how he'd feel about a spirit stalker.

Jesse starts toward his car, but turns around. "I got meetings all afternoon and most of the night. But if your lights are on when I get home, I'll stop by. And we can finish our conversation."

Note to self: don't get ready for bed early.

Chapter Fourteen

While my first morning was the definition of slow, my first afternoon was the deluge I dreamed of. A steady stream of phone calls and walk-ins have filled my appointment book for the rest of the week. On Tuesday I'm meeting with a Jack Russell mix, a Basset Hound and a Havanese (I had to look that one up online). Later in the week, I'll meet everything from a twelve-year-old Boxer to a six-week-old Schnoodle. I wonder if Nelson has a book on dog breeds.

The phone's been quiet for almost thirty minutes and I figure people are focusing on what to eat for dinner, so I clean up Midge's mess and get the place ready for the next day.

I'm locking the front door when Nelson hollers at me from the doorway of the bookstore.

Midge and I dart across the street, avoiding the one car that is parked in front of the dry cleaners. Belmont has turned back to the sleepy town from this morning.

"So, how was your first day?" Nelson bends down and greets Midge. He seems to have either forgotten Midge's strange behavior this morning, or forgiven her for it.

I smell the now familiar hint of liver treat as he rises. "It was amazing. I made a whole slew of appointments."

Taking Midge's leash, Nelson leads the way inside his shop. "I thought you looked pretty busy this afternoon."

"Um-hmm." It's the first time I've been inside Nelson Brantley's Rare and Essential Books. The building's façade is deceiving. The small storefront extends much further back than the building I rent, and soars two stories high. Books line every inch of wall space and library ladders are positioned throughout. Sections are clearly marked and meticulously organized. Comfy chairs fill the center of the space and I can smell tea brewing in the back corner.

"June?" Nelson is staring at me, his dimple betraying a hidden grin. Apparently, he asked me a question.

"This is just so..." I don't even know how to finish the sentence. It's nothing like I imagined. I had pictured a cramped space, books piled and strewn in disarray, a musty smell pervading everything. Now I realized that was ridiculous. From what I know about Nelson, his shop would look exactly like this: pristine, orderly and clean.

Nelson leads me to an overstuffed chair and offers me a cup of tea. I'm too distracted to take a sip. He settles into the armchair across from me.

I'm scanning the shelves, searching for what I am now positive I will find.

"Back left corner, third shelf from the bottom, on the right."

How did he do that?

Sure enough, there's a whole section of books on dog breeds. I take several down and return to my chair.

When I drew up my business plan, I did some cursory research on dogs in general, but primarily I was going on my limited knowledge from watching Westminster with Ally's family growing up. Well, that, and the almost habitual viewing of *101 Dalmatians* and *Lady and the Tramp*.

I can feel Nelson's eyes on me. Occasionally his spoon taps the side of his cup, but otherwise it's completely quiet inside the shop. It's unnerving really. Maybe I should suggest some background music. You know, nothing too distracting, just something with a little beat.

Selecting the book I'm going to spend my last pennies on, I look up and catch him staring. He doesn't look away or seem embarrassed.

Nelson finishes his tea and carefully sets the cup on the table beside his chair. Crossing the space between us, he reaches out his hand. In one fluid motion, he pulls me to my feet and kisses me.

Now this kiss is a far cry from my hasty peck near his mouth Friday night. This kiss is firm, certain even, and melts me clear to my toes. Nelson isn't a big guy, but he holds me firmly, despite my melting.

When he releases me, I sink back into the chair. Honestly, I can't support myself in that moment.

He doesn't say a word, just gathers up the books I've left on the floor and returns them to their proper location. Then he slips the book I've chosen from my hands and moves to the front counter where he carefully wraps it in paper and slides it into a bag.

My breathing begins to return to normal and my legs un-jello-fy themselves. I stand, and then look around for my dog. She is curled up; sound asleep, in the corner of a loveseat. I hate to disturb her, but my brain is complete mush and I need to get out of the store before I say something to completely ruin the moment.

Clearly unhappy to be disturbed, Midge glares at me as I attach her leash and drag her from the couch.

Nelson's sitting casually behind his desk, flipping through some papers. He's looking down, but I can see the smile on his face.

How can he just sit there and not say anything? And damned if I know what the heck to say.

I offer my business check card, but he shoos it away and places the bag in my hand. I mumble something that I hope resembles "thanks" and flee the shop.

"Ally. Where the hell are you?" She's never around when I actually need her. "Ally!" I hate the pleading in my voice, but I really need to talk this mess out with someone. Granted, Ally may not be the best choice for relationship advice, but she's all I've got at the moment.

I grip the steering wheel tighter to keep my hands from shaking. My gut twists with anxiety and an ache spreads up toward my chest. One benefit of my self-induced stomachache is I won't be able to eat my dinner of—you guessed it—ramen noodles. Hopefully by the end of the week I'll have enough money to go buy some real food.

"Just keep playing your cards like this and you'll never have to buy another meal again." As usual, Ally appears in her own sweet time and with her own warped opinions.

"I can't keep dating both of them. It's too confusing."

"Not confusing—exciting!"

This much excitement could kill a person.

"You're not gonna die from a couple hot kisses."

"No, I'm going to die from the stress-induced heart attack." The muscles in my forearms are starting to protest my tight grasp on the steering wheel.

Ally jabs the A/C button and a cool blast of air attempts to penetrate the heat creeping up my neck. "Junie, chill out." She's a riot, huh? "I don't understand what you're so stressed out about."

No, she wouldn't understand. In Ally's short life, she had no shortage of guys fawning over her, and typically dated as many of them as she could fit into her busy social schedule. It wasn't until just before her death that she had settled on the jerk. But a three-week relationship can't be defined as monogamous. "Ally, I'm twenty-eight years old." Something else she'll never understand. "I want to find one person to spend the rest of my life with. I'm ready to settle down, start a family. I can't do that if I'm dating two guys."

'Then why'd you go out with both of them in the first place?"

Why indeed? To prove to Ally that I could? To prove it to myself? Believe me, I never imagined that I would end up liking them both, and certainly not that they would both like me.

I pull into my apartment complex. I can see Jesse's door from where I park. 14C. The fake brass numbers taunt me. Jesse wants to finish our conversation. How am I supposed to explain anything to him when I can't explain it to myself?

"He's not home yet anyway."

How does she do that?

Ally laughs. "I'm not teleporting through his door or anything. I just don't see his car."

A snort of laughter erupts from my mouth (or maybe my nose?). The pressure recedes from my chest and I can breathe normal again. Maybe I am getting too worked up over all this. It's just a couple of kisses. It's not like I agreed to marry either of them. Not that anyone's asked.

"Are you gonna sit in the car all night?" Ally is standing outside my window, tapping the glass with her knuckles. With one hand perched on her slender hip, she looks bored.

Midge precedes me out the door, and strains toward a patch of grass.

Her business taken care of; she heads up the steps to the apartment. I may not be able to take action, but between my dog and my dead best friend, at least I'll make it home.

Chapter Fifteen

I'm sitting in my living room, ramen noodles congealing on the coffee table in front of me. I've turned the light on and off about a dozen times.

Rising from my indentation on the sofa, I flick the switch off once again.

"You better leave that light on, missy!"

Missy? Who's the adult here? I flip the switch back to the on position to find Ally sitting cross-legged on the console table behind the couch, a la *I Dream of Jeanie.* Luckily for me she has yet to master electricity with the mere nod of her head or twitch of her nose. Believe me, she's tried.

"I don't think I'm ready to face Jesse tonight."

"You were ready to talk to him this afternoon."

I squint at the clock on the microwave and flick the light switch off again. "But that was before Nelson kissed me."

"Technically that doesn't change what you would say to Jesse." The light turns on again, and Ally is standing right in front of me.

"Actually," plunging the room into darkness, "it changes everything."

I feel her hand brush mine, but I tighten my hold on the switch. "No, it doesn't. It's just a convenient excuse to avoid confronting your feelings about Jesse."

Whoa. When did Ally earn her PhD in Psychology? Do they have college in heaven?

My inquiry into her extra-June life is interrupted by a knock at the door.

"June Bug? You up?" Jesse knocks again. "I saw the light flickerin'. Is everything alright?"

I bring my hand up to cover my eyes and Ally turns the light back on. Damn. Now he knows I'm here. Taking a deep breath and glaring at my ever-helpful friend, I open the door, plastering a smile on my face. "Jesse. Hey."

"Somethin' wrong with your lights?"

"Huh? Oh, must be a short or something." In hopes of distracting him from my little fib, I steer him toward the couch. "How was work? It's too bad you had to stay so late."

He waves his hand dismissively. "No big deal. I'm just glad you're still up. So we can talk."

It's only eight-fifteen. Awkward silence ensues.

Ally attempts to fill it. "Just tell him you're hot for him."

I can't begin to refute everything that is wrong with her suggestion. Especially with Jesse in the room.

"Or, if you aren't sure what to say, just jump him."

Well, that's much more helpful.

Okay, I should say something. "This afternoon got really busy."

He looks relieved. "Yeah? That's great."

"I made a bunch of appointments for the rest of the week."

"It's gonna be a great business, Junie." His voice lowers on my name and he moves closer to me.

My instinct is to move away, but my back is already glued to the arm of the couch. There's nowhere else to go.

He's going to kiss me. And while I fear it will only confuse me further, at least I won't have to talk about my feelings.

Jesse cups the back of my head and leans in. He is both tender and forceful. No, that's the wrong word. Confident, maybe?

I might enjoy it more if I wasn't comparing it to Nelson's kiss. How can I not? After all, the kisses are only separated by a span of a few hours.

Both kisses make me weak (in a good way). Because this one is taking place on the couch, at least I don't have to worry about falling down.

Both kisses make my mind go gooey and my belly knot with anxiety.

Is kissing supposed to be this stressful?

He's settling into the embrace, but I am far too distracted to hold on for much longer.

When his lips migrate to my neck, I grab the opportunity. "Jesse?"

"Yeah?" His reply is muffled. And he's doing this delightful nibble-thing to my ear.

Reluctantly, I press both hands lightly against his hard chest.

"I knew his chest would be hard." Ally is practically on top of us.

"Jesse," I press more firmly, moving him off of me. "I think we should talk." While I know this is the rational thing to do, my ear is still tingling and I'm not even sure what I'm going to say.

He straightens up, looking a little stunned and as flushed as I feel. "Aw man, I've screwed it up again, haven't I? I'm sorry, Junie, I—"

"No Jesse, honestly, it's okay." I gently rub my ear, trying to cease the distracting tickle. "It's really nice, in fact."

His body visibly relaxes and he grins. "Yeah, it was."

I struggle to gather my scattered thoughts and emotions and make sense of them.

"Do not tell him about Nelson."

Get out of my head, Ally.

She plops down on the couch between us. "Don't screw this up, Junie. You don't even know who you like better. Do you want to risk losing Jesse when he could be the one?"

I hate it when she's right. Leaning forward, I attempt to make eye contact with Jesse. It's hard with a dead best friend in the way. "Jesse, about this weekend. I guess it freaked me out that we were moving so fast." Completely true, if not the complete truth.

Jesse reaches across the couch and takes my hands. I try not to notice that Ally still sits between us. "June Bug, I didn't mean to scare you. That's the last thing I'd wanna do. I really care about you. We can go as slow as you need to."

"Seriously, Junie. What more could you ask for? He's hot, he's smart and he's sensitive. DO HIM ALREADY!" Another tender moment shattered by my insightful friend.

"Thanks for understanding, Jesse."

He tugs on my hands and pulls me toward him. Luckily Ally has the sense to move. Settling under his outstretched arm, I cuddle up to him and try to relax. I feel his lips on the top of my head and his hand swirls a lazy pattern on my shoulder.

Midge hops up on the couch and inserts her compact body in the sliver of space remaining between Jesse and me.

Closing my eyes, I try not to think about the eventual decision I will have to make. For now, I'm determined to block out Ally's fervent speech on the joys of foreplay and enjoy the moment.

Chapter Sixteen

Juggling two men is exhausting. Especially when combined with running a new business.

My typical day consists of getting up way earlier than I would normally choose to, dragging a sleeping Midge to the car and arriving at work by seven-thirty. Yes, AM. My first customer of the day is usually greeted by a half-comatose, generally-unhappy-before-ten woman disguised as a cheerful, pleasant doggie daycare owner. The coffee pot brews continuously.

From seven-thirty until nine-thirty, I check in dogs (of which I typically have five to six a day—not bad for my second week). Ten o'clock is breakfast time for the dogs, who like Midge, weren't awake in time to eat it at home. I, on the other hand, have been eating breakfast since I sleep-walked out of bed.

Then I take the dogs, two or three at a time, down to the park for a brisk walk and any "business" they might need to attend to. I'm considering stock in the pet-waste-baggie company.

My favorite time of the day comes after the walks. This is when we all go into the largest play area and let loose. Tennis balls, squeaky toys, and bubbles come out and we play to our hearts' content. One o'clock heralds lunch for me and naps for the pooches. And even though I would love to join them in a quick snooze, this is my chance to return phone calls and set up appointments for new dogs. I try to meet with new customers in the afternoons, after everyone has expended most of their energy for the day. Of course, there's another walk in there and maybe a snack or two. The dogs, not me, I swear.

By five, dogs are being picked up and I'm gathering stuffing and discovering hidden "presents". Hound'n Around officially closes at 7:30, but I lock the door as soon as the last tail goes through it.

Exhausted, I either flop in my comfy chair (which I did not remove from the lobby as suggested by the evil Dr. Walton) or I head across the street to Nelson's comfy chair and a cup of tea.

The sign on the door of Nelson Brantley's Rare and Essential Books says that the store closes at 6pm, but his new closing time now appears to be whenever I show up. I honestly can't figure out how the man makes a living, because I see maybe two people wander through the shop on any given day, and several of those leave empty-handed. Luckily, I don't have much time for random thinking or I'm sure I would come up with some convoluted theory about an underground ring of first-edition book smugglers.

Okay, so maybe I've thought about it a little.

I rarely eat dinner alone these days, and I absolutely do not eat ramen noodles. Damn if Ally's "prophecy" didn't come true. Jesse and I tend to order in and curl up on the couch to catch whatever trashy reality TV is on that night. The nights I eat with Nelson are always an adventure. If it's exotic, we've probably eaten it. In his travels to procure rare books, Nelson has sampled the world's fare and loves it all. I, on the other hand, liked the first place he took me (a tame Japanese place where I tried sushi for the first time) and since then have practiced my polite smiling. Midge loves our forays to new restaurants, because invariably it means leftovers amounting to most of my meal.

Tonight is a Nelson night and I'm dreading the new food I will have to sample. If I wasn't so hungry at the end of these long days and I didn't enjoy Nelson's company so much, I'd probably sneak to my car and pick up a pizza on the way home. But I am, and I do, so I head across the street to take my evening nap in his comfy chair.

I'm surprised to find not one, but two customers browsing when I enter the store. Nelson is hunkered down behind his computer, tracing his finger along a row of numbers. He looks up briefly and smiles, but his attention is drawn back to the glowing screen. Relieved to postpone the taste adventure, I fix myself a cup of tea and settle into my chair to wait.

I'm just starting to doze a bit when I hear a tiny trill of laughter. Peering one eye open, I see one of the customers, a petite woman in her thirties, leaning across the counter, one patent leather pump in the air. As both eyes come fully open, I witness the vixen reach out and stroke Nelson's arm with her perfectly manicured hand. Looking down at my own bent and broken nails, I realize it's been months since I had the time, money or inclination for any sort of pampering.

When I look back up, Nelson's dimple has appeared and he's leaning toward the brazen hussy, no doubt peering straight down her low-cut silk blouse. Another trill of laughter and I'm out of my chair. Indignant, I march across the room, ready to have a showdown with little-miss-trim-and-fit. About three steps from my target, I realize that I have no claim on Nelson. He has every right to flirt with whomever he wishes. To go out with anyone he pleases.

I quickly divert my path to the left and end up in the men's fitness section. Flipping through a book on prostate health, I listen to the click, click of heels and the tickle of the bell over the door. Replacing the book, I migrate back toward my chair, hoping against hope that Nelson didn't witness my little tantrum.

The other customer, a man in his late fifties, makes a purchase and leaves the store.

I sink into the chair, trying to be an inconspicuous as possible.

Nelson locks the door and begins his routine of closing down the register and straightening up the counter. He doesn't say a word. Which is bad, because usually Nelson is quite the talker.

He completes his tasks and then heads straight for me. A smile is pulling at his lips, but he doesn't let it completely loose. Still not speaking, he plants a kiss on my forehead and picks up my empty cup. I swivel in the chair to watch his progress to the back of the store where he rinses the cup out and places it on a rack to dry.

"So, we're a little jealous, huh?" I can hear the laughter in his voice and I can't say I'm too happy about it.

I face forward in the chair, arms folded across my chest. I can do silence too.

My face is flushed and I'm trying hard to hold a scowl, but when Nelson's arms circle me from behind, I give up and lean into him.

"You," he plants a kiss on my neck, "have absolutely nothing to worry about."

I can't help but feel relieved and hypocritical at the same time. Here I am dating two men, and *I'm* jealous? And there's the teensy little fact that neither of them knows about the other. Well, I mean, they've met, and they know I know the other one, but they don't know I *know* the other one. Like *know* in the way of kissing on a regular basis.

"Junie's a player!" Thanks Ally, like I need more guilt.

Ignoring Ally, who is spinning around the room, singing a song about me sitting in a tree with two guys, I tilt my head back and grin at Nelson.

He traces his finger along the line of my chin and down my neck. Tingles follow his touch all the way down. As he leans in to kiss me, his hand migrates further down my collarbone to my chest. Holy crap, Nelson just grabbed my boob.

"Hell yeah, he did! That was awesome!" It's like I have my own little cheering section, only she's not rooting for the same thing as me.

I shift in the seat, trying not to draw attention to my evasion. I manage to turn and face him, kneeling on the chair, never breaking the kiss. Which conveniently positions his hands on my back. A nice safe place.

Somehow the idea of a new, and possibly disgusting, ethnic food adventure sounds delightful compared to the stress of avoiding Nelson's roaming hands or continued talk of my jealousy. Not that I have a problem with a little groping, but the closer I get to these guys, the more confused I become.

I've given both of them the I-want-to-take-things-slow-my-life-is-really-com-plicated-right-now speech and thus far they have been extremely respectful of it. Jesse seems especially sensitive to "offen'ing" me.

Pulling away from Nelson's embrace, I slide out of the chair and to my feet. "I'm starved. Where are we going tonight?" Maybe he'll believe my enthusiasm is for the upcoming culinary delight.

"Oh, there's a great new Cajun place in Uptown. The crawfish are amazing." He leads the way to the door, turning out lights along the way.

Crawfish? Can't get much further down the evolutionary chain than a fish that crawls. Yum. Patting my purse, I feel my trusty orange Tic-Tacs. The flavor can conquer most any offensive taste. Well, those and a strong beer.

Chapter Seventeen

Saturdays are for sleeping in, padding around in my jammies until noon, and the absence of responsibility or stress.

So, when the knocking begins at ten, I can't say I'm feeling especially charitable toward the perpetrator of my ire. The racket continues, despite my attempt to ignore said individual. Jesse has been explicitly instructed to call first on the weekends, and certainly never before lunch (well, breakfast for me, lunch for strange people who wake up at a normal hour). So, when I finally drag myself out of bed and into the living room, I may not be awake, but my annoyance has reached maximum capacity.

Wrenching open the door, I have no regard for my safety, appearance or friendly reputation. The unsuspecting salesman I assume to encounter on the other side is going to get a sales tip from me. And it won't be in the form of a motivational speech.

Only I'm not fortunate enough to be visited by the Oreck guy, or even a bicycle-wielding Jehovah's witness. On my doorstep, standing right on my "Wipe Your Paws" welcome mat, is none other than Helen Hinderson. And her vertically-challenged friend, Harry.

Now, my mother has been to my apartment approximately two times. I say approximately, because the last visit lasted exactly three minutes.

"Sweetheart, it's so good to see you. Are you doing something different with your hair?" My mother looked distractedly around the living room, her eyes settling on the towel on my head.

I pulled my robe tightly across my chest. "No Mom, I just got out of the shower."

"So you did." I hadn't seen my mom look this nervous since she had to give a luncheon for a visiting missionary.

"What's up, Mom?" I didn't address the obvious.

Her hands continued to flutter around her throat, grappling with the strand of pearls there. "I'm sorry I didn't call first, but I felt like I had to talk to you about this dog thing."

Ah, the unannounced, two-hour trip suddenly made sense.

"Your cousin Kendra tells me you're going to quit your job. You have to have a job."

I had expected this. Which is why I didn't bother telling her about my plans for the daycare. Kendra was officially on my hit list. "I will have a job, Mom. I'll be running the daycare."

"A daycare? For dogs?" She started pacing, which made Midge so nervous she began to growl. "First you tell me that your dead friend is communicating with you somehow and now this. Honestly June, I'm worried about you."

Before she started discussing the benefits of mental health drugs (which she became a little too familiar with after Dad's death), I pushed Mom to the door and scooped up Midge to calm her. "Mom, we're going to have to discuss this later, because I have to get ready for work." And I needed a few more paychecks from copy hell before I gave my notice.

Seeing her here now, two months later, unannounced yet again, and this time wielding a middle-aged man in a cardigan, doesn't do anything for my already altered mood.

"Mom? What are you doing here?"

Gripping at her pearls, my mother looks from Harry to me and back again, a smile clearly plastered on her anxious face. "Well, honey, Harry and I just decided to take a trip down here, you know—spur of the moment. I thought about calling before we left, but I didn't wait to wake you, sweetie." Despite her angst, she manages to shoot a disapproving look at my appearance, or the fact that I was still sleeping, or both.

Her use of the sappy endearments signals trouble. Words like "sweetie" and "muffin" only come out when my mother wants something. Suddenly the image of Harry and my mother planning a day trip to Charlotte over their morning prune juice and bran muffins invades my consciousness.

"I told you Ma was getting more action than you." Ally has appeared at the possibility of drama unfolding. "Shouldn't you invite them in?"

I'm getting hostess advice from a girl whose parties used to consist of spin the bottle and beer stolen from her father's stash in the garage.

I start to close the door. "Maybe you guys can stop back by on your way out of town."

At this my mother steps through the doorway and grabs me by the arm, guiding me away from the door. "June. I have never known you to be so rude. And in front of my friend." Her voice is a whisper, but the forcefulness of it surprises me.

I can't think of any way out of this, so I plaster my mother's smile onto my face and go back to the door to invite Harry in. "I'm just going to jump in the shower, but please make yourself comfortable."

Jesse chooses that moment to jog by my front door. "June Bug! You're up."

It seems Jesse has some kind of sixth sense about catching me in my pjs, bed head and all. My mother has returned to the door and is eyeing my neighbor with a mixture of fascination and fear. After all, Jesse's a big, manly guy, and he's not wearing much on this warm summer morning. I can't focus on how good he looks in his running shorts and no shirt though, because I'm dreading the fact that I now have to introduce my mother, and her "friend," to (one of) my half-naked boyfriend(s).

"What a great morning!" Ally is rubbing her hands together and grinning like the Cheshire cat. "It's like a matinee!"

I'm so glad someone is enjoying themselves. A girl shouldn't have to go through this before her shower and at least a Pop-Tart. Everyone is looking at me expectantly, so I suppose it would be noticed if I slammed the door and hid in my closet. Breathing in deeply, and almost choking on my morning breath, I decide to get it over with so I can flee to my toothbrush and a bar of soap as quickly as possible.

"Mom, this is my neighbor Jesse. Jesse, this is my mom and, um, Harry." I barely know Harry, so I don't feel qualified to properly introduce him, but honestly, I don't want to know how my mother would.

"He's her sex monkey."

Can you choke a dead person?

As I return my attention to the conversation between the real people, I hear my mother invite Jesse to lunch with us. I will Jesse to say no, but apparently only Ally can read my mind, because he agrees so fast my mother is squealing in delight before I can interject. Not only do I have to spend the day with my mother and a strange man, but now I get to be grilled about and in front of Jesse. I had such big plans for today. Plans to do absolutely nothing. If I had moved like I wanted to a few weeks ago, this never would have happened; because you can be assured, I wouldn't have sent my mother a change of address card.

"You need to have a work emergency." I'm cuddled up next to Jesse in the backseat of Harry's station wagon. Yes, the man drives a station wagon. Faux wood paneling and all.

Jesse drapes his arm around my shoulders and gives me a squeeze. I feel his hot breath in my ear as he whispers. "No way. I'm excited about meetin' your ma. Parents like me."

Oh, I have no doubt that my mom will like Jesse. My concern is that she will be planning our wedding before the salads arrive.

"Oh, Harry, look how cute they are back there, snuggling." My mother has reached across a center console the size of a small lake to squeeze Harry's wooly-brown arm.

I can see his grip tighten on the steering wheel. Apparently, my mom's death lock on his arm is threatening his ten and two positioning. "Yes, Helen."

These two have gotten way too comfortable if he's already pulling out the pacifying-not-paying-attention phrases like, "Yes, dear."

"Oo, June. Isn't that the exit for that sweet little town you opened your business in?"

It's a mile to the exit. Maybe I can stall.

She begins furiously patting Harry's right shoulder. "We have to go see June's little business. You simply must exit, Harry."

Must. Find. Excuse. Must not go to Belmont. "Um, Mom, it's really busy there on the weekends, we'll never be able to find a parking place. We should go straight to the restaurant."

"Nonsense. We're right here."

I hear the turn signal ticking to the beat of the pounding in my temples. Why the sudden interest in my "little business?" All I can hope for is that Belmont actually is busy on this Saturday. Especially Nelson's store.

Chapter Eighteen

Belmont looks like a ghost town. If ghost towns had cheery flower baskets hanging from every other light post.

Jesse gives directions to Hound'n Around as I sit sulking against the window. When Harry turns onto my street, my heart stops and a groan escapes my lips.

"Look how cute this is. And look at that young man sweeping the sidewalk. So fastidious." My mother is practically clapping at the sight of Nelson's OSD (Obsessive Sweeping Disorder).

Harry pulls into a blank space in front of my building. Luckily there isn't a car on the entire block, because I wasn't sure how he was going to manage parking this boat.

"Look, Junie, it's that book guy." Jesse is leaning across me to point out the window.

If I close my eyes, I can go back to sleep.

Before I know what's happening, I'm in the middle of the street with my mother, Jesse, Nelson, Harry, and of course, Ally, who is so excited she's doing cartwheels.

As introductions are made all around, I keep eyeing Nelson's broom, in the hopes that he won't see the need to use it as a weapon.

My mother is tittering on about how proud she is of her little girl. Harry's arm is perched on her shoulders. I'm nauseous. Jesse repositions himself between Nelson and I. Nelson is eyeing me with a look that clearly says, "What the hell is he doing here?" And Ally continues to dance around us singing about "Sweet Dreams." (We were children of the nineties, but we always preferred classic 80s tunes.)

Before I realize what's happening, my mother is inviting Nelson to join us for lunch. Seriously, did God wake up today and say, "What's the worst thing I can do to June Hinderson?"

"Sure. I can close up shop for an hour or two." Nelson makes a move toward his building.

I duck past Jesse and chase after Nelson. "You can't close your store in the middle of a Saturday. What about all of your customers?"

"I haven't seen a soul all day. The weather's too nice, I guess." He flips the sign to "Closed" and locks the door. Leaning toward me, he lowers his voice, "Besides, I'm excited about meeting your mother. But what is your neighbor doing here?"

Shrugging my shoulders, I hold back a whimper. I think I might cry.

After a cursory glance inside Hound'n Around, we pile back into the time machine. Now I have the pleasure of sitting between Jesse and Nelson. On the hump. Which is quite fitting, metaphorically.

I glance nervously between them, careful not to move my head. As long as no one speaks, this might be okay.

"It's a Junie sandwich." Ally is in the way back, arms perched on the back on my seat. "I feel like I'm dreaming."

I wonder when I will awake from this nightmare.

We pull into the parking lot of R.J. Gator's. My mother turns to face the backseat. "Harry found out about this place on the Inter Web. It looks like so much fun."

"Mom, it's the Inter*net*."

"Oh, so have you been on their e-mail before?"

I bite my tongue and let it go. Technology and my mother parted ways when we got our first computer.

We pile out of the car and head for the front door. Jesse reaches out to put his arm around me at the same time that Nelson grabs for my hand.

"Mom!" I shoot forward to catch up with my mother, and escape the dilemma behind me. I don't dare look back. "Did Harry tell you they actually serve alligator here?"

Her hand flies to her chest. "Goodness, no. He told me it was a seafood grill." She shoots an accusatory look at Harry.

I almost feel sorry for setting him up like that, but I needed the distraction.

While the hostess finds a table for us, Harry speaks to my mother in a soothing tone. He caps off his appeasement with a kiss that's a little too long for my comfort level.

Between my mother kissing well, anyone, and Nelson and Jesse talking like they're old friends, my stress-free day has turned into an anxiety-fest. I can feel the cortisol piling up in my stomach. My chest is tight, my head is still pounding, and I'm pretty sure those are pains shooting down my left arm.

"And you call me a drama queen. Pah-lease." Ally has found a perch in the rowboat that is mounted to the wall above our table.

The south Florida décor of the restaurant, combined with the smell of fish from the next table, is making me feel seasick. The spinning in my head isn't helping either.

My mom is keeping up a running litany of questions for both Nelson and Jesse, but she's restrained herself from asking if they prefer a cummerbund or a vest.

Harry and I sit quietly, him, I assume because he's fallen asleep with his eyes open, me, because it appears my tongue has frozen to the roof of my mouth.

"So, do either of you boys have a girlfriend?"

I'm ready to fake a heart attack if the real thing doesn't happen when the waitress shows up. Jesse and Nelson look equally confused, but neither comment as Stella, our Everglades Guide, takes our order. I will personally see to a generous tip if my Mango Mojito arrives within thirty seconds.

My apparent alcoholism distracts my mother enough to keep her from repeating her question. "It's barely noon, June."

I thought I was doing well to not order a Cherry Cheesecake Martini too.

Searching for a diversion, I settle on the only innocuous person at the table. "Harry," he startles a bit, proving my theory correct. "What do you do for a living?" Anything to keep my mother from going back to her previous question.

"Well, I retired about a year ago. But before that I managed a hardware store."

Her hand is back on his arm. "That's how we met. I went into the store to buy some ant poison." She turns to me. "You know how bad the ants are in the spring, June."

Getting rid of the ants was a project I helped my dad with every spring. I'd cut up a piece of cardboard into little squares and he'd pour the Torro onto each one; then let me place them around the kitchen. He called me his "little exterm-ant-ator."

"Harry is very handy. He's helped out so much around the house."

Returning to the present, I realize this means they have been dating for over a year. And keeping it from me. I can't begin to process it, because my mother has turned back to the young men across the table from her. My young men. Both of them.

"So, tell me—"

"Mom! Did I tell you that Kendra lost five more pounds?" I may be reaching a bit.

Our appetizers and my Mango Mojito arrive in time to save me from telling her about Uncle Larry's ingrown toenail.

Mom won't even allow the Alligator Tail on her side of the table. Compared to some of the foods I've tried with Nelson the past two weeks, it's quite tasty. Especially when chased with Mango Mojito. I'm feeling much better by the time my second drink arrives. I avoid my mother's dirty look.

Somehow, we make it through the entire meal with me interrupting my mother's attempts to completely ruin my life. Nelson and Jesse don't look very happy with me, but they're a little blurry anyway after the Key Lime Martini I had for dessert.

The car is surprisingly silent on the way back to Belmont to drop Nelson off. Bumping on the hump is not mixing well with my multiple liquors and fried meal. Me getting sick all over both of my boyfriends would certainly top the day off.

I practically push Nelson out the door when we pull up in front of his bookstore. I can't risk him attempting to kiss me goodbye.

Thrilled to move to a concave seat and to let down my guard about the boyfriends finding out about each other, I relax against the window on the way home. Jesse is watching me intently, but is respectful enough not to grill me about Nelson in front of my mother, and her "friend."

After we arrive back at the apartment complex, I shoo Jesse to his abode, claiming I need to spend some quality time with my mother. It's like having to choose between Chinese water torture and electric shock. But I can't risk my mother and Jesse together for another instant.

When Harry, Mom and I return to my apartment, Midge insists on taking a walk, so Harry turns on the baseball game while my mother and I head outside.

"Honey, you're probably wondering why we came all the way down here today."

Uh, yeah.

She struggles to keep up with me as Midge pulls toward her favorite spot, a dogwood tree near the dumpster. "Well, first of all, I want you to know that I'm sorry I wasn't more supportive of your business."

Reason #1: Guilt.

"Secondly, we haven't really had a chance to talk about Harry, and I need to know that you're okay with me dating someone."

Reason #2: Approval.

Her hand flies back up to her neck and begins fidgeting with her necklace. This one must be a humdinger. "Harry and I are going to take a trip." She turns to face me. "To Europe. For a month."

Reason #3: Undetermined.

"And we were wondering if you could take care of his little dog, Roxie."

Reason #3: ~~Undetermined.~~ Babysitting.

Well, this certainly explains the sudden interest in my business, and the sugar-coated endearments.

Chapter Nineteen

Monday morning my mother and Harry arrive at Hound'n Around before I can get all the lights turned on. Exactly what time did they leave Asheville?

Turns out they've been planning this trip for months now and my mother just couldn't get up the nerve to tell me. Since I didn't even know Harry existed two weeks ago, it stands to reason that I may have been a little shocked.

They are meeting their tour group at the airport at nine and Harry is "worried about the crazy Charlotte traffic." So, they leave the fattest dachshund ever in my care and hurry out in a flurry of "love you, June, sweetie" and "make sure you feed Roxie three times a day."

Roxie should be the size of a cocktail wiener, but in reality, she's a kielbasa. I decide to feed her once a day and walk her three times. If her toothpick legs can keep up.

Dog care aside, I'm quite happy my mother is leaving the country. At least I don't have to worry about her getting in the middle of my complicated dating life for a few weeks.

After lunch on Saturday, I spent the rest of the weekend holed up in my apartment ignoring both of my phones and the knocking on my door. I'm hoping that if I avoid Jesse and Nelson long enough, they will forget about the group date and my mother's strange questions.

As I'm checking Leo, a spaniel mix, in, I spot Nelson pull to the curb in front of his building. I attempt to engage Leo's owner in a conversation about the tropical storm in Haiti, but she's in a hurry to get to work. I quickly grab for the phone, but it's not on the receiver where it belongs. When I look back up, Nelson is already at my door. Drat. Why can't I put things back where they go?

"Nelson. Hi. Let me get this dog settled and I'll be right with you." I release Leo into a play area with Koby, a small black dog resembling Yoda, and Mazzy, a Jack Russell Terrier that jumps up and down constantly, as if she has her own personal trampoline. Luckily, she doesn't jump *over* things. I'm starting to understand what Dr. Walton meant when she said my fencing should be taller.

I may be fussing with the dogs a little more than necessary, and I might be encouraging Midge to have one of her barking fits by moving her to a kennel adjacent to Wilbur, a mournful bloodhound who howls uncontrollably.

Nelson waits patiently by my desk while I check that all the dogs have water (he doesn't need to know I just filled the bowls six minutes ago) and mop up an area where Chester, the hundred-pound lab, peed last Friday.

I'm running out of things to pretend to do.

"I tried to call you this weekend," Nelson shouts over Wilbur and Midge's duet.

I almost feign that I can't hear, but I don't think I can bear to have him repeat the statement. I work my way back to the front, hushing Midge along the way. She settles into a low whine. "Yeah, I was out all day Sunday, and I forgot my cell phone." I guess I'm back to lying.

"I enjoyed meeting your mother on Saturday. But I'm confused about why that guy was there. And why was your mother asking all of those strange questions? Does she not know we're dating?"

"Well, Harry is this guy that my mother has apparently been dating for like a year and didn't even bother to tell me about. So, obviously we don't discuss our social lives much."

Nelson narrows him eyes at me. "I wasn't talking about Harry. I was talking about your neighbor. Jason?"

"It's Jesse. He just kind of jogged by as we were leaving for lunch, and Mom invited him." Kind of like we just happened to run into you and ask you along.

"Well, it was almost like she was trying to set the two of you up or something. I kept waiting for you to tell her that you're taken." At this, he grabs my waist and pulls me toward him.

I have never been happier to see the obnoxious barking Quincy walk in. I run over to enthusiastically greet the Westie and his owner. This dog is even more reactive than Midge, but he's super cute and I need the business. His arrival begins a steady stream of drop-offs and after the fourth dog shows up, Nelson gives a wave and disappears. Thank goodness for a busy Monday.

Monday nights are for pizza from Brixx and Bachelor reruns. Jesse shows up at my door at eight, pizza in hand, and as much I want to continue avoiding him, the aroma of savory garlic and tomato win me over.

I allow myself to be briefly smothered in Jesse's embrace, but it's hard to enjoy when I know it will be followed by questions. Maybe tonight would be a good opportunity to practice Ally's avoidance-of-all-things-serious-by-kissing ploy.

But when Jesse sets the pizza box in the dining room instead of on the coffee table, I know he's not in the mood for cuddling.

"So, lunch on Saturday was a little weird."

I set two plates on the table. "Yeah, alligator. Who knew?"

He opens the box and stream rushes up to burn my already overheated face. "I wasn't talking about the food, June."

He almost never calls me June. And he never pronounces his "g"s.

"What was up with your mom's questions? Have you not told her about us?" He's removed a slice from the box, but is making no move to bite into it.

I cut a bite off the end of my piece and blow on it. "I don't really talk to my mom about the guys I date."

"Guys?" He shoves half the piece in his mouth and stares at me while he chews.

"You're not the first guy I've ever gone out with, Jesse."

After a long drag on his root beer, Jesse places the bottle carefully on the corner of the placemat. "What was Nelson doing there, June?"

"I don't know. Mom invited him." I quickly cram a too-large bite into my mouth, the cheese burning the sensitive area behind my top teeth.

His first slice devoured; Jesse rises from his chair. "I saw the way he looked at you, Junie." He leans down and cups my face in his hands. "Like he wants you."

My chewing grinds to a halt as I wonder if he can see straight through me. Do I look as guilty as I feel?

"I can't do it anymore. Did you see the look on his face?" I'm laid across the bed, head buried in my pillow, but I know Ally can hear me.

"So, you break up with Nelson."

I wish it was that simple.

"Do not tell me you are in love with that book geek."

I roll onto my back and find her standing over me, arms laced across her chest. "I don't know. I really like them both, but Nelson does make more sense to me."

Ally rolls her eyes. "He doesn't make a lick of sense to me. Always rambling on about what some dead guy meant when he wrote some book like a million years ago. Seriously, it's weird how obsessed he is with dead people."

How can I argue with that? Ally never spent much time with her studies in high school and never understood the fascination I had with learning once I reached college. The intelligent exchange of ideas would be a tad over her head.

"Are you calling me stupid?"

I have got to find a way to get her out of my mind.

She cocks her head and grins. "Good luck with that."

"Aargh!" I jump off the mattress and head into the bathroom to get ready for bed. While Nelson does seem like the logical choice, I love my time with Jesse, just hanging out and being goofy. And the food is definitely better. Besides, he lives two doors down, so it would be awkward to see him all the time if we broke up.

"So, you keep dating them both. Easy as pie." Ally is balancing on the edge of the tub, like a tightrope walker. Apparently if she had lived, she would have joined the circus.

"It may seem easy from your perspective, but for someone who doesn't want to hurt either of them, it's not so simple."

"They're big boys, they can handle it. Guys date more than one woman all the time."

"I don't have a problem with dating them both—it's the keeping-it-a-secret part that's getting to be an issue." I flip the light off as I leave the bathroom, and Ally trails behind me.

She flops onto the bed, right where she knows I was headed. Propping herself up on one elbow, she picks at a loose thread on my pillowcase. "You know, if you really want to know how to decide between them, you're going to have to break that silly no-sex-until-marriage rule. A girl can't truly decide until she gets to test drive the car. Vroom, vroom." She pumps imaginary handlebars.

I refuse to argue with her about cars, motorcycles or sex this late at night. Besides, I don't know anything about two of those things.

Chapter Twenty

Wracked with indecision, I spend the next week in a holding pattern. Work, dinner with Nelson, work, dinner and TV with Jesse.

During the day, I manage to let the stress go and just enjoy my time with the dogs. There is truly nothing more therapeutic than playing with dogs all day. Business continues to be brisk, so much so that I may need to hire help soon. My business plan didn't account for that for another five months. Funny how so much of my life lately has been off course with my plans.

Evenings are another story entirely.

The moment I lock the door at Hound'n Around, my shoulders tighten up, my heart rate quickens and my stomach rolls in agony. Nothing calms me. Not Nelson's comfy chair and chamomile tea. Not a slice of greasy pizza and two hours of reality TV.

I spend each evening in fear that one or both of the guys will put the pieces together and figure out what I've been up to. And that when it's all said and done, I'll be alone. Without either great guy.

It's like two adorable puppies have followed me home and while I thought I could keep both of them and love them equally, I've realized that they are growing at an alarming rate and pretty soon I will only have room for one.

My work is starting to affect the way I think.

On Tuesday I find myself with an unusual free evening. Nelson's grandfather has summoned the entire family to the country estate for a special dinner. It appears that my book smuggling theory may not be correct. Turns out Nelson's family is loaded. His grandfather was some sort of diplomat who traveled the world and made wise investments. The bookstore was Nelson's present after earning his graduate degree.

Delighted to have a stress-free night to myself, I pick up Chinese and a movie on my way home. I'm going to relax with Moo Shu Pork and Matt Damon.

Jason Bourne is tracking a sniper and I'm cracking open my fortune cookie when I hear music. The sound is muffled, but it almost sounds like "The Way You Look Tonight." There's a loud explosion on the screen, and when the sound dies down, I no longer hear the music.

A few minutes later, I feel a sensation underneath me. Like the couch is vibrating, and I didn't even insert a quarter. Hitting pause on the DVD player, I jump off the couch and lift the cushion to find Jesse's phone doing a little dance along the springs. I figure he's calling the phone to figure out where it is, so I flip the phone over to find a text message on the lock screen.

Flight lands @ 9:07. Can't wait to see you baby.

I lower the phone and find Ally leaning over my shoulder. "Looks like you're not the only one with a little something on the side."

"You can't break up with him because he's seeing someone else, Junie. That is so hypocritical." Ally has been raving like this all morning. There's been a steady stream of customers, so I haven't had the time or privacy to argue with her.

But drop-off appears to have slowed down, so I risk answering her. "I am not breaking up with him because he is seeing someone else. I only want to be dating one person. Now I know he'll be able to handle it."

"I can't believe you're choosing that weenie Nelson. I'll never understand you." With a flourish of her hands, she's gone. She's been practicing that Endora bit for the last week. Apparently, they show *Bewitched* reruns in Heaven.

Last night was a whirlwind of emotions. After seeing the text, I was so upset I couldn't even finish watching Jason Bourne outsmart the CIA. Before long I realized that I had no right to be upset with Jesse, so then I felt bad about betraying him. After a long, restless night, I finally realized that this was the sign I had been waiting for. This was my chance to break up with one of them without feeling guilty.

Now I feel relieved. And a little sad. I certainly don't fault Jesse for seeing someone else, but I'm really going to miss him and our time together. I've never had so much fun mocking reality show contestants. It's not nearly as enjoyable when you're alone. We'd especially been looking forward to the new season starting in the fall.

But it's definitely for the best. As much as I like both of them, the stress of keeping them apart is starting to wear on me. It's gotten to the point where I can't enjoy myself at all.

So, tonight while we're watching *America Idol*, I plan to tell him that I've chosen Nelson.

Well, I probably won't word it that way. Gosh, I guess I should plan what I'm going to say. I don't want it to sound like it was a contest.

It's two o'clock and I'm walking my second set of dogs when my cell phone rings. It is not easy to get a cell phone out of your pocket when you have four leashes tangled around your legs. I didn't count on having this many dogs so soon. It takes me almost two hours to walk them all.

I finally manage to get the phone up to my ear, but it's stopped ringing. Jesse's name flashes on the screen, but before I can call him back, a voicemail message pops up. I press play.

"Hey, June Bug. I hate to do this, but somethin' came up last minute and I'm not gonna be able to make fun of awful singers with you tonight. Maybe we can watch people eat bugs tomorrow night? Call me."

While I'm listening to the message, another one comes into my inbox. I press play again.

"And thanks a ton for droppin' off my phone this mornin'. It felt like my right arm was missin'. Later."

Apparently, the little hussy's flight is coming in tonight and he had to blow me off to meet her. But I'm fine with it. Honestly.

It will give me time to get back to Matt Damon. I kind of left him hanging last night.

It's an hour later and I'm on my last group of dogs. My phone rings again and when I reach for it, Wilbur's leash slips through my fingers. Luckily, I've let go of the slowest dog in the history of the planet. He walks maybe two steps, sticks his nose to the ground and seems content to smell the bushes for the rest of the day. I drag Moe and Curly, a pair of retrievers, toward the sniffing hound. Retrieving his leash, I tap my phone to see who called.

The screen flashes Nelson's number at the store. I decide to stop by on my way back.

The dogs complete their business and we head back, Moe and Curly straining ahead, and Wilbur being dragged behind. I'm afraid he's going to get road burn on his snout.

Stopping outside the bookstore, I tap on the window; then indicate the three reasons I'm not coming inside. These boys will lift their leg on anything that doesn't move.

Nelson steps out the front door, but keeps his distance from me and the stooges. Wilbur is still the full length of his leash behind me.

"Sorry I couldn't answer when you called. I was tied up." I nod my head at the dogs, who have lived up to their reputation and are watering the nearby mailbox and lamp post.

"No problem." He backs a little further away from Moe, who is straining to reach him. "I felt bad about having to cancel on you last night, so I wanted to see if you were free to grab a bite tonight."

So much for me and Matt. "Sure, I can do that. I'll head over after everyone leaves."

"Well bring an appetite, because there's a new Moroccan place on South Blvd. I hear they have belly dancers."

I'm pretty sure Moroccan food is eaten on the floor, with your hands. And we get to watch some woman shake her hips the whole night. "Sounds great."

I cross the street back to my building yearning for a hamburger and cheese fries. The next time we go out, I'm going to suggest the pub down the street. I smell yummy grease every time I walk by there.

Chapter Twenty-One

I'm seated on a red satin pillow, sandwiched between Nelson and a large, somewhat exuberant woman. The restaurant only seats parties of eight or more, so we have been included in what can only be described as an eating support group. There are seven of them, all well over three hundred pounds, all voraciously attacking the bowls of meat and rice set out before us. The meal is served family-style, with everyone dipping their hands into shared serving bowls.

I can't tell you what the food's like, because I'm terrified to reach my hand into the mix, lest it be mistaken for a chicken leg.

Nelson seems oblivious to the feeding frenzy around us and is happily sampling food from the various bowls set out on the tablecloth. Notice I said tablecloth, not table.

Add some clanging, twinkling music and a ninety-pound woman covered in bells, who shakes like a Chihuahua confronted by a Great Dane, and you've got dinner.

After I break up with Jesse and only eat meals with Nelson, I'm going to waste away to nothing. Maybe I can find an all-night Chinese and pizza place.

The group has been relatively quiet, save slurping and chewing, but the bowls are nearing empty and the natives are getting restless. The hairy, sweaty guy across the breadbasket from me starts in on how the portion sizes aren't big enough. Seriously, the bowls are bigger than Nico, the Newfoundland's, food bowl. Luckily, the waitress appears with what can only be described as a feeding trough and pronounces it the third course. How many courses does this meal have?

The woman to my right leans toward the trough, her left breast squishing out from her under her arm and creeping toward me like the blob. I lean closer to Nelson. Doesn't she have control of those things?

"Hey, isn't this great?" He wraps his arm around me and I scoot as close as possible.

Keeping one eye on the wayward boob, I squeeze in even closer. "It's definitely an experience." Is he in the same restaurant?

Wiping his mouth with a napkin, he readjusts on his pillow. Probably to unstick me from his side. "So, do you have any plans this weekend?"

Well, if I break up with Jesse tomorrow, then probably not. "No, not really."

"My family is going down to the beach house first thing Saturday morning. For the holiday."

Holiday? I strain to recall what holiday I'm missing. I vaguely remember fireworks from earlier in the summer, so it's not the Fourth of July. And it's not cold enough to be Halloween. What other holiday is there?

"You are going to close the daycare for Labor Day, aren't you?"

Labor Day. Of course. Is that considered a holiday? "I hadn't thought about it."

Leaning closer, Nelson nibbles on my ear. I can smell pork on his breath. It almost makes me hungry. "You've got to come. I've told them all about you. Mother is especially excited."

Suddenly the overbearing smells, and noise, and seven-person eating contest is too much. I've got to get out of here. "Sure, that sounds good. Listen, I've got to go, I'm not feeling too hot." Before Nelson can answer, I jump off my pillow and flee the eating frenzy.

The next day I call Jesse to confirm our *Survivor* and burrito date. I spend naptime making notes and practicing my break-up speech. The wastebasket is overflowing with rejects. Mostly sure of my decision, I head out as soon as the last dog leaves.

When I arrive home, the parking lot is unusually full and I am forced to park two buildings away. As I'm trying to get out of the car, juggling my accounting binder, several trade magazines and my laptop, Midge darts out of the front seat and takes off after an orange tabby cat. Quickly stuffing everything back into my car, I slam the door and chase after my crazy dog.

Dusk is beginning to settle, but I can just make out Midge's purple leash fluttering behind her as she darts between cars and medians and an unusual number of VW buses. What is this, a Phish reunion?

Up ahead I see the cat dart up Midge's favorite tree and my beast slows down to jump and bark and carry on. I slow my steps as well, figuring she's not moving from her target, but am watching the scene before me when my left foot hits something hard and I go down.

Pain is rocketing through my foot and up my leg as I lay scratched and bruised on the asphalt. I crane my neck back to see the culprit—a concrete parking stop. As I lay there cursing all things concrete, Midge tires of her hunt and trots over to me. Sniffing my head and neck, she barks once; then licks my nose. She's probably wondering why I spend so much time laying on the ground.

After a few minutes, she bores of me as well, and starts to take off toward our building, but with my last bit of energy, I manage to grab her leash and hold tight.

I struggle several times to rise, but even sitting up is difficult. I have never felt such concentrated pain. Besides, it feels kind of nice to just lay here. Surely someone will see me between this SUV and this minivan.

Darkness falls and I'm still lying on the ground. Midge alternately sleeps and barks, most likely out of frustration at being restrained. She may also want her dinner. Me too.

I'm just about to drift off to sleep when I hear my name being called in the distance. Midge strains at her leash and lets out a stream of canine, "Help! Save me! My leash is stuck on this woman's hand!"

The sound gets closer and I realize its Jesse's voice. He's looking for me. He probably has my burrito.

My eyes are closed against the pain, but I feel strong arms lift me and soothing kisses along my face. I curl into his solid chest and succumb to sleep.

What is that awful pain in my foot?

I snuggle deeper into the covers, trying to ignore the throbbing. I can see flashes of the night before: Midge, chasing the cat; me, falling to the asphalt; Jesse rescuing me. I think I remember the emergency room, doctors, Jesse eating a burrito.

Oh crap. I shoot up in bed, nearly paralyzed by the agony of moving my foot so suddenly. The daycare. Frantic, I look at the clock. It's after ten.

As I attempt to swing my legs out of the bed, I see a note propped up on my nightstand. In Jesse's neat script, it says simply, "June Bug." He's even drawn a small, spotted beetle.

My heart rate slows considerably as I read the note. Not only did this wonderful man save me from the parking lot, take me to the hospital, bring me home and put me to bed, but he took the day off work to run my business.

SWEET JUNIE,

I HOPE YOU'RE FEELING BETTER TODAY. THE DOCTOR SAID YOU WERE LUCKY AND IT'S ONLY A SPRAIN. BUT YOU SEEMED TO BE IN A LOT OF PAIN, SO THEY PRESCRIBED YOU SOME PRETTY INTENSE PAIN KILLERS. DON'T WORRY ABOUT MIDGE, OR THE DAY-CARE. I TOOK YOUR KEYS AND WILL TAKE CARE OF EVERYTHING. CALL ME THERE WHEN YOU WAKE UP. MY ASSISTANT IS GOING TO BRING YOU SOME LUNCH.

LOVE, JESSE

Love? These pain meds must be distorting my vision. Reading back over the note I realize that his actions show exactly that. Love.

Double crap. I made the wrong decision. I chose the wrong guy. Wait. I haven't broken up with Jesse yet. I never had the chance to. Wahoo!

"Good. Now you can break up with the book weenie." Ally drapes her body across the end of my bed.

"Nice of you to show up in my time of need."

She flips her hair. "I knew Jesse would take care of you. The man *I* chose for you."

As much as I hate it when Ally's right, I guess I should end it with Nelson. But I'm supposed to meet his family this weekend.

"Seems to me you can't traipse off to the beach with your foot all out of whack."

Also true. She's on a roll. "Yeah, I should probably call him and let him know."

"And tell him you found a real man."

Chapter Twenty-Two

After I check in with Jesse and arrange for lunch, I dial the bookstore. Please let the machine pick up.

"Nelson Brantley's Rare and Essential Books, this is Nelson." No such luck.

"Hey, Nelson. It's June."

"June! Are you alright? That Justin fellow told me you sprained your ankle."

I bite down my irritation. I've told him Jesse's name plenty of times. "Yeah, I'm pretty much stuck in bed. That's why I called. I won't be able to make it to the beach this weekend."

He doesn't answer for a full sixty seconds. I'm beginning to think the connection has been lost. "You're not coming."

"I'm sorry, but I wouldn't be able to get around."

His voice takes on an edge that I didn't know Nelson possessed. "It's not even broken. I told my family you were coming, June."

Why is he acting like this? It's not like I don't have a valid reason for canceling. "Nelson, surely you understand that I hurt myself."

"This is because of that John guy, isn't it? That's why he's at the daycare."

"This has nothing to do with Jesse." My voice rises to an angry shout. "I sprained my ankle. I'm on Percocet for gosh sake."

Silence answers my angry cry.

"I'm sorry I yelled. I guess the drugs are affecting my mood." Why am I the one apologizing?

"No, I'm sorry, June. I don't know why I feel so threatened by your neighbor. I guess it's because I think he has a thing for you. It kills me to know he's the one who found you last night. The one who rescued you. It should have been me."

I have never felt smaller than I do at this moment. "Listen Nelson, when you get back from the beach, we need to talk."

"Did something happen between the two of you last night?"

How did I get myself into this mess again? "Sort of. Let's talk more next week."

"No, I'll come over tonight. Bring you dinner. I'll stay home this weekend. Take care of you."

"Nelson, that's really sweet, but you should go to the beach like you planned. My cousin's coming in tonight to stay with me for a while. Until I'm back on my feet."

When he speaks again, his tone is distant. "Yeah, okay. Next week."

My stomach churns in agony as I end the call. I'm still clutching the phone when I hear an unfamiliar voice call out my name.

Jesse's assistant is an attractive, middle-aged woman who immediately starts telling me about her husband and three kids. At least I don't have to worry about an inter-office romance.

She brings my lunch into the bedroom, straightens up my sheets, and asks if there is anything else I need.

Um, to travel back in time and *not* date two guys at once? "No, I'm fine, thanks."

I hear her banging around in the kitchen for a few minutes before she calls out that she's leaving. Then I'm alone again. Alone with my misery. Somehow, I don't think the Percocet can help the pain I'm feeling.

Around five o'clock my cousin, Kendra, shows up.

"What in the world have you done darlin'?" Kendra is as southern as biscuits and gravy. Turns out she's quite fond of eating them as well. She settles her ample frame on my bed, causing me to roll in her direction.

I've just awoken from a drug-induced sleep, so I'm a little fuzzy about the events of the last few hours. "I was chasing Midge and I tripped."

She throws back her head in a fit of laughter. "I'm not talkin' about your foot, June. I'm talkin' about the sexy man who answered your phone down at the daycare."

Abruptly I'm reminded of the misery unrelated to my ankle. "That's Jesse. He's my neighbor."

"Oh, honey, he is *definitely* more than just a neighbor. That man has got it bad for you." Kendra speaks in a rolling lilt, stretching her words out and using pauses like they are seasoning.

I feel a flush rush into my cheeks.

"Oo, looks like he's not the only one with a problem." She pokes my shoulder with a bright pink nail.

"Oh goody, Delta Burke is here." Ally appears on the other side of the bed.

Nodding in that direction, I address Kendra. "Ally says hi."

A shadow briefly crosses my cousin's face, but she quickly covers it up with a smile. "Always good to hear from the beyond."

Kendra is the only person who knows about Ally and actually believes me. My sophomore year of high school, Kendra came to live with us because her parents were in Africa doing missions work. A year older than Ally and I, Kendra regaled us with stories of college boys and antics her parents would have been appalled of. The three of us got pretty close that year, until the spring dance, when Ally's boyfriend asked Kendra to go. Things were tense that summer, but Kendra returned to Raleigh in the fall and Ally dropped the rivalry.

When I told Kendra that Ally had appeared to me, her exact words were, "doesn't surprise me a bit. That girl wouldn't wanna miss a thing."

"Tell her how I introduced you to Jesse."

"That's not exactly what happened, Ally."

Kendra draws her legs up on the bed, getting comfortable. "What tall tale is that girl spinning this time?"

"She says she introduced me to Jesse."

"Jesse's the one with the yummy baritone?"

"Tell her how hot he is!"

"Ally says to tell you he's hot."

Kendra sweeps a nonexistent hair from her forehead. With all the hairspray my cousin uses, she could be the primary cause of the hole in the ozone. "Honey, you don't need to tell me that. The man oozes sexuality."

Gosh, I hope Jesse wasn't oozing sexuality to Kendra. Or anyone else for that matter.

"Kendra, I've gotten myself into quite a pickle."

"Looks like you're sittin' pretty to me, darlin'. Got that man so whipped, he's down there runnin' your business."

I flop back on my pillows. "It's a tad more complicated than that."

"Yeah K, she's got two men. Well, if you can count that book weenie."

I shoot a glare in Ally's direction before turning back to Kendra. "I'm kind of seeing someone besides Jesse."

Kendra narrows her eyes. "Besides, or in addition to?"

As usual, my cousin zeros right in on the problem. "In addition to."

"Two men at once. Wow, June. When it rains it pours. How long'd that last drought go on for?"

Ally pipes up. "Three years. Pathetic if you ask me."

"Well, no one did. Stop ganging up on me."

Kendra jerks her thumb in Ally's direction. "That girl actually agreein' with me? Well, tickle my britches."

Hands over her ears, Ally jumps off the bed. "Make it stop. I feel like I'm stuck in *Fried Green Tomatoes*."

Kendra's sappy Southern speech wears on me a bit too. "Kendra, do you mind getting me a glass of water? I feel like I've got cotton mouth."

"Sure thing, but don't you gals talk about me while I'm gone." She poses in the doorway. "Unless you're talkin' about my new, trimmer figure." Kendra saunters out of the room.

"Why you'd have to call her? Jesse could have taken care of you."

Briefly, I wonder if I don't agree with her. But southern fried or not, I love my cousin, and I'm glad she's here.

Chapter Twenty-Three

Kendra fixes me a dinner of grilled cheese and sliced tomatoes and while I'm waiting for Jesse, I find myself drifting off. Darn Percocet.

When I awake, it's dark outside. I struggle into a sitting position and fumble with the lamp on the nightstand. It's a little after one, and the apartment is quiet, so I imagine Kendra is in bed. It's too late to call Jesse, but I'm anxious to know how the day went—and to thank him profusely.

Once again, I'm dying for a glass of water, but the drop in the tumbler on my nightstand doesn't quench my thirst. Pulling myself out of bed, I cling to the wall, dragging my lame foot behind me. I'm doing alright for myself until Midge hears me and starts dancing around my feet. I make the mistake of bending over to pet her, and down I go—taking a framed picture with me.

Kendra comes rushing out of the spare bedroom, hair perfectly coifed, closing her robe around her. Ally's right, she does belong in that movie.

"Honey, what are you doin' out of bed?" She carefully pulls me to my feet and helps me limp to the couch.

I sink into the cushions gratefully, happy to be out of bed. "I'm sorry to wake you. I needed some water."

Kendra flitters into the kitchen, pouring me a glass from the water pitcher in the refrigerator. "The dreamboat came by, but you were asleep. He's even yummier in person."

"Did he say how things went?"She hands me the glass and retrieves a note from the console table just inside the front door.

This letter is a far cry from the love note of this morning. The outside bears a scribbled "June."

I HANDLED EVERYTHING AT THE DAYCARE TODAY. THERE WERE 12 DOGS. I'M RETURNING YOUR KEYS. LET ME KNOW IF YOU NEED ANYTHING

JESSE

"Did he *say* anything?" I look up at Kendra, hoping she can fill me in on the expansive gap between the two notes.

"Not much, although he seemed relieved that you were asleep, which I thought was a bit odd. What's the note say?"

I hand her the paper, numb with disbelief. What happened? Did Nelson say something to Jesse? Does he regret helping me out?

Kendra looks up from the note. "Maybe it was just a long day. He seemed tired."

"Yeah, maybe that's it." But I'm not convinced. Something is very wrong.

Another pain pill allows me to sleep through my anxiety and the rest of the night. Saturday dawns bright and clear. Not that I see it dawn or anything, but it's nice at ten when I wake up.

Kendra is making French toast, which she knows is my favorite. I've spent the night on the couch, so it's the smell that rouses me. Not a bad way to wake up.

I try Jesse's cell before I take the first bite, but it goes straight to voicemail. Figuring he's out running, I leave a message, hoping I sound upbeat. "Hey Jesse. You really saved my butt yesterday, oh, and the night before. Thanks so much. Call me."

By twelve-thirty, I'm ready to drag myself down the hall to his apartment.

"Now honey, you don't want to seem desperate." Kendra is making lunch, although we've barely finished breakfast. No wonder she's a size 16.

"I just need to know that everything's okay."

She comes into the living room and squeezes me from behind. "Of course everything's okay. You're an amazing woman, and he'd be a fool not to see that."

I'm spinning my cell phone in my hand when I remember the text message. "It's her."

"Her who? Is Ally here?" Kendra looks around the room.

"No, her the hussy." I explain about finding Jesse's phone and my decision to break up with him. And my decision to not break up with him.

"So, let me get this straight. You figure he's got a little something on the side, so you're gonna break up with him and go for Nelson, who you've got on the side. But then, Jesse pulls a knight-in-shining-armor move and so you decide to break up with Nelson and stay with Jesse. But you can't break up with Nelson because you're stuck at home and he's on a beach trip with his family, that you were supposed to go on, and now Jesse's actin' like he's got a carrot up his ass and you don't know why."

"Basically."

"Girl, you got a mess."

I hang my head. "Thanks, I wasn't aware of that."

Sunday is more of the same: Kendra feeding me continuously and Jesse ignoring my calls. At least the pain in my foot is receding, or I'm becoming dependent on pain meds.

I have Kendra retrieve my laptop and accounting binder from my car, where I shoved it before the falling-down-debacle in the parking lot. Sitting out on the balcony, I catch up on my books and crunch the numbers since Hound'n Around opened. If business stays this steady, I can definitely afford to hire some part-time help. And being crippled, I can definitely use some.

When Kendra returns from checking on Roxie, the rotund dachshund, she's got a sly smile on her face.

"What are you up to?"

She purses her lips together and raises her penciled eyebrows. "Nothin'."

I close my computer. "Kendra..."

"You ready for some supper?" She makes a move toward the kitchen.

"Kendra, it's only four o'clock. No, I am not ready for supper."

Unable to cook, Kendra looks lost. She cracks. "I met Nelson."

"Nelson's at the beach."

She shakes her head vigorously, dangled earrings slamming into her cheeks. "Not so much."

I point at the chair next to me, indicating that she should plant it. "What was he doing?"

"Well, I was comin' out the door of the daycare with little Roxie—my goodness isn't that just the cutest little thing you've ever seen?"

"Kendra, focus."

"Yes, well, so I was comin' out the door and this skinny fella is comin' out of the bookstore and I figure it's Sunday and besides, Nelson's at the beach, right? So just who is this? So, I 'too-ta-lee-do' and head across the street."

The image of shapely Kendra, dragging the portly Roxie across the street to meet Nelson is too much to bear. A giggle bubbles up and escapes my lips.

Kendra scowls briefly. "Now you hush, June." She taps my leg in mock punishment. "Anywho, so I said, 'Is the bookstore open today?' And he says, 'No, sorry.' And looks down at Roxie and back up at me and says, 'Do you know June?' I slapped him on the shoulder, which nearly knocked him down—June you should feed that boy more, honestly."

If she only knew just how much Nelson eats. Of course, maybe if he ate real food like pizza and hamburgers, he would beef up a bit.

"Anyway, I knock him on the shoulder and say, 'Of course I know June! She's my cousin, silly!' And then he looks like his mama just died, because his eyes get this faraway look in 'em and he's bitin' his lip. Goodness, girl, what did you do to that poor boy?"

Kendra takes a rare breath and I figure I better interject while I can. "I told you, Kendra, he thinks there's something going on with me and Jesse."

"Which there is."

"Well, yeah." At least, I hope.

She looks out over the commons area. I can tell she's avoiding my eyes.

"Kendra, is there something else?"

She doesn't look at me right away. "That Nelson's a sweet boy, June."

Flopping my head backwards, I stare up at the balcony above mine. "I know, K."

"Good!" She jumps out of her chair and steps back into the living room. "'Cuz he's comin' here for dinner tonight."

Chapter Twenty-Four

I haven't showered since the accident, so Kendra helps me wobble into the bathroom and I'm able to clean away the grime of being homebound. She offers to "do up" my hair and "put on" my face, but I decline and push her out of the bathroom. I refuse to see Nelson, or anyone for that matter, looking like a poofed and teased Julia Roberts.

It's almost six when the doorbell rings. I'm still in my bedroom, because Kendra hasn't helped me waddle out yet, so I strain to hear what's being said.

For once, Kendra is speaking at a normal decibel, so I can't hear a word of it. Frustrated to be missing out, I reach across to the dresser and pull myself over to the door. I've just gotten it open when Kendra comes flying down the hall, ducks inside and slams the door shut again.

"Now, sweetie, you can't be tryin' to get around on your own. Remember what happened Friday night?" She leads me back to the bed.

"Kendra, I'm ready. Let's go to the living room." She seems to be in even more of a tizzy than usual. Maybe she inhaled too much Extra Hold.

My cousin perches on the edge of the bed and places her hands on mine. She's making me nervous. "Now, honey. I don't want you to freak out..." She pauses as if trying to ratchet up the tension.

Well, that's a real effective approach to keep me from freaking out.

"...but Jesse's in the living room."

I don't have time to freak out about that, because the doorbell rings again, and now I'm freaking out about Nelson and Jesse being here at the same time.

"Well, crap." Kendra rises calmly from the bed and leaves the room.

Sprained ankle, or no sprained ankle, I am not staying in here. I jerk off the bed, and fling myself toward the open doorway. I've completely miscalculated the strength of my ankle, because I immediately crumple to the floor in a heap of agony. I may have screamed something vulgar.

Within moments, Jesse, Nelson and Kendra appear in the hallway. I'd say there's a good chance, I did, in fact, scream.

The three of them rush the doorway, creating a massive jam. It's not a huge space to begin with, but with the width of Jesse's shoulders, the breadth of Kendra's hips and the, the...oh crap, they've squished Nelson.

After untangling from the mass, Jesse reaches me first and without a word, scoops me tenderly into his arms.

Normally I would be extremely comfortable here, but at this moment it's impossible because of the look on Nelson's face. He turns to leave.

My dear, sweet cousin—God bless her—grabs that poor boy by the elbow and he boomerangs back toward her. "Oh no, honey. You're not goin' nowhere."

Caught in Kendra's grasp, Nelson has no choice but to follow her back into the living room. Jesse and I bring up the rear. He settles me on the couch, propping my throbbing ankle up on his lap.

For a solid five minutes, no one speaks.

The oven timer dings and Kendra's face explodes in a smile. "Appetizers!" She vaults out of the chair, and into the kitchen. Within moments she returns with an arrangement of fried stuff on a platter. She's obviously decided to personally take on the task of fattening Nelson up.

When no one makes a move toward the platter—well, except for Midge, but it's at her level—Kendra scowls and begins handing out plates laden with food.

If we're eating, we don't have to talk, so I bite into a greasy mozzarella stick. Slowly, the others join in and soon we're all chewing in unison. No, this isn't awkward at all.

Neither of the guys will meet my eyes and I'm beginning to wonder how Jesse ended up here. Did Kendra purposely invite him too? If so, I need to remember to kill her later.

"Well, isn't this quite the little party? Thanks for inviting me, Junie." Ally doesn't look happy to have missed out on the action, but honestly, when would I have found the time to summon her? Not that she ever shows up when I want her to anyway.

Soon, we've run out of appetizers and the guys have gone back to darting their eyes around the room.

"Somebody talk already! Better yet, just kick some book-weenie butt, Jesse." Ally is bounding around the room pumping her fists as if she's boxing.

I roll my eyes.

Kendra must see my look of frustration. "So, June, have you talked to Ally lately?"

"Yeah, just a bit ago." This has always been our code when there are others in the room.

Jesse leans forward slightly. "Who's Ally? You've mentioned her before."

Kendra jumps in to save me. "Oh, June and that girl have been friends since they were wee high." She gestures with her hands.

"Really? Does she live around here?" He's absently stroking my feet now, truly intent on the conversation. Which is odd, and ticklish.

I speak up before Kendra can get me in trouble. "No, but she visits a lot."

"Funny that I've never met her." Jesse's finally looking me in the eye, but now I don't want him to.

Nelson pops into the conversation. "Yeah, me neither."

The guys exchange a look that might precede a duel.

Kendra titters from across the room, drawing the attention in her direction. Thanks, K. "Well, the girl is a bit flaky, so she just kind of pops in and out randomly."

"Flaky? I'm flaky? I'm not the one who decided I didn't like my perfectly nice boyfriend anymore, because I wanted my cousin's best friend's!"

Okay, apparently Ally still holds a grudge about the spring dance.

Jesse looks back at me. "Well, regardless, I'd like to meet her. If she's important to Junie—"

"Hold on a second." Nelson rises from his chair. "I think there's something more important to address here than some friend who may or may not exist."

On the one hand, I'm glad the conversation is moving away from Ally, but on the other hand, I don't think I like where it is heading any better. And it totally freaks me out that Nelson is questioning whether or not Ally exists. That's just weird.

Jesse's hands cease their movement over my feet. He folds his arms across his chest in a defensive posture. "Yeah, okay."

Damn, why did they have to notice the elephant in the room? I tried to dress him so he would blend in. "Kendra? Didn't I hear the timer go off?"

"Junie, it's time to deal with this." Jesse reaches across my lap and takes my hands.

Nelson doesn't look happy and moves to sit on the coffee table, where he reaches out and places a hand on my knee.

I feel like my world has come crashing down on me and I'm suffocating. I send a soundless plea across the room to Kendra, who has apparently been stunned into a rare silence.

Nodding once, she springs into action. "Okay boys, back off. Give the woman some space." She steps bravely into the middle of our love triangle and shoos the guys away from me.

"J-E-S-S-E! J-E-S-S-E!" Ally is campaigning from her spot on the dining room table.

The guys are arguing with one another and with Kendra, but everything is running together. I bury my head in my hands, unable to bear the chaos.

"Look what you're doing to her." I glance up and Kendra is pressing the guys apart, although they don't look ready to come to blows.

The room goes silent, except for Ally, but I've trained myself to ignore her. The guys take their seats again and everyone looks at me.

"Kendra, can you please get me a pain pill and some water?" She nods and takes off down the hall. I look at Nelson and then Jesse and try to address them both, which forces me to repeatedly turn my head from side to side. It's making me dizzy. "I've created a mess and I intend to deal with it. But can I have until after we eat? Maybe by then my foot won't hurt so bad and I'll have a little clarity about what I want to say. Is that okay?"

"Yeah, sorry Junie."

"Of course."

Kendra returns with my pill and I gratefully swig it down with the water. I inform her of the plan to eat before we talk and she sets about getting dinner on the table. Nelson reaches out to help me off the couch, and Jesse respectfully allows him to assist me. Throughout dinner, everyone is quite civil.

Kendra has outdone herself. I didn't realize my kitchen could be used to create such a meal. The most I've ever gotten out of it is a macaroni and cheese casserole.

She's prepared fried chicken (without any help from the Colonel), mashed potatoes (with the lumps still in so you know they're real) and gravy, and three different kinds of vegetables. Made-from-scratch biscuits round out the feast. Kendra keeps the conversation safe by talking about her job as a Mary Kay representative and her travels as the child of missionary parents. She and Nelson could have a passport contest.

After dinner, Jesse carries me back to the couch and the guys settle in chairs opposite me. Kendra offers to give us some privacy and takes Midge out for a walk.

All through dinner I've been planning and debating and praying. And since the earth hasn't swallowed me whole yet, I guess I've got to do this.

Chapter Twenty-Five

"**I**'ve been dreaming of opening this daycare for years. So, I had a plan. To focus on the business for the next year—no distractions." I look up from my lap at these two amazing guys sitting across from me. "Then I met Jesse." Distraction #1. "And I thought, 'we'll just be friends,' but well..." I turn to Nelson. "And then, like three days later, I met you. And you rescued me." Distraction #2. "And you're so smart, and witty and it's nice to have someone who understands running a new business."

Turning back to Jesse, I continue. "And Jesse, you're so sweet and the time we spend together is so easy, so comfortable."

Tears are building up in my eyes, but I try to contain them. "Before I knew it, I was dating both of you. And really liked both of you. And I couldn't choose."

"But you did choose." I hear a catch in Jesse's voice.

Confused, I look toward him.

"I found the notes at the daycare. You chose him." He tilts his head in Nelson's direction.

I cover my face with my hands and try to wipe the tears without being obvious. "I saw the text on your phone." There's no anger in my voice, only sadness.

He looks momentarily perplexed; then his face falls. "Junie, that was my mom. She was just stoppin' over on her way to New York."

Feeling like a fool, I stop fighting the tears. "I figured it'd be easier, because you had someone else. But then, the way you took care of me—of everything—after I fell, I knew I couldn't *not* choose you."

Nelson's been quiet the whole time, but I haven't forgotten about him. "I really did want to go this weekend, to meet your family, Nelson. But this foot..." I nod my head at my ankle, wrapped and still throbbing despite the Percocet, which is starting to make me sleepy.

"No, of course. I had no right to get upset over it, June. It wasn't the weekend—it was realizing that I had to worry about losing you."

"I'm so sorry I kept it from both of you." Between the emotion of the situation and the effects of a pretty serious pain killer, I've completely lost it. I'm sure my tears have destroyed the little make-up I had applied, and snot is pouring from my nose. The heaving sobs soon give way to hiccups that shake my whole body. Jesse and Nelson leave their chairs and flank either side of me.

Jesse smoothes my hair back from my face. "Junie, calm down. It's not so bad. We'll figure it out."

Nelson wipes my face with a tissue and strokes my back. "Yeah, sweetie. It's not the end of the world."

"Now you've got 'em right where you want 'em." Ally is standing directly in front of me with a calculating look on her face. In that moment, I realize she doesn't get me at all.

I wake up, snug in my bed, and try to remember the evening before.

Before any grand resolution could be made, I floated off in a medicated haze. I'm not even sure how I ended up in my jammies in bed. But there's a box of tissues on the nightstand, so I know Kendra had some part in it. Hopefully the jammie part.

As I'm trying to ease of out bed and test my foot, Ally pops into the room. "You fell asleep on me before we could talk about what happened last night."

"Percocet will do that to you sometimes." Placing my foot flat on the ground, I apply a little pressure. Not too bad.

"Well, you may not remember, little-miss-stoner, but you did not break up with the book weenie."

The pain in my ankle is nothing compared to my pain in the ass, who is now sitting atop my dresser. "Don't call him that. His name is Nelson."

She flops her hand through the air as if to say, "Whatever."

"Seriously, Ally. I don't know what I'm going to do yet, but I might end up with him—and I will not have you calling him the book weenie for the rest of eternity."

Ally holds her hands up in mock surrender. "Okay, okay. Nelson." Turning her wrist, she begins to examine her nails. "I'm just glad you're not going to end up alone. I was starting to wonder..."

"Wonder what?" My tone may be getting combative—and loud—because Kendra shows up at the door.

"Everything okay in here?"

I jerk my thumb at the dresser.

Kendra sighs and stares at the top of the dresser as if she can see Ally herself. "Ally dear, why do you have to give our June such a hard time?" She turns to me. "She never did treat you quite right. Almost as if she was just keeping you around to make her feel better about herself."

"Oh please. I'm not the one who constantly tried to get you to curl your hair or wear more make-up. That was Tammy Faye's job." Ally is standing directly in front of Kendra and pokes her finger right into her chest.

Kendra actually flinches. "Holy hell! She just touched me!"

It's the first time Ally's contact has been felt by anyone but me. She's honing her skills and it terrifies me.

"Ally, you need to go now. I can't deal with this."

"Okay, I'll go. But remember, Junie. I'm the one who cares about you. I'm just trying to make sure you don't spend your life alone like K. She peaked in high school and now she spends her time painting old ladies. This is your chance, Junie. You've got two guys who want you—don't blow it."

As her parting words sink in, I realize what I have to do.

I dated two men to prove to myself that I could. Now I have to break up with both of those men to prove to Ally that I don't need a man to complete me. And I certainly don't need a dead worst friend.

It's turning into an incredibly painful day—and it's not just because I've stopped taking the Percocet.

Apparently in my drug-induced haze, I agreed to a Labor Day cookout at Nelson's house—with Jesse offering to man the grill. Kendra is zipping around my tiny kitchen creating potato salad, baked beans and a peach cobbler. I feel completely useless.

The worst part is the dread of knowing that after dessert, I have to end it with both Jesse and Nelson. No way am I going through that hell without some peach cobbler to fortify me.

At five-thirty, Jesse knocks at the door, here to carry me to the car. I have no idea how I'm going to make it around after I dump him. And I'm supposed to be open for business tomorrow.

"Kendra. Jesse's here."

She scurries back into the kitchen and carefully stacks the casserole dishes in a box.

"Do you need help with that, Kendra? I can make two trips." Jesse's already got me in his arms and I'm quite enjoying my last visit with his muscular chest.

"Don't be silly, I'm just fine. You take care of Miss June, and I'll take care of the food."

Midge is jumping around Jesse's feet, leash in her teeth.

I look up into the face I've become so familiar with the past few weeks. Damn, I'm going to miss him. "Someone thinks she's going with us."

"Why not? Nelson's not afraid of dogs, is he?" Jesse bends down, as if I weigh absolutely nothing.

Trying to hook the leash to a moving target isn't made easier by my awkward position, but I'm milking this as long as possible. "No, I think he bribes her, though."

Jesse laughs, taking the leash from my hand and straightening back up. He plants a kiss on my cheek and smiles. I'm going to miss that chipped-tooth grin.

The four us of tramp out of my apartment, the smell of baked peaches giving me the courage to face my fears.

We're gathered around Nelson's patio table on an expansive deck which circles his home. It's hard to imagine someone our age owning a home so large and extravagant.

"Nelson, the house is great. Reminds me of my place back in Texas. I can't wait to get out of that cramped apartment the company put me up in." Jesse covers my hand with his own. "No offense, June Bug, but those apartments are awful. You wouldn't know I work for a multi-national corporation based on the likes of that place."

My head is spinning. These two have more in common that I thought. First the loafers, now houses.

"This home belonged to my Aunt Hilda. She didn't have any children, so she left it to me."

Kendra strains her neck to look up at the three stories towering above us. "Big house for one person."

Nelson follows her gaze. "Aunt Hilda never spent much time alone. She always had the family over." He takes off his glasses and begins chewing on the earpiece. I know him well enough to know a story is coming. "Hilda met her husband just before World War II. She was barely eighteen, but they married right away and he was shipped out two weeks later. He never returned. Hilda said he was the love of her life and she never even dated another man. I hope to fill this house up with children one day. Hilda would have wanted that."

"Wow. What a story." Kendra's eyes are the size of a pair of Frisbees. I know how much she loves historical romances, so Nelson's tale is right up her alley.

"Sounds like he's trying too hard if you ask me."

I squeeze my eyes shut. I was hoping Ally wouldn't show up here. I can do without her commentary tonight.

"You okay, June?" I open my eyes to find Nelson watching me intently.

Forcing a grin, I pat his hand to reassure him. "Yeah, I'm fine. Just a sad story."

Jesse rises to check on the steaks and Nelson joins him at the grill.

Kendra leans closer to me. "I've got to go with Nelson, sweetie. He's so romantic." She gestures toward the house. "And look at this place. Whew."

I haven't told her my plans, because I didn't want her to talk me out of it.

The guys return to the table with a platter full of meat.

For the next few minutes, dishes are passed and plates are filled. I've just stuffed a bite of steak in my mouth when Jesse speaks up.

"June, I just want to let you know that I'm alright with the way things are. I've thought about it a lot, and it's okay with me if you wanna keep dating both of us."

Before I can finish chewing and respond, Nelson lays down his fork and adds his two cents. "I agree. We never said this was exclusive and I don't have a problem taking our time and seeing where this goes."

"Wow, Junie. You did it. They're so enamored that they're willing to share you. Damn girl."

I swallow my bite, glare at Ally and set down my fork. I had hoped to wait until after dessert. "I appreciate that, guys. The fact that you're willing to forgive me for my deception is such a relief." I pause, swallowing over the words in my throat. "But I can't, in good conscious, continue to date both of you."

Chapter Twenty-Six

This is where the civility ends.

The meal forgotten, Jesse and Nelson resort to what can only be described as caveman antics. I'm fearful one of them is going to bonk me over the head and drag me away at any moment, and with my ankle continuing to throb, I won't be able to escape.

"Junie, you can't tell me you're as attracted to this guy as you are to me." Jesse jerks his thumb at Nelson.

Nelson puffs up like a peacock. "She's intellectually attracted to me, you dumb jock."

"Just because she likes to have fun with me doesn't mean we don't connect intellectually."

"I've introduced her to new things—to culture. What have you introduced her to? Football?"

Kendra is watching the exchange like it's a sporting event, which is appropriate, because Ally continues her "Jesse" cheer from last night. I look on, unable to interrupt, but more convinced with each jab that I'm making the right decision.

Both men are standing now, arms waving in wild gestures, insults flowing more readily.

"I have more money than you do. I can offer her more."

"Well at least I *earn* my money. I don't rely on daddy to give it to me."

"June can see the world with me. Where are you going to take her? Texas?"

"Do you actually think she likes those pretentious, exotic restaurants you take her to? Junie's favorite food is pizza. And she'd rather eat it on her couch."

Wow. These two sure have learned a lot about each other in the past two days. Where have I been?

"I can assure you that June prefers books to television. She only watched that garbage to please you."

"Yeah, I could tell she was just miserable when she laughed so hard soda blew out her nose."

I'm so glad they're focusing on my most attractive features.

They move closer with each verbal sling and while I still don't believe they'll turn physically violent; I can't take it anymore. If my foot didn't hurt so much, I'd stand up in my chair. I'll just have to use my voice.

"Okay, that's enough."

They don't even blink.

"Guys! Cut it out!"

Nothing.

"I don't want to date either of you anymore!"

That gets their attention. Faces that were a moment ago distorted in anger now look crushed. Nelson's lip is trembling and Jesse eyes might just have tears in them.

They return to their chairs, shocked into utter silence.

"I'm sorry. This is all my fault. The last thing I want to do is hurt either of you, because I like you both so much." I push back from the table and rise, balancing my weight on my good foot and the back of the chair, all thoughts of peach cobbler gone. "But I can't choose one of you, so I have to choose none of you." I look to Kendra, who quickly gets up and helps me wobble away.

Kendra and I don't speak on the way home, which I'm extremely grateful for. Unlike Ally, K has always given me space.

She knows when I'm ready for her opinion, I'll ask—and until then, I need to process my own feelings.

Ally, on the other hand, hasn't stopped talking since we left Nelson's. She's delivered a 25-minute soliloquy on how I've ruined my life and blown my chance to be with a great guy—or at least the "book weenie". Her last shot as I'm hobbling up the stairs is that I'll "never get laid."

Once safely in my apartment I turn to face her.

"Ally, I'm only going to say this once, and then I expect you to leave." I take a long look at this person—this thing—who I once considered my best friend. It's hard to remember why. "Obviously we have a very different view of life. I'm sorry yours was cut short, but that doesn't give you the right to try to control mine. I will forever cherish the memories I have of you, but I can't take this anymore.

"You died. Ten years ago. I can't live my life for you. I have to live it for me. If you care for me at all, you'll leave me alone." The emotion of the past few hours catches up with me and I collapse in a heap on the couch.

The cushions beside me sink down and Kendra's arms encircle me. It's so nice to be comforted, by someone I can *feel*. My tears spent, I look up, searching the corners of the room.

"Is she gone?" Kendra's voice is a whisper.

I nod my head slowly, wanting to believe it's true. "For now."

When we arrive at work the next day, there's a sign on the bookshop door. Kendra jogs across the street to read it.

Panting, she returns, eyes avoiding mine.

"Well, what's it say?" I fumble with the lock, trying to balance on one foot and hold Midge's leash.

Kendra grabs the keys away from me and kicks the bottom of the door. "Closed until further notice."

My heart sinks into my stomach. He can't close the store. Not because of me. It's his passion, his dream.

Taking my arm, Kendra helps me inside and settles me in a chair. I direct her from my spot in the lobby and she goes about opening the daycare. She's staying the whole week to help me while I'm healing. I can't thank her enough, but I have insisted on paying her. I needed help anyway.

Throughout the morning, I find myself staring out the window at the dark shop across the street. Inside, I can picture my favorite comfy chair, and the teapot in the corner.

"K, do you think I made the wrong decision?"

She's sitting on the floor, playing tug-of-war with Percival, a black pug mix. "About Ally? Or about the guys?"

"The guys."

Her back is to me, but I can see her shoulders hunch up and then fall, as if in a sigh. "I don't know, June. But about Ally—definitely."

It is so nice to have someone who knows about Ally, and who understands everything I had been through with her. Why didn't I call Kendra when this whole thing started with Jesse and Nelson? Maybe if I had talked it out with her from the beginning, I could have avoided this mess. Instead, I relied on someone who is eternally seventeen. She can never understand what it's like, as an adult, making your way in this complicated world. Ally gets to pick and choose—if she doesn't like something, she just disappears for a while. She doesn't have to deal with reality. By relying so much on her, I guess I wasn't either.

Suddenly the loss hits me. The three people (well, sort of) that I spend the most time with, love the most, are all gone from my life in one day. By my design. There's a gaping hole in my heart. What have I done?

Chapter Twenty-Seven

I go through the week like a zombie, directing Kendra and staring out the window. By Thursday, the pain in my foot has subsided enough that I can hobble into the play areas and sit on the floor with the dogs. At least from that position, I can't see the shop across the street.

Kendra has a group of small dogs on their afternoon walk and the big dogs and I are napping. I have my head resting on Moe (or is it Curly?) and my legs splayed out across the floor. I hear the bell over the door tinkle, but I don't bother to open my eyes, assuming it's K.

The dogs are more attune to a stranger entering the building. With little ceremony, Moe leaps up, causing my head to bonk onto the floor. Soon all the dogs are standing at the fence howling and barking. Wilbur is leading the impromptu chorus.

I struggle to sit up, but can't see who is standing on the other side of the fence. It must be a kid, or something.

Pulling myself up without putting weight on my injured foot is awkward at best. At worst, I end up back on the floor.

There's an apology on my lips as I finally become upright and can see my visitor. But at the sight of the ill-tempered Dr. Susan Walton, my mouth clamps shut.

"Well, hello, Miss Hinderson. Having a nice nap?"

My eyes dart around the room, checking to see if anything is amiss. I pray that Kendra returns soon, so I won't have to let on that I'm hurt.

"Yeah," I force a small laugh, "we just had a pretty intense play session. Needed a rest." I pat the top of the closest canine head to demonstrate my bond with the dogs. "My, um, employee is out with a group of smaller dogs on a walk. She should be back any minute." Any minute, K.

Dr. Walton stares at me over a pair of bifocals perched on the end of her nose. "I've come back to make sure everything is in order." She narrows her eyes, her look assuming that I've failed somehow. "You did complete my list of suggestions?"

The list is sitting on the corner of my desk, out of my reach. I yearn to run to it, scoop it up and show her all the check marks. Instead, I stay where I am behind the fence. "Yes, ma'am. Every last thing I was *required* to do." But not the silly stuff that you wanted done for no reason.

"Um hm." Her response reminds me a stern school teacher waiting, ruler in hand, for me to answer incorrectly.

"If you look at the area behind my desk, you'll see the cubby system—complete with airtight bins—for the dogs who bring their food." I gesture toward the wall.

She looks at the bins, and back at me, but doesn't move an inch. "Why don't you show me?"

The woman is trying to goad me, and I know it. But I also know those stupid regulations backwards and forwards, revised version and all, and I'm not falling for it. "I'm sorry Dr. Walton, but I can't leave the play area until my staff member returns. Can't leave the dogs unsupervised." Ha! I showed her.

"Very good, Miss Hinderson. I see you've been reading." She strolls over to the cubbies and begins removing the marked bins, checking that each one seals tightly. Man, this woman is a stickler. Without turning around, she addresses me once more. "And your records? I assume they are organized properly?"

"The files are in the bottom drawer of the desk, just behind you." I'm not budging, lady.

She pulls out several of the files, lips pursed. Looking up, her eyes land on the comfy chair in the lobby. The one she instructed me to remove.

At that moment, Kendra comes bursting through the door, six little yipping dogs trailing behind her. "June, you should've seen the pile that Oscar just..." Her voice trails off as she notices the ancient woman behind my desk. I've warned her about Dr. Walton, so she's prepared. Leading the dogs to the kennel area, she arranges them in two groups of three. She remembers the instruction about no more than four dogs playing together unsupervised.

"I'm glad you're back, Kendra. I was just going to show Dr. Walton the new isolation area we set up in the back room. Maybe you could take her back there?"

Dr. Walton takes another look at the chair, but follows Kendra. Yeah, she better not say anything. There isn't a darn thing in those regulations about me having a comfy chair in my lobby.

By the time they return from the back, it appears my cousin has charmed the ornery old bag. They're laughing like long-lost friends—or granddaughter and great-great-grandmother.

"Miss Hinderson, I'm delighted to see that you've hired such a delightful young lady. Everything looks fine here." She completes another of the pink forms and hands it to Kendra. "I'm afraid this will be my last visit."

"Oh, are you retiring?" One can only hope.

Dr. Walton looks startled behind her bifocals. "Of course not. What would lead you to believe that?" She looks to Kendra as if she can explain why I've lost my mind. "I only do the initial assessments. You will be assigned an area inspector. They will stop in at least once a year, unannounced. Be ready."

My dear, sweet cousin walks her to the door. Leaning down, Kendra whispers something and the two share a final laugh.

As soon as the door closes, I blurt out my disbelief. "What the hell did you say to her?"

K shrugs her shoulders and smiles. "I slipped her some free overnight eye cream. Told her I was in my fifties."

Kendra is leaving today. I'm dreading the quiet apartment, frozen dinners and having to crawl to my bedroom and back. Okay, maybe I'm overdramatizing a tad, but Ally's not around to do that anymore. I haven't seen or heard from her since Monday night when I asked her to leave. I'm still getting used to having a conversation with one person at a time.

My ankle is much better, although it hurts to move too quickly. Walking the dogs by myself next week should be an adventure.

This afternoon K bought a HELP WANTED sign at the hardware store, and now it sits in the window, pleading for someone to stop.

As the last dogs leave for the day, and Kendra sweeps and mops the play areas, I stare out at the darkening street. Most people are headed for the pub, but one couple lingers in front of the display in Nelson's window. Just before Labor Day weekend, I helped him spread fake red and gold leaves in the window. The books he chose all centered on the upcoming season. He even took my suggestion and included a collection of poetry containing Emily Dickinson's tribute to autumn.

The couple moves on, most likely because of the dimming light. I wonder if they would have wandered inside, lingered over the table of classics near the front counter. Nelson loved to watch the process of his customers finding just the right book. The exclamations, the stroke of the spine. He was like a matchmaker, not a salesman.

"Hello..." I look away from the window to find Kendra, a squirming Midge in her grasp, obviously waiting for me.

"Sorry, K. Guess I spaced there for a minute." She sets Midge down and circles my shoulders with her arm. "Are you sure you're gonna be okay here, without me?"

"Yeah, I'll be alright." I glance back across the street before reaching down for Midge's leash.

Kendra doesn't look convinced, but she keeps it to herself. "Well, I'm sure gonna miss this place. What a fun job!"

It's hard not to smile at her enthusiasm, despite the sadness in my chest. "Anytime you want to come back, you're welcome to. I've certainly loved having you here."

"Darlin', you need anything, I'll come a'runnin'!"

"I might take you up on that."

Chapter Twenty-Eight

The next day, I wake up and realize that I am completely alone. There will be no more home-cooked meals with Kendra spouting off skincare tips. There will be no more burritos or mockery of reality television. There will be no more exotic restaurants and stories of world travel. Ally's not even around to insult me.

I sink back under the covers, prepared to spend the day right here, in this bed.

Until I feel Midge pounce on my chest and her tongue dig past the comforter to find my face. Okay, so I'm not completely alone.

I throw on some clothes and head toward the dumpster so Midge can do her business, but change my mind and pass right by her favorite tree. She doesn't look too happy that I've failed to stop, and pulls on the leash to go back. But I've made a decision. We're not just pottying this morning. We're walking.

I continue along the path that snakes around my apartment complex, literally dragging her for the first fifty feet or so. Eventually, she catches on and starts trotting along beside me. It's been so long since I took her for a walk without five or six other dogs coming along that she's most likely forgotten what it's like.

It's a beautiful day, and while still warm, a hint of fall lingers in the air. The pending change in season gives me a ray of hope. Soon I can put this summer behind me and look forward to the next phase of my life. My business. I'll just focus all my energy there. Like I planned.

My stride takes on the sense of the determination I now feel, and Midge's short legs struggle to keep up with the faster pace. A short bark knocks me from the zone my mind had entered.

Slowing down, I stop near a row of bushes. "I'm sorry, Midge. I didn't even let you pee, did I? I'm kind of in my own world, I guess."

A man jogging past me eyes me with a funny look on his face. What? Are people not allowed to talk to their dogs?

Relieved, Midge strains on the leash, now excited about the prospect of an adventure.

I take three more steps, and then remember with startling clarity, and a shooting pain, that my ankle is not fully healed. I really should think things through better. Leaving the path, and heading straight across the parking lot, I limp home.

The only thing I was supposed to do this weekend was continue to rest my foot. My brain isn't functioning properly. Digging through the medicine cabinet, I'm relieved to find one last Percocet.

I flop down on the couch, ankle propped up, and flip through the channels. Saturday morning cartoons remind me of Ally, although these are wildly different than the cartoons of our childhood. Reruns of Survivor make me long for Jesse, and when one of the contestants fails a challenge, it brings me to tears—instead of the laugh we would have shared. Flicking the television off, I reach for a book from my end table, but of course, Nelson gave it to me and I can't bear to flip through the pages.

I close my eyes and hope the pain pill will take effect soon, so I can sleep through the loneliness.

I spend the weekend planted on that couch; except the few times I venture out to let Midge pee. On Sunday, I don't even bother to change out of my pjs to walk her.

Breakfast is dry cereal, because I've run out of milk. Lunch is a bag of Doritos, because they are the first thing I see when I open the pantry. By dinner I figure I need some protein, so I eat peanut butter straight out of the jar.

Only two times in my life have I experienced this type of numbing grief. The first time was when Ally died, but I had my father to comfort me. The second time was when my dad died, but Ally was around to ease that pain. The sense of loss threatens to overwhelm me.

At eleven, I'm watching the news and I see a piece on the rate of divorce in our country. "Idiots. Why would you throw away love when you had it?"

Now I'm talking to the TV.

The pajamas I wore to bed last night are now covered in orange Dorito dust, a smear of peanut butter and little brown dog hairs from the couch. My hair is half up in a ponytail, the other half sticking out the bottom. And I haven't brushed my teeth today. Yet I find myself walking out the front door and down the hall to 14C.

There are no lights on inside and the blinds are closed. He's probably in bed. Like a normal person who hasn't slept on and off all day. I lean my forehead against the door, picturing the room beyond. Remembering all the nights curled up on his couch, in the comfort of his strong embrace. Tears slide down my cheeks and again I agonize over the decision I've made. It doesn't seem any easier now, almost a week later, but if I could've just chosen...someone. Then I wouldn't be alone.

Wait. I lean back from the door. What a stupid thing to think. Choosing someone so I wouldn't be alone? What about choosing someone because I love them? That would have made sense. But to choose for the sake of choosing?

I march back down the hallway to my apartment and strip on the way to the shower. Washing away the grime of the weekend, I resolve that there isn't a thing wrong with being alone for a while. It will be good for me. I can figure out who I am—apart from Ally, apart from a man. This will be great.

Well that attitude lasted for maybe a day. Tuesday, I have 22 dogs and being alone really sucks. For very practical reasons, of course.

It takes me almost four hours just to walk them all. And my ankle is throbbing again. By the time I get home, I'm tired, I'm achy and I'm cranky. So, my mother's cheery voice on the answering machine grinds on my last nerve.

"Bonjour! Oh sweetie, we are having the best time here! We just went to the Eiffel Tower and oh, June, it was magnificent! We have some very exciting news and we'll be home on Monday! Can't wait to see you, honey. Arrivederci!"

The number of sappy endearments, paired with the exclamations after every sentence makes my stomach churn. Exciting news? Is she kidding me? Here I am. Alone. With no one to love me. And I have to listen to my mother and some man named Harry's exciting news? Now I can't even eat that Lean Cuisine lasagna I chipped the freezer burn off this morning.

Without undressing, I head straight to bed, burrow under the covers, and fall into an agitated sleep.

So, my new thing is that I'm not sleeping well. The doctor says it's probably a withdrawal symptom from the Percocet. Or maybe the stress. He doesn't feel comfortable prescribing me anything over the phone. He'd be happy to see me the second week of November.

Tonight, I'll try a stiff drink before bed.

My crankiness from Tuesday night turns into a full-on funk that lasts through the week. Work is busy and distracting, luckily, except that every time I walk out the front door, I have to see Nelson Brantley's Rare and Essential Books.

I fantasize about what my life would be like if I had chosen Nelson. Or Jesse. Or kept dating both of them. Or packed up and moved to Hollywood and married Matt Damon. Oh wait, he's already married. Basically, I am now convinced that I have chosen incorrectly, but can do nothing about it, because Nelson has disappeared and Jesse doesn't answer his door. (I've only been down there three, or seven, times since Sunday night. I'm starting to get worried.)

The only person I haven't tried to contact is Ally. As much as I miss her, I think it's important to live in my world without her for a while. Like a normal person whose best friend has died.

I put on a happy face for my human customers, but the dogs are excellent therapists and are helping me work through my grief. They are also excellent snot rags if there isn't a tissue close by. On Friday night, I'm sad to see the last little guy go home, because now I face another weekend—just me, Midge and my pajamas.

Chapter Twenty-Nine

I awaken on Saturday to a drizzling, sunless day. Kind of how I feel inside. Normally I would relish lingering all day in my pjs, but today they feel oppressive somehow, as if they are responsible for my sad mood. I shower, hoping to wash away my funk (emotional, not the smelly, physical kind), but it persists through a breakfast of Cocoa Puffs and Toaster Strudel.

I can tell it's bad when comfort food does nothing to comfort me.

Needing to get out of my head, and my rut, Midge and I hop in the car and head to Asheville. With Mom still in Europe, the house will be all mine. Maybe if I concentrate hard enough, I can find my dad there. He'll make everything better.

The drive itself is therapeutic, easing my anxiety and allowing me to focus on the simple task of keeping the car on the road. Pulling into town, I find myself tempted to visit the places I frequented as a teen. Memories rush at me as I pass the coffee shop where I had my first espresso; Barley's, where we ate pizza and played pool; Mast General Store where my father took me for Teaberry Gum. I'm saddened to see the changes in the center of town and new buildings towering over the Thomas Wolfe house. Continuing up Merrimon Ave, I turn right at The Hop, but it's gone. I vaguely recall my mother telling me it had moved.

I pull into the driveway of my childhood home, but I don't go inside. Instead, Midge and I take a once familiar route to the park where Ally and I played as children. The homes along the way haven't changed much in the years I've been gone, a fresh coat of paint here, a new planting there. But as I round the corner to the park, I notice something startling.

Changing direction, I head up Ally's old street, my breath catches in my throat. Before me lies devastation. It's as if the entire street has been flattened. Where stately homes used to grace large lots, now endless rows of cookie-cutter townhouses dot the landscape. Further up the street, I realize that most of the original homes remain, their lots reduced to barely a ring of grass surrounding the houses. Lingering in front of the two-story clapboard that I used to consider my own, I watch as a tire swing sways in the breeze, back and forth, back and forth.

It's a new addition—the plank swing we played on as children removed years earlier when Ally's parents moved. The yard behind the house is bare dirt, foundations already laid for the next row of townhomes. Gone is the strip of woods, gone is our fort, gone are our memories.

"I hope you won't forget me entirely." Scanning the quiet street, I search for my friend.

I shake my head firmly, my eyes filling with tears. "Never." Finally, I spot her. Perched in the oak tree in her front yard. Nudging the tire swing with her foot.

"A tire swing would've been fun, huh?" There's a hint of sadness in her voice, a yearning almost.

"Wanna go to the park with me?"

Ally leaps gracefully from the tree—something she never would have accomplished if she was alive—and meets me on the street. "You sure you want me around?"

Leaning toward her, our foreheads meet, and I can just barely feel the pressure. "I think we were growing apart."

"Well, with Jesse and Nelson around all the time, you didn't need me as much."

We start down the hill toward the park, stepping in a comfortable rhythm. "I mean before that. When you died."

"Oh."

We reach the small park and I tie Midge's leash to a dogwood tree. The playground is deserted on this overcast Saturday—as if saved just for us. I settle onto a swing and begin to pump my legs up and down. Ally takes the swing next to me, and for a while we just push back and forth, soaring into the air.

Slowing the swing, I turn to my best friend. "If you hadn't died, would we have stayed friends?"

She doesn't answer immediately, and when her gaze meets mine, it's filled with tears. I never knew angels could cry. "I hope we would have."

"You were so eager to grow up, to move fast, to be different. It scared me a little."

"It scared me a lot." Sticking her feet into the sand, she stops the motion of the swing and turns to me. "We've never talked about that night."

I can't look at her, or I'll lose it. "No, we haven't."

Her voice is a whisper. "Junie?"

I turn to meet her gaze, tears streaming out of my eyes before I can even attempt to stop them.

"You asked me what my obsession with sex is." She bites her bottom lip and looks down at her feet, twirling though the sand. "If I had sex that night, I might still be alive."

Chapter Thirty

That's when the rain starts. Not just a light drizzle, but a threatening, soaking downpour. I grab Midge and the three of us take off toward my mom's house.

By the time we arrive, two of us are drenched to the bone. I'm toweling Midge off and wringing out my clothes when I notice that something's different about Ally that I hadn't noticed before. In place of the low-slung jeans and sequin top, she's dressed in a worn pair of Levi's and a battered tie-dyed tee. It was her favorite outfit in the days before boys entered our world.

Our eyes lock and soon we're laughing and crying at once.

Upstairs, Ally flings herself across my bed while I search for dry clothes. I hold up a t-shirt from band camp. She scrunches her face into a grimace and shakes her head. Then, at the bottom of the drawer, I spot a soft yellow tee, faded from multiple washings. Drawing it on over my wet head, I proudly turn around.

"Little Miss Sunshine!" Ally dissolves in a fit of laughter as I drop onto the bed beside her. "I'd forgotten all about that shirt."

Stroking the soft fabric, I close my eyes. "Me too."

We were twelve, and having one of those spats girls sometimes have when they're as close as sisters. I think this one was over whether I liked the new girl, Penny Masters, better than Ally.

She had invited me—and not Ally—to a sleepover in her rec room, but there were like seven other girls and I maybe talked to her for twenty minutes the whole night. Penny Masters was just using me to get to Robbie Stuart, who sat next to me in math class.

Once I explained all of that to Ally, she mellowed out, but not before destroying my favorite New Kids on the Block t-shirt (which I later thanked her for, by the way). Jordon had suddenly grown a permanent purple goatee that reached to his belly button, Danny had sprouted red devil's horns and Joey's ears rivaled Dumbo's. Sharpies had long been one of Ally's favorite weapons. I still own jeans that she'd written on.

So, to make up for the misunderstanding, her mom dropped us at the mall and Ally picked out the "Little Miss Sunshine" shirt from Spencer's Gifts. She knew how much I had loved the Little Miss and Mr. books as a kid. And she told me that I was sunshine in her life.

As I trace the round character on my shirt, with her braids sticking out and freckles dotting her cheeks, I wonder how I could have ever forgotten why Ally and I were friends. Are friends.

I reach beside me and grasp her hand, which feels more solid than before. "I'm ready."

"Brad and I were at that college party I told you about. Over off Hillside." I nod, and she continues. "He did like six hits from the beer bong real early on, and planned to stop well before we would leave. So, around ten o'clock, he takes me upstairs and we find an empty bedroom and start making out.

"Things were getting a little hot and I asked him to slow down, but he was pretty worked up. It was like he couldn't hear me. When he tugged my pants down, I knew I didn't want him to, so I kneed him in the groin. That got his attention." Ally is staring at the ceiling, as if watching the moment unfold.

"He told me I had led him on and that he should have taken Olivia Sanders to the party, because she would have put out." She pauses, and a tear runs down her cheek. "I was so hurt that he only went out with me to get sex. I mean, I had broken it off with like three other guys to date him. I thought he probably would be my first. But not like that."

I squeeze her hand tighter and I can feel her respond. This is the most alive she has felt to me since she died.

"I wasn't thinking straight, so I demanded that he take me home." She's sobbing now, the tears wracking her whole body. "It was only a couple of blocks. I should've walked."

Or called me.

She turns her head to look at me, a small smile on her face. "But I was afraid you wouldn't approve."

I pull her into a tight embrace, and I can feel her in my arms. Actually feel her. Like she never left me. We're holding each other and crying, and I can feel the moisture from her tears soaking through the thin cotton of my shirt. How is that possible?

As our tears subside, she pulls back and wipes her face. "I've been such a bad friend to you. It was so selfish of me to not let you go."

"No, no." I shake my head.

"Yes, Junie. I've held you back from so much. And I've pushed you into things you didn't want to do. I'm so sorry."

We embrace again and I try to process everything she's told me. "Ally, you don't really think having sex that night would have saved your life, do you?"

She pulls back and stares at me so intently, it's as if she's looking into my soul. "I used to. But now I think if I had gone through with it, I may have lived, but it would have ruined my life."

When I wake up on Sunday morning, in my childhood bed, I'm saddened to find that my friend is gone. But she has left me a note.

Junie,

You have been a great friend to me for 23 years. And I died at 17. Now I'm going to try to be the same to you. I will always be here for you, but on your terms, not my own. You need me, just let me know.

Love Always, Ally

P.S. Admit it, you need me. At least for fashion advice.

Chapter Thirty-One

On Monday morning, I step out the door of my apartment and almost run into a man in coveralls carrying a bucket of paint and a roller. Apologizing, I watch him walk down the hallway and enter what appears to be Jesse's apartment.

Giving Midge's leash a tug, I head down the hall and stop short at apartment 14C. In the window sits a VACANCY sign and a team of men are inside spreading plastic over the carpet. The living room is empty, save one candle perched on the ledge over the fireplace. One of the painters grabs the candle and shoots it into a nearby trash can, shouting, "Two points!"

Turning, I head back down the hallway, past my door and to my car. He's gone too. First Nelson left and now Jesse.

Once at work, I distract myself from all thoughts of both men. But then I remember that Mom and Harry are returning today and they have "exciting news." I'd rather think about the fact that I'm going to die alone.

Work is busier than ever and if I don't get some help soon, I'm going to pull my hair out. Luckily, two people stop in and fill out applications, but I'm not sure how to make a decision about who to hire. I mean, sure, I was once assistant to the assistant of human resources. But I never even saw applications there. I just copied memos and made coffee. I feel completely unprepared to make this decision. Honestly, I feel unprepared to make any decision at this point.

But I can walk dogs. Which I spend most of the day doing lately.

Finishing with my last group, I arrange everyone into the kennels for naptime and turn down the lights. I flop into my comfy chair—this was the necessity of having a comfy chair—and close my eyes. For exactly seventeen seconds. I know, because I've been counting dogs in my head to make sure I walked everyone.

My count is interrupted by a pounding on the glass behind me. Twenty-one dogs' naps are interrupted by the banging.

Planting my best "I am a small business owner and therefore have to be pleasant at all times" smile on my face, I rise from the chair and turn around. There in the window is my mother and Harry. Who is wearing a beret. Seriously.

They have on matching Eiffel Tower shirts and goofy grins. The tuna I had for lunch rolls in my stomach. My mom's hands are clenched behind her back and she's nearly hopping with excitement.

I open the door and step out onto the sidewalk, hoping the dogs will settle back down. "Hi guys."

Mom doesn't step forward to hug me, instead she sidles up beside Harry squirming and giggling. "Are you ready for the surprise?"

Closing my eyes, I can see Harry in a powder-blue tux and my mom in a ruffled gown. I can't believe my mom is getting married and I'm all alone. It's so not fair. Forcing the smile back onto my face, I open my eyes, ready to fawn and gasp over the ring she is holding behind her back. I'll try to act happy for them, but I am not calling him Dad.

"Tada!" From behind her back, my mother produces, not a ring, but a small wiggly thing with pointy ears.

"A dog? The surprise is a dog?"

A French Bulldog to be exact. Now that I look closer, I can pick out the distinctive features of the breed. But a dog?

"Isn't he just the cutest?" My mother, who has never, to my knowledge, owned a dog, is holding this wrinkly little puppy up to her face and making kissing noises.

I can't deny that he's cute. Solid white, save for a brown spot on his left side, his ears standing at attention and little nub wagging, he's pretty much the cutest little puppy ever. But I don't need another dog. Especially not a puppy. Midge would not be happy.

"Mom, it's really sweet of you, but I don't think I can handle a puppy right now, on top of the business." But unable to resist his cute face, I reach for the little fella.

Her eyes nearly bugging out of her head, my mom turns away, cradling the puppy. "He's not for you. He's mine." She looks up at Harry, that ga-ga look in her eyes. "Well, he's ours."

Oh. They got a puppy. "So, you're not getting married?"

"Married?" She lets out a snort—wonder where I get it from? "Heavens, no! What were you thinking, June? We've only been dating a few months. We haven't even discussed marriage."

Harry's got the familiar deer-caught-in-the-headlights look common to men when the "M" word comes up in conversation. I didn't realize guys that old were still so affected by it.

"Well, I don't know. Paris, the city of love, exciting news..." So maybe I jumped to a conclusion. The wrong conclusion. Thank goodness. I reach out and pet the little guy's head. "I'm happy for you, Mom. He's adorable. What's his name?"

"Pierre. We did get him in Paris, after all."

I can hear Wilbur starting to howl from inside. Apparently, naptime is over. "Harry, you're probably anxious to see Roxie. Let me get her."

The trimmer Roxie is somehow managing to sleep through Wilbur's serenade. She's probably exhausted from all the playing and walking of the last month. I wonder if Harry will notice that she actually has a waist now.

Gathering her bed and food, we head outside.

Harry's face lights up at the sight of his little dog and her long body vacillates back and forth quivering with excitement. Crouched down, he's rubbing her belly when he looks up at me. "She's so thin! What did you do?" His tone is on the verge of accusatory.

I start to defend myself when he backpedals.

"I mean, how did you do it? I've been trying to get the weight off her for a year!"

Feeling quite proud of myself, I wish I'd thought to take before and after pictures. "Well, she played a lot. And we walked three times a day. I also cut her food in half. You were feeding her a little too much." Not wanting to sound harsh, I add, "I think she'll enjoy having another dog around to play with."

He's scooped her up in his arms and is kissing her on her little brown head. Mom holds the wiggling Pierre out to meet his new sister—or is she a half-sister? I'm not sure how joint custody of a puppy works. But whatever, they seem to like each other.

I can hear the rest of the dogs inside joining Wilbur in his discontent, so I politely shoo Mom and Harry and their canine children off on their way.

Back inside, I switch on the lights, turn up the radio, and release the dogs into the play area. And we dance and play the afternoon away. Because my mom got a dog—and not an engagement ring.

Chapter Thirty-Two

Today I'm interviewing Geoff, who reminds me of one of those guys that follows bands like The Grateful Dead around and says "dude" a lot. His interview clothes consist of torn shorts that hang down to his calves—at least I think they're shorts; I hope men don't wear capri pants—and a t-shirt with what I think is an anarchy symbol on it. I swear he didn't scare me this much when he stopped in to fill out the application.

"So, Geoff, it says here that you attended Davidson College for three years." Seems like a fancy school for a deadhead. "May I ask why you didn't complete your degree?"

He stops picking at his beard to answer me. "That school was bogus, dude. I just went there 'cuz my folks made me. But I had to break that oppressive tradition 'cuz it was stealing my soul, you know whadda mean?"

"Um, sure." I keep my eyes focused on the application so I won't stare at what appears to be actual twigs in his shoulder length hair. "And you worked at The Gap for a couple of months?" According to the dates, it was seventeen days, but I don't want to make him feel bad.

"Also, for the folks, but I just couldn't work for the man, you know?"

'Cuz he was stealing your soul? "So, why do you want to work with dogs?"

At this point in the interview, Geoff stretches his arms behind his head and really starts to get comfortable. His shirt is straining across his chest and I can't take my eyes off what are unmistakably nipple rings underneath the thin fabric. If a dog jumps on him and gets a claw hooked in one of those...

"Dude, my folks said they'll stop sending me money if I don't get a job, and I figure dogs are cool. They won't steal your weed, right?" He finds this amusing.

I find it disturbing beyond words. Did he actually just talk about weed during a job interview? "Okay then. I have a few more people to interview and then I'll be making my decision. Thank you for coming in."

He's halfway out the door when he turns around. "Hey, if it helps, you're hot." He does a pistol-motion with his hand and winks.

I run his application through the shredder as soon as the door closes.

If the girl coming in tomorrow is even semi-normal, I'll hire her on the spot.

At home later, I pop a frozen lasagna in the microwave and slap some butter on a slice of bread. The food I'm eating lately tastes like crap. I miss Kendra's cooking. I miss Nelson's fancy restaurants. I miss Brixx pizza with Jesse.

Plopping down on the couch, I flip through the channels looking for something to take my mind off being alone. *The Biggest Loser—Couples Edition.* No. *The Amazing Race.* No. *Love Connection.* Absolutely not. Wait. *Love Connection* is still on? Nope, just reruns from the eighties. Chuck says they'll be back in "two and two" and I click the TV off.

"Ally! I'm lonely. Can you please come here?"

She appears beside me on the couch. "What's up?"

I like this summoning thing. "There's nothing on TV and I have to eat this crappy frozen dinner." I stab a noodle with my fork.

"Junie, I said I would be a better friend to you, but I'm not a genie. I'm an angel. We don't have magic powers."

"I know. I guess I just wanted to complain a little."

She settles against the arm of the couch, facing me. "Oh, well that I can do. You know what sucks the most about being dead?"

"Ally, that's not exactly what I meant."

"What?" She slaps her palm against her forehead. "Oh, I see. This being a good friend thing is hard to figure out."

I can't help but smile. "Ally, you were always a good friend to me. It's about love, and we've always had that."

She kicks me playfully with her foot. "That's for sure, Junie." Pulling her legs back up to her chest, she gets a serious look on her face. "Can I give you some advice? Grown-up stuff, I swear."

"I guess..."

"You need to move on. You're wasting your time pining over Nelson and Jesse. Get out there. Meet new people. Go on a date." She leans toward me. "You're too cool to be sitting at home alone talking to me."

The morning has been even crazier than usual. Midge won't stop barking at the new dog, Percival just pooped out a Lego, and Mazzy has finally succeeded in vaulting herself over the fence. I haven't even had time to look at the big dogs.

If this Sarah-chick I'm interviewing today has two arms, two legs and no obvious metal stuck through her nipples, I'm hiring her.

The bell over the door tinkles. Maybe that's her now.

Unless Sarah is about 6'2", wearing a suit that is obviously Armani—and I don't know anything about men's clothes—and has a goatee, this probably isn't her.

"Hi. May I help you?"

"Yes, I think I'm probably supposed to call first, but this is kind of an emergency. My mother had to be taken to the hospital this morning, I have her little dog in the car, and I have a meeting in five minutes. Is there any way you could take Gigi for the day? I'll pay anything." He pulls a checkbook from the inside pocket of his jacket as if to prove that he's serious.

"Oh, that's awful about your mother. Of course, we can help out with her dog. I'll just need you to fill out some paperwork. Do you know which vet your mother uses?" I get him started on the new dog registration form while I hush Wilbur. He's probably feeling neglected because I've been so focused on the little dogs this morning.

Mr. Armani signs the release form and sprints outside. Within moments, he's deposited a small black schnauzer on my desk and is back out the door, barely getting in a "thank you." Despite all the checkbook waving, he's failed to pay me.

Gigi is shaking and when I reach for her, she pees—all over the pile of bills I plan to pay later today. Isn't this a dandy morning?

I've just finished cleaning off my paperwork and Gigi has finally stopped shrieking when the door opens again. Mazzy chooses that moment to hop over the fence and head straight for the exit. A short, frumpy blonde snags the Jack Russell by the collar and slams the door shut. "Where do you think you're going, missy?"

Please let this be Sarah.

Chapter Thirty-Three

Sarah may not have the best fashion sense, but she has excellent dog sense. Within five minutes I know that she will be perfect for the job and basically save my life. Well, the business part of it at least. I doubt she can do anything about my social life. I doubt Dr. Phil could do anything about my social life.

I hired her on the spot and she is just returning from her last "walk and scoop", as she's termed it. I've been able to clear off my desk, pay my pee-soaked bills and eat lunch without having to share it for the first time in over a month.

Once the majority of the dogs have gone home for the day, I hand Sarah a schedule and send her on her way as well.

As the clock ticks closer to seven, I begin to worry that Gigi has been dumped on me. After her initial shaking-peeing-shrieking trauma, she has settled into quite a pleasant little dog. She and Midge are even getting along.

At two minutes to seven, Mr. Armani reappears.

Determined to get my money before he lays a hand on the dog, I stand firm behind the desk. I'm surprised to see him drop into the chair across from me and bury his head briefly in his hands. Now I notice that his suit is crumpled, his tie has a mustard stain on it and a five o'clock shadow is creeping along his jaw line.

"Hard day?" I settle into my chair, now more concerned about this man than my money.

He looks up at me, a smile tugging at the corners of his full lips. "Yeah, pretty bad." Sitting up straighter, he attempts to smooth his jacket, but gives up; probably realizing it's a lost cause. "I can't thank you enough for helping me out with Gigi. I hope she wasn't any trouble."

"No, not at all."

"My mom had a stroke this morning—they say she's going to be just fine—and there's this merger going on at work so I had to be there, and the last thing she said to me was 'don't forget about Gigi.' She loves that little dog." Letting out a breath, like it was the first chance he'd had all day just to breathe, Mr. Armani closes his eyes.

I'm worried he's fallen asleep, he's silent for so long. "I'm glad to hear your mom's okay."

He opens his eyes and I notice they are a startling grey. Leaning across the desk, he grasps my hands in his. "How can I ever repay you for your help? I just threw poor Gigi at you, and I didn't even pay you." He looks shocked to realize this. "Let me take you to dinner, please."

Dinner? "Don't be silly, I'm just doing my job."

"Um, Junie, I hate to butt in, but it's obvious that you're not seeing the opportunity here." Ally is beside me, whispering my ear, which is odd, and completely unnecessary. "This man is obviously flirting with you—"

"He is?" Armani-suit-guy drops my hands. Did I say that out loud?

"—and now he's looking at you like you're a nut job. But regardless, he asked you on a date. We were just talking about how you need to move on."

I'm staring at her dumbfounded and I'm sure Mr. Armani will be retracting his invitation at any moment. If in fact, he did ask me out, which I doubt.

"I don't know what's wrong with me today. I haven't even introduced myself. You must think I'm a lunatic. Who wants to go to dinner with a lunatic?" He reaches out his right hand. "I'm Luca Morrow, the lunatic."

Wow. I think Ally's actually right. He is kind of flirting with me. And dinner doesn't appear to be off the table.

I shake his hand, which is so large it engulfs mine. "I'm June. And I doubt that you're a lunatic. You've just had a stressful day." Because who am I to accuse anyone of being crazy?

I'm sitting across the table from Luca, who is clearly not a lunatic. He's quite brilliant, actually. Turns out he's a financial hotshot who mediates merges and takeovers. Just a tad over my business-degree-from-UNC head.

We are eating prime rib, which is a huge leap up from my lunch of pretzels dipped in peanut butter. The bread alone is making me loopy, it's so good.

"Um, Junie, I know I'm not supposed to interrupt you during your date, but you look like you're making out with the bread." Ally is crouched, elbows on the table, looking like she'd much rather flick the bread out of my hand than reason with me. "Step away from the garlic butter."

I lower the baguette to the plate and try to play off the fact that I was staring at the edge of the table while Luca was telling me about summers at the Outer Banks.

"If you haven't been to Hatteras, you should try to get down there. Beautiful coastline."

Folding my hands primly in my lap, I try to remember enough of what he said to make a proper comment. "I think we visited that lighthouse when I was little. It's the black and white striped one, right?"

"So, you have been there, good. Every kid should spend time on a real beach, without all the commercialism and high-rises. Our family still keeps a place down there. I hope I can get away one more time before winter." He's looking at me, this wistful look in those sterling-grey eyes. Surely, he's not hinting that I should go with him to the beach? I just met the guy. Maybe he is a lunatic.

"Yeah, with the new business, I guess I won't be taking a trip anytime soon." I try to mimic his wistful look, but I'm actually checking him out for signs of serial killer.

By the end of dinner, I'm once again convinced that I'm the only crazy person on this date. Luca genuinely seems like a nice guy. And he bought me a very nice meal.

We return to Hound'n Around and I go inside to get Gigi and Midge. Gigi does this cute dancing and shrieking (but obviously happy ones this time) thing and Luca scoops her up and plants a kiss on her nose. No lunatic worth his salt would kiss a dog's nose.

I lock the door and we walk the dogs toward my car.

We're standing at my car and he says something about having fun, but I can't stop staring at the dark windows of Nelson's bookstore.

So, I'm completely blindsided when Luca leans down and gently kisses my cheek. Which is totally appropriate and would have been quite pleasant if I hadn't turned my face too quickly and slammed my forehead into his. Well, my guilt probably hampered my enjoyment of the moment as well.

Being a good sport, Luca laughs and rubs his head.

"Sorry I'm so hard-headed." Is there a course I can take on how to end a first date well? Because I seem to be a master at messing it up.

"No problem." He's got a great smile. "Okay if I drop Gigi off again tomorrow?"

"Of course. And tell your mom I hope she's up and about real soon." Climbing into my car, I'm wishing I hadn't parked under a street lamp, because my face feels like it's on fire. Why am I such a doofus around men?

"Oo, oo, I can answer that one!" Ally's in the backseat, raising her hand like we're back in Ms. Powell's first-grade classroom, which is where we met.

I start the car and pull away from the curb. "Thanks anyway, Ally, but I don't think I can bear to hear the answer right now. Maybe later." I creep along, until I'm past Nelson's shop, and then speed up to reach the highway. It's obvious that I blew my chance with two men who liked me anyway.

Chapter Thirty-Four

Luca brought me a latte when he dropped Gigi off this morning. Either he's sucking up to me because I'm taking care of his mom's dog, or I didn't completely blow it last night. I'm going to allow myself to believe the latter might be true.

Sarah shows up a full ten minutes early, which turns out to advantageous because Mazzy's back and is trying to escape every time a customer walks in the door. Now Sarah's in the back play area, entertaining the little dogs and keeping the fence-hopping Jack Russell on a short leash. Literally.

I continue to check dogs in and can't remember how I was managing by myself. My social life might be in complete disarray, but in business, I seem to be doing something right, because the dogs keep coming and I'm able to pay the bills. I shouldn't complain about a thing.

Sarah and I switch off, and I play fetch with the little guys while she starts taking the big ones for their morning walks. I'm parked on the floor, playing tug-of-war with Oscar (de la Renta, in case you've forgotten), when the phone rings. I reach it just as the machine kicks on.

"Hello? Hound'n Around, I'm here." I wait for the message to end. "How can I help you?"

"Well, for starters, you can tell me why you don't return my phone calls, missy." My cousin's tone belies the angry words. Besides it's hard to take someone seriously when they call you "missy."

"Hey, Kendra, I'm so sorry. Things have been crazy here at work. There are twenty-eight dogs here today." Having worked here for a week, K will understand the significance of that number. "But I hired someone yesterday, so it should get better."

"I'm glad to hear that business is going so well, June. But that doesn't explain why you can't call me after seven-thirty p.m. Unless one of those boys has shown back up in your life—and if that happened and you didn't call me, well I oughta—"

I cut in before the threats start flying. "K, I can assure you that I would call if that were to happen. Honestly, I've spent most of my nights moping. Well, until last night, that is."

She jumps on my last statement like it's a plate of biscuits and gravy. "What happened last night? Spill, girl."

I fill her in on meeting Luca and trying to determine if he's a lunatic. She agrees that most crazy people can't afford Armani and insists on meeting him if we make it to a third date.

"What about Ally? She back yet?" There's caution in my cousin's voice.

"Kendra, you won't believe it. I went back home last weekend, and she showed up and we talked, really talked. About our friendship then and now and about the night she died. K, Brad tried to force himself on her that night. That's why they left the party early. She was convinced that she caused her own death by saying no."

There's silence on the other end of the line.

"You there, K?"

"That poor girl. She's been blamin' herself all these years?"

I see Sarah through the window, so I know I need to wrap this up. "Yeah, but we talked and things are good now. She's being very supportive and not at all intrusive."

'Well, ain't that somethin'."

"Hey, K, I gotta go. But I promise to call if anything else happens."

"You better, 'cuz I know where you live, honey."

The rest of the week flies by and on Friday as Luca is picking Gigi up, he invites me on a picnic the next day.

It will be my first non-moping Saturday since the break-up(s).

Imagine my disappointment when I wake up to not just rain, but thunder and hail. The storm is battering my building and I try to hold Midge over the toilet so I won't have to go outside. She's not getting it.

I haven't been able to find my raincoat since I moved into this apartment. I asked Ally to do the final check at the last place. There's no telling what else I left behind. Midge is doing the doggie equivalent of crossing her legs, so I cut a hole in a trash bag and stick it over my head. Shouldn't matter, I'm sure the picnic is off.

My Hefty bag can't compete with the stinging wall of water and hail that greets us outside the door. The building can barely compete.

Before we even make it down the stairs, I'm soaked to the bone. So much for washing my hair last night. Midge seems completely undeterred by the storm and strains to go to her normal spot. She steps off the curb and is nearly carried away by the rushing river now flowing through the parking lot. Never much of one for swimming, Midge jumps back on the sidewalk and pulls me toward the steps. Apparently going potty isn't worth braving the rip tides.

As soon as her little feet are back inside the apartment, my adorable little dog squats. Glad to know I didn't go outside in a tsunami for nothing.

I've just finished wringing out my clothes when the doorbell rings. You're kidding me, right?

Gathering my dingy, 10-year-old robe around my body, I peek out the window beside the door. Sure enough, there's Luca, wearing a trench coat *and* carrying an umbrella—basically taunting my complete lack of preparation.

I crack open the door. "Luca, hi."

"I'm sorry, am I early? Did you just get out of the shower?"

"No, I just got in from trying to walk my dog. I figured we'd have to cancel the picnic." I realize it's rude to not invite him in, but my formerly-white robe is disgusting. I'm trying to hide as much of it as possible behind the door.

Luca looks over his shoulder at the sheet of rain. "I didn't want to cancel, so I made alternate plans. Should I leave?"

"No, please don't. I just need a few minutes to get into some dry clothes. Do you mind waiting?" I swing the door open wide enough for him to enter. Screw the robe. Look at that smile.

Midge is shivering by the couch and doesn't even make an effort to bark at Luca. She's probably deciding where to poop.

Not bothering with my hair, which will just get wet again the moment I step back outside, I throw on a casual skirt and t-shirt. Not too thin, as I'm sure it will also be getting wet.

When I enter the living room, Luca has got Midge wrapped in the afghan from my couch and he's rubbing her down. What a sweetie. But couldn't he use a towel and not my fake velvet throw?

"Well, I'm ready. Do I need to bring anything?"

"Nope, just that pretty face."

What a line.

Luca sets Midge down on the floor and rises from the couch. "Shouldn't you get a raincoat?"

What a smart idea. "I can't find mine. I think I left it behind when I moved."

As we step outside, Luca opens his trench coat and pulls me close to him. The walk to the car is awkward and I still get pretty wet, but cuddling up to a man is not entirely unpleasant. He settles me in the front seat of his Porsche and races to the other side.

"So, where are we going?"

He taps the end of my nose with his index finger. "That's a surprise, sweet June."

Chapter Thirty-Five

We're in the heart of uptown when Luca pulls into the garage of a towering glass and concrete structure. It's not a building I'm familiar with, but I don't get uptown much.

It's nice to be out of the driving rain and bruising hail. Stepping from the car, I shake off the moisture still clinging to my legs and hair. Luca leads me to an elevator, and as we step inside, I'm reminded of my last elevator ride and Ally's reference to "hot elevator sex." Luckily the new Ally won't pull a stunt like that, but just thinking about it brings a flush to my face.

Luca inserts a key into the panel and presses a button marked "Penthouse." Is he taking me to his apartment? That seems awfully presumptive.

Smiling at me as the elevator whisks us up nearly thirty floors, Luca explains. "One of the companies I consult for keeps a condo here for visiting associates. I thought we could have our picnic inside." His eyes are sweeping up and down my body, and I suddenly feel exposed in my knee-length skirt.

What do I really know about this man other than he helps his mother with her dog? If he actually has a mother. Maybe Gigi is just a prop used to lure unsuspecting doggie daycare owners to strange penthouses. I step back into the corner of the elevator.

"You're not afraid of heights, are you?" Now he's teasing me. The nerve.

Ally appears beside me. "Junie, I think you're being paranoid. He just sounds concerned to me. Probably because you're glued to the back of this elevator, and your face is as pale as a geisha's."

When did Ally take on this role of rational, "talk Junie down from the ledge" friend? Not that I'm not grateful.

I force myself to unclench my hands from the railing lining the car and step toward Luca. "No, not afraid of heights, just surprised the elevator travels so fast." I have no idea if this elevator is moving any quicker or slower than a typical elevator, but I'm thinking on my feet.

Luca takes my hand and pulls me close to him. "You can hold on to me."

He's coming closer to my mouth. Oh crap. He's going to kiss me, and not on the cheek this time. His lips cover mine, gently pressing while he tilts my head back. Closing my eyes, I try to give in to the kiss, but images of first Jesse, and then Nelson flash through my mind.

He releases the hold on my lips, but not on my head. "Is something wrong?"

Yes. Everything is wrong. There's a perfectly nice (or maybe a lunatic) man kissing me, and I can't kiss him back because I can't stop feeling like I'm cheating on the two men I was cheating on with each other before. Okay, that doesn't even make sense to me.

"I'm sorry, Luca. Can we slow things down a bit?" He lets go of my head then and takes a step back. "I just got out of a pretty complicated relationship and I...I need to take it slow." I step toward him, placing my hand lightly on his chest. "Is that okay?"

"Of course, it's okay. We'll take as long as you need." He squeezes my hand as the elevator dings and the doors slide open.

Okay, I was wrong. That was the longest elevator ride ever.

We step inside the most luxurious condo I've ever seen. Floor-to-ceiling windows expose an expansive view of the skyline, the floor is tiled in rich marble, and the furniture looks like it was plucked right from a designer's sketchbook.

Rain washes down the windows, but no sound from the storm penetrates the glass.

Luca has already been here to set things up.

Spread on the floor in front of the fireplace, which is lit to stave off the chill, is a checkered blanket and a full spread of food. An actual picnic basket sits off to one side.

I sink onto the blanket, which I now realize rests on a fluffy shag rug.

Luca pours a glass of wine for each of us. Raising his to mine, he taps the edge. "To taking things slow."

In the movies, this is where the heroine says, "Oh screw that," and proceeds to straddle the suddenly bare-chested hero. In this real-life version, Luca offers me some cheese and crackers. And keeps his shirt on.

"So, do you want to tell me about this relationship you were in?"

No. Not at all. Not even the teensiest-tiny bit. "Maybe another time."

He holds his hands up in mock surrender. "Okay. Slow."

"Thanks."

The rest of the meal we talk about safe things, like his mother, and Gigi, and the company that he just bought and broke into little pieces and sold again.

And I try to put Jesse and Nelson as far out of my mind as possible.

Luca and I have been on six dates. We've gone to dinner, the theater, a little league game (his nephew's) and Carowinds. The little league game was when I knew once and for all that Luca isn't a lunatic. The man ran out of the stands and onto the field when his nephew scored the winning run.

The amusement park was the most fun. I've lived in Charlotte for six years, and I've never been to Carowinds. We ate junk food, rode roller coasters and shot ducks with a water gun. I beat Luca. He says he let me win, but I know better. That was the day I kissed him. Without a single thought of old-what's-their-names.

It's so much less complicated dating one man. I don't have to keep straight whose night it is, or which name I moan as they're nibbling on my ear. Not that I've done any moaning with Luca yet. We're taking it slow.

Sarah and I have just settled the dogs for their nap when the bell over the door tinkles. A huge bouquet of roses is followed in by a scrawny guy with a ponytail.

"Delivery for June Hinderson."

Okay, I was dating *two* guys and never had flowers delivered. "I'm June." He lowers the vase to the surface of the desk and I can see his pock-marked face.

"Sign here." He sounds bored, but his eyes are traveling over the room and all the dogs. They settle on Sarah, who is in the back eating her lunch.

I hand the clipboard back to him, but he doesn't take his eyes off my employee.

Sarah giggles and covers her mouth.

It's like watching two teenagers at a dance.

Delivery guy is shifting his feet back and forth, and Sarah is swiveling on the stool, eyes lowered, looking up through her lashes.

I'm looking back and forth between the two, feeling like I should leave them alone.

Finally, delivery guy glances down at his clipboard and shuffles out the door.

"Ohmygosh. He was so cute." My dependable, no-nonsense staff member morphs into a giggly teenage girl right before my eyes.

I'm the one who just got flowers. I'm supposed to be giggly.

Sarah rushes to the front of the room and peers out the window, watching the flower shop van drive away. Once it's out of sight, she turns around and sinks into the chair opposite my desk with a huge sigh.

"Oh. You got flowers." Well that only took her six minutes to deduce. "Who are they from?"

Now to Sarah's knowledge, I only date one man at a time, so common sense should tell her who they are from. Any minute now...

"Oh! I bet they're from Luca!"

Laughing to myself, I open up the card.

"Happy two-week anniversary. Luca"

What kind of guy remembers a two-week anniversary? That's not creepy, is it?

Ally pops onto the desk and smells the roses. "Not creepy, June. Ro-man-tic."

I'm not five, Ally.

Sarah skips back to finish her lunch and I send Luca a quick text thanking him for the flowers.

"You know, you were never this paranoid before you dated Jesse and Nelson."

"Sarah, I'm going to step outside for a second and make a call." This is how I have conversations with Ally now that Sarah's here all day. Let the people on the street think I'm crazy, but not my employee. I need her.

Once outside, I put the phone up to my ear. "I'm not paranoid."

"Um, yeah you are. You're talking on a phone with no one on the other end."

"Well, not about guys."

She's twirling around a lamp post like she's in a musical or something. "Remember the whole I-think-Luca's-a-lunatic thing?"

"He brought it up."

"And the elevator thing?"

She had me there. I was a little freaked out in the elevator. "You can never be too sure in this day and age. Most psychopaths are charming. Like Ted Bundy."

"I'm just saying. That whole thing with Jesse and Nelson totally screwed you up. I think you made the right decision dumping both of them. And I'm glad they haven't been around to confuse you."

"Confuse me?"

"Yeah, if Nelson was still across the street, or Jesse down the hall, you would've have broken down and gone back to one or both of them weeks ago."

I wave the phone at her. "That is not true. I stuck by my decision. And I moved on. With Luca."

An old man crosses the street, most likely to get away from the crazy woman waving her phone and blessing out the lamp post.

I raise the phone back to my ear. "Maybe I was confused. But I'm not now. I like Luca a lot. It's that simple."

Chapter Thirty-Six

Sarah's out walking Moe, Curly, Wilbur and Sparky, a boxer mix, who's visiting for the first time today. Ally's playing with a group of little dogs, but if anyone walked in it would just look like Percival was playing fetch with himself. I'm catching up on e-mail.

Outside there's a rumble, and a UPS truck stops in front of the building. I haven't ordered anything, so I turn back to the computer screen.

The bell over the door tinkles and in walks the most magnificent thing I've ever laid eyes on, all wrapped up in brown. And he's carrying a package.

Ally is at my side instantaneously. "Junie, forget about Luca. You want that."

I think my mouth is hanging open, but I no longer have control of my muscles.

"June Hinderson?" His teeth gleam white against his rich, cocoa skin.

Am I breathing?

Ally nudges me.

"Oh, I'm June."

He leans across the desk, and indicates I should sign on the small screen he is holding.

"Junie, I can assure you. That is the finest man on the face of this planet or elsewhere. And I know."

"I believe you."

"Excuse me?"

Oh crap. I have got to stop saying this stuff out loud. "I said, 'thank you.'"

"Okay then, you have a great day." With a wink he hands me the package and turns to leave.

"That view is even better going than coming." Ally starts to follow him out the door.

As soon as it clicks closed, I snap out of my stupor. "Ally, get back here."

"But Junie..." She's sticking her head through the front door, which she knows I hate.

I can't argue with her though, because I've just looked at the package in my hands.

When I don't answer, Ally appears behind me and peers over my shoulder. "Who's N. Brantley?" Suddenly her hand flies to her mouth. "Oh..."

I'm back to being completely confused. And I haven't even opened the package yet. Turns out Ally is right again. Just seeing Nelson's name has got me all in a tizzy.

Sarah came back shortly after the chocolate dream left and I shoved the package in my desk drawer where it's been taunting me from ever since.

Pick-up time has begun and we're both running back and forth getting dogs ready to go home. I don't have time to think about the package. Only it's all I can think about.

I stop long enough to text Luca, saying there's been an emergency and can we please reschedule dinner? Yes, I'm going to miss my two-week anniversary dinner with a wonderful man who is actually in the same city as me so I can stay home and focus on a package from a man I broke up with a month ago who is apparently in Nevada. I never claimed to be sane.

Next, I call Kendra. "K, I need you."

Apparently, my tone conveys everything, because she answers without hesitation. "I'm on my way."

Three hours later, I'm sitting on my couch staring at the package. I've memorized how Nelson forms his "J"s. I've memorized the zip code of Paradise, NV. Nelson's in Paradise. And I'm in hell.

"This is nothing like hell. We took a field trip there once. You know, it's not nearly as hot as everyone says." Ally has been doing this all evening. Trying to snap me out of my daze. So far it hasn't worked.

The door flies open and Kendra breezes in. "Okay, which one is it?"

I just point to the package on the coffee table.

"K, you've got to do something. She's been like this for hours." I've never seen Ally so excited to see my cousin. She's forgotten that Kendra can't see or hear her.

Kendra picks up the simple brown package and turns it over in her hands. "Nevada, huh?"

"Paradise." The first tear of the night slips down my cheek. I've done so well up 'til now.

She lays the parcel back on the table, as if it contains something fragile, or explosive. I'd guess the latter.

We sit side by side on the couch, in silence, for nearly another hour.

"Have you eaten?" Kendra rises, and heads toward the kitchen, where she feels most at home.

I shake my head. More tears stream down my cheeks. "Two weeks. Dinner." I'm sobbing now, the words coming out in between sniffles.

"You haven't eaten dinner in two weeks?"

"No, doofus! She canceled out on her two-week anniversary dinner with Luca because of stupid Nelson and his stupid package." The sight of Ally standing with her hands on her hips, getting all riled up about Nelson turns my sobs into laughter.

Now I'm laughing and crying all at the same time.

Kendra looks irritated. "It's her, isn't it?"

I nod my head, trying to control my laughter so I can speak.

"Well, I don't know what's going on, but I could sure use some brownies."

Chapter Thirty-Seven

Kendra and I have eaten an entire pan of brownies. And washed them down with a bottle or two of wine. But who's counting?

I finally feel ready to open the package.

I tear the plain, brown wrapping off, careful not to rip the writing on the front. I may be tipsy, but I'm still sentimental.

The moment I held the parcel in my hands, I knew it was a book. But that's not the same as seeing which book Nelson deemed important enough to send me from across the country.

My breath comes in short huffs as I stare down at the familiar yellow binding.

"What'zthat? A Nancy Drew book?" Kendra is leaning into my lap, the wine causing her words to slur slightly.

Specifically, it is a first edition of *The Secret of the Old Clock*, the first in the series. A book that Nelson knows is very dear to my heart.

Flipping through the pages carefully, I search for a note. Something telling me he's coming home. There is none.

Sarah opens Hound'n Around for me. I drag myself in around ten, hoping Luca has already dropped off Gigi. His mom is getting out of the hospital this weekend, so if I can avoid him for two days more days, I should be in the clear.

If I just change my business, home and cell numbers.

He keeps leaving these concerned messages on my various answering machines and voicemail. I guess it has something to do with my emergency excuse for missing dinner last night. So maybe it wasn't an emergency in the classical sense of the word.

I send him one more text insisting that everything is fine, but my cousin came into town and I need to entertain her for a few days. Kendra, of course, doesn't mind me using her as an excuse, but she'd like to meet Luca before I kick him to the curb.

I'm breaking up with Luca. Nelson sent me a Nancy Drew book. I don't know what it means, but when I saw the cover, it was the happiest I've been in over a month. Regardless of picnics, baseball games and roller coasters.

This is truly a case of it's-not-you-it's-me. I'm just putting off the inevitable. The roses are still taunting me from my desk. I consider having Sarah return them to the flower shop. Then she can run into delivery guy. But I can't figure out what my reason for return is. They're too beautiful? They smell too good? The guy who sent them to me is too perfect?

I've spent the last ten years of my life trying to downplay my craziness. I can't imagine this would help my cause. So, I keep the roses and my guilt grows with each whiff.

Sarah wants to know how dinner was. I guess she thinks my coming in late is a sign of a good dinner, and even better dessert. Come to think of it, I never even had dinner. Kendra and I skipped straight to the good stuff.

"My cousin came into town, so I hung out with her instead."

She gives me a look that clearly says, "The guy sent you like a million roses and you stand him up?" Or maybe I'm reading too much into things.

I sneak out at four, lest Luca shows up early to get Gigi. I hope I'm not taking advantage of my brand-new staff member.

Kendra and I spend the evening watching *Survivor*. We make fun of how skanky the contestants are and chant "batter, batter, swing batter" during the challenges. It's almost as fun as it was with Jesse.

I'm lying on the couch, feet stretched out in Kendra's lap, drifting off. "K?"

"Yeah, June?"

"Thanks so much for coming. Don't know what I'd do without ya."

Just before sleep overtakes me, I think I hear her say, "Probably starve."

Kendra opens the daycare on Friday, as I continue my covert working style. Avoidance hours: 10:00-4:00.

"Hey K. Where's Sarah?"

"She's out with some little ones. I think it's her last group." Kendra is throwing a tennis ball for the big dogs. Curly and Moe are tripping over each other trying to get to it.

I sit down at the desk and scan the appointment book. "We've got a new dog coming in this morning?"

"Yeah, it was a last-minute thing. Should be here any minute."

I'm checking my email when the bell tinkles. A skinny kid dragging a shaggy mutt comes through the door. He looks awfully familiar. The kid, not the dog.

"Come on, Jasper. Get in here." The dog's giving him a hard time, so I grab a Snausage and approach the door.

The treat gets the dog's attention and he trots over to me. "Good boy." When I look back up at the owner, I realize why he looks so familiar. It's the flower delivery guy. Who knew getting flowers would earn me a customer? "So, you're interested in daycare for your dog?"

Delivery guy is looking around the room, craning his neck to see over the fencing. He drops the dog's leash and Jasper follows me back to my desk. "Um, yeah, I guess."

Just then the door opens and Sarah enters with the group she was walking. Upon seeing delivery guy, she starts giggling uncontrollably and runs to the back, dragging six little bodies behind her.

As delivery guy stares after her, I think I understand why he made the appointment.

He's filling out the application for Jasper but keeps glancing back at Sarah who has relieved Kendra in the big dog area. Sarah is absently throwing the ball, but keeps one eye on the front desk, and she continues to giggle every few seconds.

K walks over to me and whispers in my ear. "What's with her?"

"She thinks delivery guy is cute."

"Delivery guy?"

I nod my head in his direction. "He delivered the flowers from Luca the other day."

"Ah." She stares at the kid's greasy head. "I don't see it."

I shrug my shoulders. "They're like nineteen."

When Austin, according to the registration form, hands the paperwork to me, I notice that most of the information about the dog is blank. "Who's your vet?"

He's looking at his feet and keeps wiping his hands on his jeans. I figure he's nervous because of Sarah. "Um, like, it's my brother's dog? I'm just watching it for a while."

"Okay..." I reach down and check Jasper's collar for a rabies tag. "I can get the vet's information off the tag, so that should be fine."

He pays for the day and with one last look at Sarah, leaves.

"That was weird." Kendra's looking at his incomplete paperwork.

I glance back to make sure Sarah's can't overhear. "If I didn't know better, I'd say that kid borrowed a dog so he could see her again. The dog doesn't even seem to like him."

"Well, I guess that's one way to get a girl."

We both stare as Sarah twirls around the play area, humming and grinning uncontrollably. "It certainly seems to be working."

Kendra comes back in toting one of her many make-up kits.

"Hey, I thought you were getting us some lunch."

"You know, I was goin' to, but I figured this was more important." She snaps open the case, extending a mirror and folding out trays full of Mary Kay.

"I'm not following."

She's digging through eye shadow and blush, selecting several of each. "I'm gonna do Sarah up. For the boy."

Of course. She's gonna do Sarah up. For the boy. "Huh?"

Sighing, and perching her hands on her ample hips, K looks at me as if I'm a few cards short of a full deck. "I'm gonna give Sarah a makeover. To impress the delivery guy."

"Ah." I look at the clock, then at the make-up taking over my desk. "But what about lunch?"

Kendra is putting the finishing touches on Sarah's face. She's already increased the volume of her hair by about 80% and my once frumpy staff member now looks ready for a night on the town. Except for the fact that she's wearing holey jeans and a t-shirt that looks like it's older than she is. Well from the neck up, she's gorgeous.

I'd love to stick around and see how Austin receives the new-and-improved Sarah, but not so much that I want to risk running into Luca. Kendra has assured me she'll give me the play-by-play later tonight.

Wishing Sarah luck, I head out the door. As I'm pulling away, I spot Luca's Porsche in my rearview mirror. Oo, that was a close one.

It's Saturday, and I've effectively avoided Luca for two days. I'm quite proud of myself, until he shows up at my front door.

Oh crap.

I yell over my shoulder as I open the door. "Kendra, we have company."

"I presume Kendra is the cousin you dumped me for."

Well, I haven't technically dumped you yet.

Somehow, in the thirty seconds it takes me to open the door and invite Luca in, Kendra has transformed herself from pajama-clad and sweaty to cute sundress and done up. Seriously, she put on an entire face and fluffed her hair to its normal state.

I, however, am reveling in my post-aerobics-video state. Little Miss Sunshine shirt sweaty and clinging to my midsection. Hair failing from ponytail. Baggy, torn Umbros almost falling off. Don't want to look too good when I tell Luca it's over.

"Luca, I presume." Kendra pushes me out of the way and grabs Luca's hand. Apparently since I'm breaking up with him, K sees him as an acceptable target. She turns on her Southern wiles. "I'm just gettin' ready to whip up some of my famous blueberry pancakes. You will join, us, won'tcha?" She's nearly dragging him into the kitchen.

Luca looks to me, eyes scared, begging me to rescue him. Believe me honey; you aren't going to like me any better. You may as well get some pancakes out of the deal. I shrug my shoulders.

While Kendra's busying herself in the kitchen, Luca escapes and pulls me into the hallway. "What's going on? Is everything okay?"

The look of genuine concern in his grey eyes almost undoes me. But then I think of Nelson. Of the book. "I'm sorry I've been so out of touch the last couple of days." I struggle to think of how I want to do this. I need to sit down. Luca should sit down. I lead him to the couch. "You know how I told you I recently got out of a complicated relationship?"

His expression falls. His shoulders slump. The man is smart. He knows what's coming.

I grasp his hands in mine. "You are the sweetest guy, and I've had a great time with you. But I'm just not over..." Nelson, Jesse, any of it, really. "...it yet."

He's searching my eyes, maybe even my heart. Apparently, he doesn't find what he's looking for, because he rises from the couch without a word.

"Pancakes are ready!" Kendra calls out merrily from the kitchen.

Luca's at the door before I can even get off the couch. I race to him. "I'm so sorry, Luca."

He tenderly cups my face with one hand and kisses me gently on the lips. "I hope you find happiness." Then he's gone.

"Wait! Luca! They're blueberry!" Kendra joins me at the door, watching his broad shoulders descend the stairs. "You couldn't wait 'til after the pancakes."

Chapter Thirty-Eight

On Monday, Sarah bounds into the daycare nearly an hour before her shift starts.

"What are you doing here so early? And why are you so happy?" I'm filling water buckets in the play areas.

Sarah's swaying back and forth, her hands behind her back, her grin filling her face. "I couldn't wait to tell you.""Tell me what?" Although I have a suspicion this relates to Austin, who, according to Kendra, asked for Sarah's phone number last Friday night, I don't want to spoil the fun of her getting to tell me about it.

Her hands fly out and she jumps straight up off the ground. "He called!"

I cover a grin. "Who?"

"Austin!" She catches me laughing behind my hand and slaps me playfully. "Kendra told you."

"Yeah, she said he asked for your number."

Sarah's absently stroking Serena, a chocolate lab mix, on the head. "He called me that night and then on Saturday he took me to the movies. Like on a date!"

"That's great, Sarah." While your new love is blooming, mine is once more on a thorn-covered trail headed for disaster.

On Tuesday, another package arrives. The postmark is from Aspen, Co.

Sarah stops mopping and stares at the departing UPS man. "Is that guy even for real?"

"He isn't an angel, or I would be all over that." Ally is leaning over my desk, a puddle forming beneath her chin. I didn't know angels could drool.

I start to ask Ally if she's even allowed to "be all over that", it being Heaven and all, but I stop myself because Sarah's standing like three feet away. I send her out to walk some dogs so I can open the package in private. Well, as private as it ever is with Ally around.

I tear into the paper, sentiment gone now that Nelson has communicated with me a second time. Well, sort of. If sending a book can be considered communication.

A copy of *James and the Giant Peach* stares up at me from inside the wrapping. I'm stroking the cover, remembering the first time I read it.

"Is there anything inside? Did the book-wienie even say hi?" Ally's regressing.

I flip open the cover, no inscription, but when I turn to the title page, I find that this is a signed copy. I trace the letters in Ronald Dahl's signature. I can see why finding treasures like this is so exciting for Nelson. Skimming through the rest of the pages, no notes appear. This doesn't surprise me. Somehow, I expected another book to arrive.

"If he's going to keep sending books, I'm not leaving this building. I'm not going to risk missing my tall drink of hot chocolate."

The magnificence of the UPS man is just a bonus for me.

Book #3 arrives three days later. Kansas City, Mo. The pattern is becoming clear. He's coming home.

"What is it?" Ally has finished mooning over Elijah—yes, the UPS man has a name—and is perched on the edge of my desk waiting for me to open the package.

The bell tinkles over the door and we are both forced to wait a while longer.

An older woman using a cane is accompanied by a striking redhead with grey eyes. Uh-oh.

"Are you this June person?" The woman is obviously frail, but that doesn't stop her from shaking her cane in my direction. "Do you always go around playing games with unsuspecting men like my Luca?"

"Mama, you really should take it easy. The doctor said—"

The redhead is abruptly cut off my Luca's mother. "Oh, pooh. There's nothing wrong with me." She turns back to me, staring me down with the same penetrating grey eyes that she obviously passed to her children. "You should be ashamed of yourself!"

"I am."

She appears to be caught off guard by my quick acknowledgment. "Oh."

I gesture to the chair opposite my desk and Luca's mother lowers herself into it, her daughter standing guard behind her. "I am so sorry about what happened with your son. He is a wonderful man and any woman would be lucky to have him. But I'm not over my last boyfriend, and I didn't feel I was being fair to Luca." I keep the possibility of Nelson coming back to myself.

"See, Mama. I told you that someone who took such good care of Gigi couldn't be all bad." The redhead pats her mother on the shoulder and then looks up at me. "Luca doesn't have any ill will toward you, I promise. Mama was just upset to see him hurt."

Feeling humbled that Luca is taking this so hard, I begin to second guess my decision. He is a great guy. And I don't even know if Nelson is coming back for sure.

"Do you really want some man that goes crying to his mama because a woman dumped him?" Ally is standing beside the desk, arms crossed, foot tapping. "Besides, Nelson is obviously coming back."

I look from Ally to Luca's mom and sister and back. They both turn to see what I'm looking at. "I am so sorry. I wish things could have been different. Maybe if I met him another time, who knows? But I'm glad to see you up and around, Mrs. Morrow. And I hope you'll give Gigi a hug for me."

The older woman's face lights up at the mention of her dog. The two women bid their farewells and leave.

I think I handled my first disgruntled mother pretty well. Hopefully there won't be anymore.

Luca texts me ten minutes later.

> Sorry about my mother. I had no idea she would show up there. Miss you.

Ugh. Dagger. Heart.

Saturday, I decide that I need to get out of my comfort zone and do something for somebody else for a change. There's a walk to benefit the local Humane Society, so Midge and I get up at eight—yes, AM, yes, on a Saturday—and head down to Campbell Creek Greenway.

It's a beautiful October day and unseasonably warm. We're about a mile into the walk and my shirt is stuck to my back. Mind you, it may just be the fact that I am horribly out of shape. Since I hired Sarah, I don't think I've even taken Midge for a walk. But Sarah's lost six pounds.

My diet has been appalling as well. Most evenings I sit in front of the television, squirting Easy Cheese onto crackers, or if I'm feeling especially adventurous, making a peanut butter and jelly sandwich. I can't remember the last time I ate a vegetable. Unless French fries count.

Resolved to take better care of myself, I quicken my pace. Midge doesn't seem happy about the new speed. But our longest walk of late has been to the dumpster and back.

There are approximately 400 people registered for the walk, so the path is crowded with people leisurely strolling, others running, and even a few power chairs. One breezes past us, a Chihuahua perched between its owner's legs. Midge is, of course, offended by the scooter and barks ferociously every time we see one.

But for the most part, she's behaving herself, and I've even managed to hand out a few business cards.

Around mile marker three, I take a seat on a bench to rest. Pulling a water bottle from my backpack, I pour some into a bowl for Midge and then take a long drink. Midge is lying at my feet, tongue darting in and out of her mouth in quick bursts. Suddenly she jumps up and starts a frenzied bark. I look for another motorized wheelchair, but instead I see Jesse jogging toward us.

My heart goes still in my chest. Midge strains at her leash. I'm so numb from the shock of seeing him that the handle slips right through my fingers.

I watch, as if in slow motion, as my dog darts across the path toward Jesse, tripping a small child and nearly taking out a Boston terrier. Jesse scoops the little dog up and cuts across the path toward me, apologizing for my terror along the way.

It's been exactly forty days since I last laid eyes on Jesse. Is it bad that I know that?

He looks even better than I remember. His hair has grown out a little and now brushes the tops of his ears and the collar of his t-shirt—which is straining against his muscular arms. His skin is golden brown and glistening from sweat. And his hazel eyes are crinkled against the sunlight streaming through the trees.

I don't know what to say. I need time to process. But I don't have time, because Jesse is now sitting beside me, chipped tooth peeking out at me through his grin.

"Hey Junie."

Junie. I blink to hold back the rush of tears that are threatening to escape. Luckily, I'm wearing sunglasses. "Hey Jesse."

Midge is standing on her hind legs in his lap, covering his face with kisses. I imagine they're sticky too, because a volunteer gave her a peanut butter and honey doggie daiquiri about a mile back. He doesn't seem to mind.

"So, you came out for the walk?" Stupid question, I realize, but my brain is functioning on very little oxygen right now on account of my heart stopping and all.

Jesse laughs—that slow rollin' chuckle that I didn't realize I missed until right now. "Actually, no. I run here most every day. But when I saw they were doin' the benefit today, I signed up." He sets Midge down on the ground and holds on to the end of her leash. "I bought a house near here."

Where he lives now. Instead of three doors down from me. He had to move to get away from the woman who broke his heart for no good reason. I'm developing a bad habit of that lately. I should probably stop dating altogether. Just for the sake of the male population.

"How's business goin'?"

"Good. I had to hire some help. We stay pretty busy."

He shifts in his seat, his thigh grazing against mine. Tingles rocket up my spine. I've forgotten the effect he has on me. "So everythin's good?" It's as if he's studying me, trying to see through the darkened lenses of my glasses into my soul.

How do I tell him that I made a mistake? That I ruined everything? "Yeah."

He leans back, as if to distance himself. "Good."

For several minutes we don't speak, just sit there watching the walkers go by. Midge seems content to lie between our feet.

"Well, I guess I should get on." He rises from the bench and places the leash in my hand. "It was right good seein' you, June Bug." His voice catches a bit on the last word, and I want to jump up and throw my arms around him and tell him I miss him.

But I sit on the bench, watching him run away, back out of my life.

Chapter Thirty-Nine

I t's all I can do to finish the walk. I can't get home fast enough.

In my mind, I go over the conversation again and again. I could have said something, anything. I miss you. I want you back. The new *Bachelor* is a schmuck.

When I walk into the apartment, the first thing I see is *James and the Giant Peach* laying on the coffee table. Nelson. For the morning, I'd completely forgotten about Nelson.

Somehow, I've managed to get right back to where I was two months ago. Two guys, both great. The biggest difference is: they were in my life then. Now, I'm not even sure I have a choice.

Jesse has most likely moved on. I should put him out of my mind.

Nelson, on the other hand, reached out to me. Maybe he'll be home soon and he'll give me a second chance.

"But are you sure you want Nelson back?" This voice-of-reason Ally is getting on my nerves.

"No, I'm not sure. I'm not sure about anything." Tears of frustration, of confusion, of sheer exhaustion run down my cheeks.

She plops down beside me on the couch and circles her arm around my back. I can feel the lightest touch, like a breeze blowing over my shoulders, but nothing like that day at my mom's house. "Junie, I wish I knew what the right answer was. I wish I could look into the future and tell you what you should do."

I manage a small smile through my tears. "You're just an angel, not a fortune teller."

"Sorry."

"Me too." Right now, I wish she wasn't an angel. I wish she had never died. I wish I could hold onto her and cry until my tears are gone.

Back at work on Monday, I'm straightening up my desk when I find the package that arrived on Friday afternoon. After the visit from Luca's mother and sister, I had forgotten all about it.

I wait until Sarah has left for a walk and scoop, and tear the paper from the book.

Charlotte's Web. Nelson is recreating my favorite childhood memories through these books. This is a brand-new copy, printed just last year. That's odd.

Flipping through the pages, a small piece of paper falls onto the desk. It's a receipt for sushi and on the back, in Nelson's distinctive scrawl, are two words.

"SOME MIDGE."

I'm chuckling to myself when Sarah returns with the new dog, Huckleberry. We tend to walk the new ones on their own the first time around so we can get a feel for how they are going to behave before we add three or four more dogs to the mix.

"What's so funny?" Sarah's got her body wedged against the doorframe and she's pulling on the leash with all her might.

"Nothing." I get up to see what the problem is. Huckleberry, a Great Dane-mix puppy, is sitting in the middle of the sidewalk, refusing to move. At seven months, he's 65 lbs, and if he doesn't want to move, he pretty much doesn't have to. "It's a good thing he's cute."

Sarah lets the leash go slack and hands it to me. Huckleberry lies down. I hear the treat jar clink and, in a few seconds, she's back at the door, Snausage in hand. He doesn't budge.

"Seriously? Not for a Snausage?" I look around to see if anyone is out on the street nearby. "Midge will do pretty much anything for a Snausage." Handing the leash back to Sarah, I step outside and over Huck. Getting behind him, I lift his back legs as Sarah pulls the leash.

Safely inside the building, Huckleberry decides he does, in fact, want a Snausage and knocks the treat jar off the shelf. Shards of glass and treats fly across the lobby. Huck happily eats a dozen or so; then wanders back to the play area.

Some Huck.

"Are you sure you don't mind watching them for us?" My mother is speaking at a volume only needed for people with hearing aids. She must be on her cell phone.

I jot Roxie and Pierre in the reservation book to board for the weekend. "No, Mom. It's fine, I promise."

"Well, I just don't want to take advantage of you with your new business and all."

"You're not taking advantage. I'll see you on Friday." I go to hang up the phone, but she's still talking.

"Maybe you could have one of those nice boys join us for dinner. You are dating someone, aren't you, June?"

So maybe I haven't filled Mom in on my dating life. She's had enough excitement of her own to keep up with. "No, Mom. I'm not dating anyone right now." For once, I'm not even lying.

"Okay. Well, Harry and I will be in town by five. See you Friday, sweetie."

My mom and her boyfriend are going to Atlantic City for the weekend. How disturbing is that? And I get to watch their dogs. If I start to board dogs regularly, I'm going to have to get more help. Sarah's already working forty hours, and I'm scared to figure out how much time I actually spend here. Because then I'll be tempted to figure out my profit so far, and then I'll determine that my hourly wage is equivalent to the minimum wage in 1944, and then I'll be really depressed. But I'm paying the bills, so I can't complain. I have to keep reminding myself.

The packages are arriving with a startling frequency. On Tuesday, it was *Where the Sidewalk Ends.* Yesterday, the entire *Chronicles of Narnia* arrived. The last postmark was Memphis, Tn. Nothing so far today. And Elijah should have been here by now.

With only two dogs left, I send Sarah home. "I'll wrap things up. See you tomorrow."

"Thanks. I'm meeting Austin for dinner tonight." Putting on a light jacket, she walks toward the front. "It's weird that it's getting dark so early."

"Yeah, that means fall has arrived." I follow her to the door. "It'll start to get chilly now. You'll probably want to bring a coat for the walks soon."

She steps out onto the sidewalk. "Hey, that's the first time I've ever seen the lights on over there. I thought that place had closed down."

My eyes move to where she is pointing. I steady myself against the doorframe. The display window at Nelson's store is lit up. The open sign is visible on the door.

"You ever go in there? It looks pretty cool." Sarah has no idea the significance of those lights being on.

"Yeah, sometimes."

"Maybe I'll check it out on my lunch break tomorrow. 'Night." She heads down the street to her car, leaving me staring at the top of Nelson's head—which I can just see behind the display.

Closing my door, I keep my eyes trained on the door of the shop, afraid that if I look away the lights will go out.

We're open for another forty minutes, but if I have to wait that long, I fear I may burst from the anticipation. I should've stopped Sarah—she could have waited with the last two dogs.

"He's back, huh?" The sound of Ally's voice startles me. Which is odd, because I'm so used to hearing her pop in out of nowhere. I'm really in a state.

I'm pacing, but it's awkward, because I don't want to take my eyes off the windows across the street.

"Junie, sit down. Chill out." There she is again, being the reasonable one. Used to be, *I* was the reasonable one. "You're going to go over there and he's going to be thrilled to see you. And things are going to be great."

"You think?"

"Yeah. If that's what you want."

I turn to look at her so quickly; I get a crick in my neck. Rubbing it, I lower myself onto the bench in the window. "What do you mean? It's what I've been waiting for. For him to come home."

"Okay."

"No, really. What did you mean?"

She sighs. "I just meant that you seemed awfully upset about running into Jesse."

"But that was just a coincidence. Nelson sought me out."

"I don't see him over here."

Is she right? Do the books not mean what I am assuming they mean? Wouldn't he have come to see me as soon as he returned?

"Unless he's giving you space. You were the one who broke up with him, after all."

I'm not used to Ally playing devil's advocate, but this time I want her to be right. "He did just send the books, as if he was afraid to communicate further. In case I wasn't interested."

"Maybe."

"Maybe," I echo. Why is it so complicated?

Wilbur's dad arrives to pick up the hound. Oscar's mom is right behind him. Now I can leave, but I'm not sure if I'm ready.

"Ally?"

"Yeah?" She joins me at the window.

I turn to my friend, who has been there through this whole mess. "If he doesn't want me back…"

"Then he's even more of a wienie than I gave him credit for."

Chapter Forty

When I reach the door of the shop, I can see Nelson working at his computer. His hair is shorter, no longer falling into his eyes, and it looks as if he's lost weight. He was already a skinny guy. I hope that wasn't because of me.

I place my hand on the knob, but it takes a full minute before I can turn it. My brain feels disconnected from my body.

As I push the door open, he looks up, eyes guarded, hands stilled over the keyboard.

I close the door gently behind me and for a moment there's silence. I think again how nice it would be to have music to fill the void.

"The books were amazing."

His hands drop into his lap and his shoulders fall as if he's just let out his breath. "I'm glad you like them."

"You didn't have to."

He smiles, his dimple making its first appearance. "Do you want some tea?"

I move toward the chair in the middle of the store. My comfy chair. "That'd be nice." Curling my feet underneath me, I sink into the plush folds, rediscovering the peace I've found here before.

Nelson hands me a cup and saucer, then sits across from me. "How have you been?"

"Good. We've been busy at work."

"We?" His tone is curious, not accusatory.

I blow on the hot tea. "Yeah, I had to hire someone. Her name is Sarah."

He nods his head; then studies his hands before looking at me again. "June, about the way I left...it probably seemed like I was running away." He pauses, thinking. "Maybe I was."

I don't know how to reply. He's been gone almost two months. I'm not sure how to act around him.

"You," his gaze lingers on my eyes, "are you seeing anyone?"

I shake my head no. I'll save Luca for another day.

"Maybe we could have dinner?" He's got this scared look in his eyes, like he's waiting for me to reject him again.

I feel a grin spread across my face. "I would love to have dinner." No pb&j tonight.

By the time the salads arrive, it's like he never left. The tension has drained away and in its place is the camaraderie of old friends catching up.

"You drove to California?" I stab a cucumber with my fork and swirl it through the dressing.

Nelson nods his head, but finishes chewing before answering. "Yeah, it was something I'd wanted to do for a long time. I figured this was as good a time as any." He fidgets with his wine glass. "It was hard to think about seeing you, after..."

"I'm so sorry I screwed everything up. Things got out of hand, and I didn't know how to fix it—"

"No, June, don't blame yourself. It's okay, honest. This trip was good for me."

Breaking off a piece of bread, I dip it in the olive oil laced with herbs. "Tell me about it."

He pushes his salad plate away, settling in for the tale. "Well, I drove straight through to California. Then started making my way back. I stopped whenever someplace seemed interesting. And everywhere I went, I sought out the local bookstore.

"I knew of a guy near Vegas that specializes in first edition children's books. Works out of his house. He put me up for the night and I was looking through his stock and saw *The Secret in the Old Clock*. I had to send it to you.

"Then I headed east and ended up in Aspen. The bookstore there is legendary. It's in an old Victorian house with all these different rooms, and library tables and even a tea shop. That's where I found the Ronald Dahl. The owner didn't even realize it was signed. Can you imagine?"

He's chewing on the end of his glasses now, really getting into the story. He pays no attention as the waitress puts our plates in front of us.

"Then it became a challenge for me. To find a book that you had talked about everywhere I went. When I drove through Kansas City, it was late and the local stores were closed, but I had thought of *Charlotte's Web*, so I found a Barnes and Noble.

"The more books I found, the faster I wanted to get home. Back to you."

He glances down, noticing his meal for the first time. Cutting off a bite, he chews it slowly. He won't meet my gaze.

"I couldn't wait for you to come home."

He raises his head, eyes widening, and his dimple appears. "Really?"

"Really." Reaching across the table, I link my fingers through his.

I'm finding it hard to wipe the smile off my face today.

Nelson's back. He's not mad at me. And I think he still likes me. I'm not 100% certain, because he didn't kiss me goodnight, but I'm pretty sure. I don't blame him for being cautious. He's been burned in the past—by me.

I haven't seen much of Ally, but with Nelson back, Elijah won't be stopping in, so what's the point in hanging out with me?

During naptime, I call Kendra to catch her up.

"I can't believe you waited so long to call me."

"I'm sorry, we stayed out pretty late last night talking and then I've been working all day."

"Um hm. Whatever. So, are you back together or what?"

I wish it was that simple. "I don't know, K. We didn't talk about it outright, but he did ask me if I'm seeing anyone."

"You didn't tell him about Luca, did you?"

"No, but I'm going to."

"I don't know if that's so smart, June."

I'm sitting on the bench in front of the building, and if I turn just right, I can see Nelson sitting at his computer. "It'll be all right. I mean, I broke up with Luca because I wasn't over Nelson, so he'll see that as a good thing, right?"

"Because you weren't over *Jesse and* Nelson. And I think it's obvious that it's best not to bring up his name at all."

"I saw him, K."

"Luca?"

"No, Jesse."

Kendra's voice rises in both pitch and volume. "You saw Jesse? When? And why the hell didn't you call me?"

I do feel a tad guilty about not calling her, but it was just too painful. "Saturday, at the Walk for the Animals."

"Saturday? You saw him Saturday and you are telling me this on Friday? Almost one week later?"

She's kind of missing the point. Besides, Nelson's spotted me sitting out here, and he's coming over. "K, I gotta go. I'll talk to you later."

"June! Don't hang—"

I end the call, cutting my cousin off, and smile up at Nelson. "Kendra says hi."

"That's nice." His eyes are fixed on mine as he lowers himself onto the bench beside me. In one fluid motion, he's got his hand behind my head and his lips over my mouth.

It's almost the exact same way that Luca kissed me that day in the elevator, except this time I'm definitely kissing back. It's starting to get really good when I imagine that I hear my mother's voice.

"June April Hinderson!"

I'm not imagining things. That is definitely my mother's voice. And yes, that is really my name. Most people don't know that. But now Nelson does. And Harry does. I know this because when I pull back from the kiss, I see my mother and Harry, each holding a dog, each with their mouths gaping open. They are extremely early.

I refrain from reminding them that this is exactly how I found them when I discovered my mother had a boyfriend.

"Well, you don't have to tell me everything about your life, June, but I expect you to at least be honest."

I have no idea what she's talking about.

Nelson jumps up and hurries over to shake their hands. Roxie tries to bite him. Dogs don't seem to like Nelson unless he has liver treats.

"Mom, what are you talking about? I didn't lie to you."

"I asked you if you were seeing anyone, and you told me no. And now I find you, in front of your place of business, no less, kissing the book fellow." She places her hand on Nelson's arm. "Which I am just thrilled about, by the way."

I throw my head back and stare up at the cloudless sky. Counting to ten, I breathe deeply and then look back at my mom. "I didn't lie. Nelson just got back yesterday. We weren't dating when I talked to you on Monday."

"Mm hm." I can tell she doesn't believe me. "Nelson, dear, where did you go?"

I'm a liar, and he's Nelson dear?

"I took a cross-country tour of bookstores."

I watch, dumbfounded, as my mom hooks her arm in Nelson's and walks into Hound'n Around inquiring about his trip. Harry and I just look at each other. I doubt he understands my mother any better than I do.

Nelson's back across the street and Harry's at the park with Sarah and a few dogs. My mom is detailing her itinerary for the weekend, including which slot machines she'll play.

I'm sort of half paying attention as I play tug-of-war with Denver, a retriever mix.

"It was so odd to pull up and see both Nelson and that neighbor of yours."

Huh? "You mean that Nelson's shop is across the street and that makes him my neighbor?"

She looks at me as if I just failed kindergarten. "No June. The nice fellow who lives down the hall from you. He was just down the street when we pulled up." She strokes Pierre's ears. "But then I saw Nelson and you kissing like that—in public—and when I looked back up, he was gone."

Jesse was here? He was here on my street? He was here on my street at the exact moment that Nelson kissed me? Seriously. What are the odds of that?

"June?"

Was she still talking? "Huh?"

"I asked you if that neighbor fellow of yours worked around here too."

"No, Mom."

She sets Pierre down on the floor and he goes running over to play with Huckleberry, who's about ten times bigger than him.

"Well, I wonder what he was doing in Belmont."

I'm wondering the exact same thing.

Chapter Forty-One

I'm guessing that Nelson didn't bargain for a dinner with the folks his second day back in town, but he's taking it in stride.

We're at—gasp!—a chain restaurant. I know how strongly Nelson feels about supporting local businesses and his general disdain for normal food. He's being a trooper.

My mother is telling him all about their trip to Europe. Nelson is politely listening while eating his blackened Cajun tilapia—the most exotic thing on the menu. Harry is concentrating on his steak. I'm picking at my potatoes, still hung up on the fact that Jesse obviously came to see me and instead saw me kissing Nelson.

When I look up, everyone is staring at me—well, except Harry, who is still staring at his side of beef—so I assume someone addressed me and I missed it. I force a smile. "Sorry. Guess I was in la-la land. It is Friday." I raise my glass of wine, to imply that maybe I've had too much to drink. To get to too much, I'm going to need my own bottle tonight.

I get another concerned/accusatory look from my mother. She will probably start sending me flyers for AA meetings. "Well, June, if you care to join the conversation, we were just discussing Thanksgiving."

We were? "Isn't that over a month away?" The idea of my mother talking major holidays with a guy I've been dating for approximately twenty-four hours is causing me to hyperventilate. No one seems to notice.

"I invited your family to the country estate for the Annual Brantley Family Brunch."

Why? Why would he do that?

"Doesn't that sound delightful, June?" My mother is practically swooning into her Cobb salad.

Delightful? No. Excruciating? Yes. "I'm not sure if I'm going to be free for Thanksgiving. I'm thinking about adding boarding for the holidays." If it will keep me from attending that brunch, I'm definitely adding it.

My mother grips her chest as if her non-existent pacemaker has just stopped. "Work on Thanksgiving?"

"Mom, it's just turkey." What's the big deal? Since Dad died, I haven't even been home for Thanksgiving.

Suddenly I realize how often I've seen my mother lately. I liked it better when she moped around the house all day. At least then she stayed in Asheville—and out of my life.

Harry is patting my mother's arm, muttering soothing reassurances.

"Besides, shouldn't you eat with Harry's kids?" Aha. That's my ticket out of this mess.

"Nah, the kids all go to their in-laws since Marlene died. I don't cook."

Drat.

Nelson rests his hand on top of mine. "June, it will be fine. Our families need to meet sometime."

Why? Why do they ever have to meet? It's bad enough this is the second meal Nelson's had to suffer through with my mother and her "friend."

I drain my glass and search frantically for the waitress—and a refill.

"How bad is it that we've just gotten back together and I'm already having a commitment crisis?" I'm pacing my bedroom, unable to lie down after three more glasses of wine and a slice of cherry cheesecake.

Ally is lounging on the bed, twirling her hair between her fingers. "I warned you not to rush back into a relationship with Nelson."

"When? When did you tell me that?"

"I thought it. But this new thing where I try to be sensitive all the time gets tricky. I'm not sure what I should say."

That's helpful. "Maybe *you* can read *my* mind, but I can't read yours."

"June, it's not that big of a deal. You've had two dinners and one kiss. Some people wouldn't even define that as dating, let alone a commitment."

"He invited my mother to Thanksgiving dinner. I'd say that qualifies as something someone in a *relationship* would do."

She gets up off the bed and puts her hands up to stop my pacing. "June, I don't get it. Two days ago, you couldn't wait for Nelson to get back so you could get on with it. Why aren't you getting on with it?"

I sink onto the bed. "I don't know. Everything was fine yesterday."

"Until Jesse showed back up."

I can feel my eyes filling up again. A sob builds inside my chest and moves upward until it erupts. "Why does it always have to be complicated?"

Ally strokes my hair. "Because love is. If it was easy, everybody would be doing it."

I'm not sure when it happened, or how, but my seventeen-year-old dead best friend grew up.

Chapter Forty-Two

It's morning, but somehow, I missed the good part. The part where I sleep.

I've been tossing and turning since I went to bed at two. The sun is now peeking through my window, so I might as well get up. My mouth has that cotton ball taste that comes with too much wine and not enough sleep. The toothpaste can't even compete.

I pull on my jeans from the night before and grab my UNC sweatshirt from the closet. So what if I'm still wearing my pj top with the monkeys all over it. Pulling my hair into some semblance of a ponytail, I grab Midge's leash and head out the door.

A thin layer of dew covers everything, and the railing is slippery as I head down the stairs. I haven't been out this early since, well, ever. Midge, not understanding why we're out in the middle of the night, does her business and we head to the car.

As I'm pulling out of the parking lot, Ally shows up.

"Where are you going this early?"

I hedge. "I'm going to check on Roxie and Pierre."

She stares at me as if delving into the deepest recesses of my brain. I try to empty my mind. "It's awfully early. Nelson won't be at the bookstore for hours." She says this more to herself than me.

"I'm not going to see Nelson. I'm going to walk Roxie and Pierre."

To prove my point, I get off at the Belmont exit.

She's looking at me as if she thinks I'm up to something.

I try my best to not think about what I'm up to.

The two little dogs are excited to see me, and I've arrived before the puppy woke up and had an accident. I guess there's at least one advantage to getting up this early—well, that, and the fact that I only saw two other cars on the highway.

The moment we step off the sidewalk, little Pierre squats and a stream flows down the street. The morning air is cool enough that steam actually rises from the puddle.

We continue down to the park and Roxie sniffs around before relieving herself. I sit on a bench overlooking the pond and try to sort out the conflicting feelings tumbling around in my head. Somehow, I thought if I purged myself of Nelson and Jesse, I'd be able to figure out what I really wanted, but after all this time without them, I'm no closer to knowing what that is.

"I knew it!" She disappeared after I got to Hound'n Around, but now Ally's back, shattering the quiet of the morning.

"Knew what?" I can't remember when I've ever felt this tired.

"You're still thinking about Jesse." She looks quite pleased with herself at this brilliant deduction.

I look sideways without turning my head. "I'm thinking about Jesse *and* Nelson. So what?"

Ally purses her lips, brow furrowed. "I don't know. I'm just trying to figure out what you're not telling me."

"I'm not telling you anything, because I don't know anything. I'm not trying to keep you out of the loop. Right now, there is no loop." I get up and begin to trudge back to the daycare.

"Well, just so you know, I checked into that looking-into-your-future thing, but it was a no-go."

I'd laugh, but I'm too tired. "Thanks anyway."

Deciding to leave Midge for the day to hang out with Roxie and Pierre, I get the three of them set up in one of the play areas with water and a potty pad, just in case. I'll check back around lunchtime.

Heading back out to my car, Ally continues to tag along. "Ally, you don't have to follow me around. If I have any epiphanies, I'll let you know."

She narrows her eyes at me as if she suspects I'm trying to ditch her. "Nah, that's okay. I like hanging out with you."

"Whatever." I start the car and head for the highway.

My windshield keeps fogging up from the temperature difference inside and outside the car. I flip the defroster on as I merge into traffic. And by traffic, I mean three cars and one semi-truck.

"Um, Junie, you missed your exit."

"I'm not going home right now."

"You're going into town looking like that?"

If I was more awake, I'd be offended. I flip the turn signal on.

"Isn't this the exit for that park you went to last weekend?"

I can't answer her, because I'm having to scrunch down in my seat to see out of the two-inch semi-circle that my defrosters have made. By the time I see the orange cones leading up to the truck pulled over on the shoulder it's too late to correct myself.

"June? June? Can you hear me?"

Why is my mother in my apartment? I finally get to sleep and she has to wake me up?

"June, sweetie." She's shaking my shoulder now and I squeeze my eyes tighter to block her and that obnoxious beeping out.

"Mrs. Hinderson, your daughter has suffered a serious trauma to the head—she may not wake up for some time."

I'm awake. I'm awake! What the heck is he talking about? I force my eyes open to bright lights, monitors with bumpy green lines, and my mother talking to a man in a white coat. Trauma? What trauma? I mean, besides my love life?

"Oh, June! You're awake." She's at my side, grabbing my hand, which I now realize is attached by a tube to something behind me. "Can you speak?"

My head is pounding and the cotton ball sensation in my mouth is even worse than it was earlier. I didn't have more wine, did I? "I think so." My voice sounds like a croak, and it hurts to talk.

"You were in an accident, sweetie. You've got a pretty good bump on your head, but the doctor says you're going to be fine."

I remember Ally in the passenger seat, and the fogged-up window. And something orange.

"Ally?"

My mother's eyes flash to the doctor and back, looking frantic. Something's wrong. "Honey, Ally died."

I killed my best friend? Nooooo!!!!!

"I didn't realize there was another passenger in the car." This from the man in the white coat.

"Obviously, my daughter is experiencing some memory loss. Her friend died ten years ago."

Relieved to remember that I can't kill someone who's already dead, I allow myself to relax. Maybe now that Mom knows I'm alive, I can go back to sleep.

When I wake up again, Nelson and Kendra are in the room.

"June. Oh my goodness, you had us worried sick." My cousin is clutching my hand in a death grip.

Nelson leans over and kisses me on the forehead. "I'm so glad you're okay."

I notice it's dark outside the window. "The dogs." My voice is still scratchy, but it's not as bad to talk. I just don't have the energy for many words.

"Don't you worry a bit, I picked up Midge and she's back at your apartment. Harry took the other dogs back to Asheville with him."

Back to Asheville? "My mom?"

"She's just down in the cafeteria getting some dinner."

I ruined my mom's escapade to Atlantic City. And her ride back to Asheville has left her here. Now I'm the one clutching Kendra's hand. "You're staying?"

My cousin laughs, rubbing my arm. "Yes, honey, I'm staying. I'm not gonna leave you alone with her, don't worry."

I love that K understands so much about me. It makes life that much easier.

A nurse enters the room, carrying a basket full of needles and other scary things. "If you two don't mind stepping out in the hall, I'll just be a minute."

"I've got to run anyway, but I wanted to see that you were okay." Nelson leans in close and gently kisses my lips. "I'll be back tomorrow, okay?"

I nod my head. Which sends shooting pains through it.

"You aren't going to want to move your head much for a few days."

That was helpful information.

The nurse straps a rubber tourniquet around my upper arm and taps around, searching for a vein.

I turn my head to the side and try not to think about the needle that'll be going into my arm. Ally? Ally! It'd be extra nice if you could show up about now.

She doesn't answer me, so I open my eyes, but she's not in the room. So much for the whole I'll-be-there-when-you-need-me plan.

I jerk my arm at the stick of the needle and the nurse glares at me. Whatever happened to "first do no harm?" I bite my bottom lip and try not to watch the syringe fill with blood.

"Okay, that'll do it." She snaps the tourniquet off my arm and yanks the needle out. Apparently, she didn't get the memo about the trauma I experienced.

My mom pokes her head in the door as the nurse exits. "You ready for us, sweetie?"

As long as they don't have needles, I should be fine. I nod. More pain rocketing through my head. I've got to stop doing that.

Kendra trails my mother into the room, carrying a paper cup. "I snuck some hot chocolate past the nurse's station. I thought it might feel good on your throat."

I gratefully accept the cup, savoring the warmth in my hands. The scalding liquid, however, does not make my throat feel better. "Thanks, K."

My mother has planted herself in the chair at the foot of my bed and pulled out her knitting. It appears she is making a black and white striped dog sweater. I wonder if she'll pair it with a red scarf and mini beret.

She seems distracted, so I wave for Kendra to lean in closer.

"Where was I?"

"When you wrecked?"

I remember not to nod. "Yeah."

"I dunno. Some off-ramp in town." She settles onto the bed, blocking my mother's view of me. "Do you not remember where you were going?"

"No, not really. It was early."

"Which isn't exactly like you."

I smirk. "Yeah, I know. I'm trying to remember what I was doing, but all I can see is Ally in the seat beside me. And she's not here to ask."

"She's probably freaked out by hospitals."

I hadn't thought of that, but Kendra's probably right. It would have been the last place she saw. "I can't help but feel like it was important."

Kendra pats my hand. "Don't worry. It will come back to you. You should try to sleep some more." She moves to the chair beside the bed and pulls out a magazine.

Sleep sounds so good, but images from this morning keep pulling at the edges of my mind. Where was I going?

Chapter Forty-Three

It's my first day out of the hospital and I feel fine, but nobody will let me do anything. I tried to get Kendra to take me to work, but she assures me that she and Sarah are handling things just fine without me. Nelson has closed the bookstore and is hovering around the couch, constantly asking me if I need anything. And my mother, who has stayed to help out, is napping in the spare bedroom.

I found a *Brady Bunch* marathon on TV, but Nelson appears to be in physical pain after three hours of it. I've determined that his parents were neglectful by not building up his tolerance to television when he was a child. I click the TV off, just as the episode where Marsha gets bonked in the nose with a football is coming on. But Nelson seems grateful.

I pick up *The Lion, The Witch and The Wardrobe*, but the words blur on the page. Apparently, my brain got a little rattled in the crash.

"You want me to read it to you?"

"Sure."

Nelson looks relieved to have something to do. He sits on the couch and I carefully spin around, resting my head on a pillow in his lap.

I read the *Chronicles of Narnia* multiple times as a child and saw the movie when it came out, but listening to Nelson read it aloud makes it seem fresh and exciting.

Despite that, I find myself drifting off before Lucy steps into Narnia. Even a great story can't compete with narcotics.

When I awake on the couch, the lights are off and I'm alone. I've slept through dinner, because I can see clean dishes stacked in the drain board. I sit up slowly and make my way to the bathroom, stepping gingerly. I don't want to jostle my head, but I also don't want to wake Kendra or my mother. It's the first time I've been alone since the accident, and I'm anxious to finally talk to Ally about what happened.

In the kitchen, I find a bowl of pasta K has left for me. Popping it in the microwave, I lean back against the counter and stare out at the empty living room. "Ally." When she doesn't appear, I raise my voice a notch, even though I know volume isn't necessary. "Ally!"

The microwave beeps. I remove the steaming bowl of pasta. Something about steam. It's right there. At the edge of my mind. On the tip of my tongue. Where is Ally?

It's unlike her to ignore me for this long. Were we fighting in the car? Did I do something to make her mad?

Maybe if I could sit in my car, or go back to where we crashed, maybe that would jog my memory. But the car is totaled, and Kendra isn't even sure which exit it was.

I swirl a noodle around in the creamy sauce and blow on it. Maybe once I'm off these pain killers, my brain will be clearer.

Harry is picking up my mom today. Knitting and watching soap operas all day just isn't that helpful.

Kendra has promised that she will come pick me up after lunch and let me go to work for a few hours. I can't wait to get out of this apartment. I love TV as much as the next person who was raised with a set as their babysitter, but even I can overdose on it. And I miss the dogs. I do, after all, have the coolest job ever.

If I feel up to it later, Nelson wants to take us to dinner. Kendra's been cooking every night, after running Hound'n Around all day, and he wants to give her a break. He's a good guy. I'm really glad he came back.

I've showered and am applying the moisturizer than Kendra insists will make my skin look ten years younger, when the phone rings.

Moving quickly is still hard on my head, and on my balance, so I let the machine pick it up. My mother's sitting next to the phone, but it wouldn't occur to her to answer it. I hear my outgoing message, and then a dial tone. I hate when people just hang up.

I finish getting dressed and by the time I make my way to the living room, Harry has arrived and my mom is gathering her yarn.

I pick up the phone and tap the caller ID button to see who called. I don't recognize the number, but it's local. I'll try it later.

"Thanks for all your help, Mom." She did miss Atlantic City because of me.

"Of course, honey. But I missed my boy so much."

I'm about to be sick, until I realize she's talking about the dog. Pierre is dangling high above my mother's head, little legs swimming in the air, while she jiggles him from side to side.

"Have a safe trip home." I kiss her on the cheek and pat little Pierre on the head.

Harry carries her suitcase to the door and Mom trails behind him. "We'll see you at Thanksgiving."

Cringing, I try to smile and wave. Something else I had forgotten about.

"Did I tell you that Nelson invited my mother and Harry to his family's country estate for Thanksgiving?" We're in the car on the way to Belmont. I am trying to sit perfectly still so the bumps in the road don't jostle my head too much.

"You mean he didn't invite me?"

"Missing the point, K."

She looks at me with a huff before focusing back on the road. "What's the big deal? It's just turkey."

"Turkey, my mother, Harry, and two hundred of Nelson's closest relatives."

"Aye."

I stare out the window, trying to remember the morning I drove along this highway less than a week ago. "It just seems so serious for our families to meet. He's been back for a week, K."

"Well, if you make it to Thanksgiving, you'll have been together a month. Plus the month before you broke up."

"When I was dating another guy."

I can see her grinning from the corner of my eye. "Yeah."

Releasing a sigh, I slowly turn my head to face my cousin. "I'm thinking too hard about all this, aren't I?"

"Definitely." She reaches across the console and pats my knee. "Nelson's a great guy. Just go with it."

"I wish I could talk to Ally about that morning. I feel like there's something important that I'm missing."

Kendra pulls off the exit and stops at the light. She turns to look at me. "You still haven't seen her?"

"No. And I miss her. I was really getting to like the new Ally."

The light changes to green and Kendra turns toward Main St. "I still have trouble picturing a mature Ally."

"Well, it was happening. She was getting reasonable and insightful and everything. And now she's gone."

As she pulls up in front of my building, K turns to me. "Well, you've got a real live friend here anytime you need one."

Chapter Forty-Four

"There was one Halloween, I guess we were about ten, and Ally dresses June up like a mummy. She's wrapped in toilet paper from head to toe. So, we're walkin' down the street and this group of boys runs by and grabs a piece of the tp that's flutterin' in the wind and keeps on goin'." Kendra pauses long enough to get a good look at the horror on my face. "And poor June is shriekin' and carryin' on. I had no idea what the problem was until they got about a hundred feet away. June wasn't wearing anything under the toilet paper!" K is roaring in delight.

Nelson is holding his hand over his mouth, trying to contain his own hiccups of laughter.

"That is not true. I was wearing panties."

"Yeah, *Wonder Woman* panties." Now Kendra's slapping the table.

I clutch my head.

Nelson reaches his arm around me, quieting down. "I'm sorry, June, are we hurting your head?"

No, but if it'll make Kendra stop telling embarrassing stories about me... "Yeah, a little."

K narrows her eyes at me from across the table. She knows what I'm up to, but she lets it slide. "Nelson, do you have any funny Halloween stories?"

"We never celebrated Halloween. My parents didn't allow me to eat candy."

"That's just sad!" Kendra's eyes light up and I can almost see the wheels turning in her head. "We should totally get dressed up and go out tomorrow night. There's bound to be something going on downtown for big kids like us."

"I don't know, Kendra. I doubt June will feel up to it." Nelson appears to be rescuing me, but I suspect he's rescuing himself.

K apprises each of us. "You two are old fuddy-duddies. Don't know how to have any fun."

"Speaking of being old, I think I need to get to bed." My head actually is starting to hurt and I can't risk Kendra remembering Halloween freshman year.

I return to the doctor on Monday for a check-up and I'm cleared to go back to work as long as I don't move suddenly, drive a car or operate heavy machinery. I'm pretty sure the last one will be easy to avoid, but the first two are going to make it hard to run my business. Kendra, my lifesaver, agrees to stay for the immediate future to shuttle me to work and take on the brunt of the physical aspect of my job.

So, at work, I get to sit at the desk or play with the little dogs. Anyone under fifteen pounds.

Today I'm on the floor in one of the play areas, throwing a teeny tennis ball for Tokyo and Thai, a pair of miniature Pomeranians. Every five minutes, Tokyo runs to the water bowl, dips both his front paws in it, and then runs back to me and jumps in my lap. He, of course, thinks this is loads of fun. I look like I had an accident in my pants.

The bell over the door tinkles and in walks Luca, carrying Gigi.

I ease myself into a standing position, but Kendra beats me to the desk.

"Luca, hi." She's looking between us nervously, as if one of us might start spewing curses or spontaneously combust. "What can we do for ya?"

Having reached them, I take Gigi from him and position her over the wet spot on my pants. "Is your mom okay?"

The little dog is wiggling with enthusiasm and I'm praying she doesn't start her excited shrieking. My head still reacts poorly to loud noises.

"She's had to go back into the hospital. She wasn't taking her meds."

Having met his mom, I know how strong-willed she is, so this doesn't really surprise me. "I'm sorry to hear that."

He's shifting from one foot to the other, obviously uncomfortable. "Mom insisted I bring Gigi here. She told me to suck it up." He cracks a smile, but his expression is guarded. "How are you doing, June?"

Kendra can't contain herself any longer, and throws herself between us. "June's great, well except for the accident, but Nelson and I are taking excellent care of her, so you don't need to worry."

Luca looks overwhelmed by my cousin. People are often overwhelmed by Kendra "Accident?"

"I'm fine, Luca. I was in a car accident a couple weeks ago, but everything's okay now." I nudge K out of the way. "We're happy to help out with Gigi until your mom is feeling better."

He turns to leave, but stops before he reaches the door. I can tell he's looking across the street. "Nelson?"

Kendra races to open the door for him and practically pushes him out of it. She lowers her voice, but for K, that doesn't keep Sarah or me from hearing. "June is with Nelson now. She's happy. I'm sorry."

Wow. And I thought Ally intruded on my love life.

If I thought it was hard to have a relationship with a dead person hanging around, having one with a person both of us can see hanging around is nearly impossible.

Kendra, Nelson and I have fallen into a pattern. After work, we hang out at the bookstore, or my apartment, playing Scrabble or Balderdash, or we all go out to eat. With K living with me and working for me and driving me everywhere, it's hard to not include her.

I love my cousin and I'm so grateful for all the help she's giving me, but I haven't kissed my boyfriend in private in three weeks. Which means I haven't *really* kissed my boyfriend since before we broke up and got back together. Which was so long ago, I barely remember it.

Kendra is having so much fun; I don't think she realizes there's a problem. And I can't bring myself to say anything. Nelson won't say that it's bothering him, but I can tell he's getting antsy. The other night when Kendra went to the bathroom, he nearly tackled me. We were so rushed, we ended up banging heads and knocking over a vase.

On the one hand, it's kind of nice not having to worry so much about the physical side of the relationship, but because K is always in the room, it's like the three of us are dating. I don't feel nearly as connected to Nelson as I did the first time we dated, and I was dating another man that time. Apparently, I can do two men at once, but not two women.

See, if Ally were around, she'd jump all over that thought.

But that's the other thing that's changed since the accident. I haven't heard from Ally at all. Which doesn't do much for my mood.

I can't drive, I can't run my business, I can't be alone with my boyfriend, and I think my best friend is dead for real this time. And I think I killed her.

I'm holding my breath, praying the doctor will give me the all clear. There's only one week until Thanksgiving and I've booked twenty dogs to board—mainly so I have an excuse to leave the brunch early.

Plus, it will mean that my dear, sweet cousin can return to her Mary Kay life in Raleigh. I'm not sure how the legislature has survived without their makeup.

"Well, Ms. Hinderson, everything looks good on the scan. If you're feeling up to it, I think you can resume life as normal."

The doctor looks surprised when I hug him.

I head out of the office and find Kendra sitting in her molded plastic chair, sound asleep.

I sink into the chair beside her. I'm a horrible person. This woman put her life on hold for a month to come and help me and I'm just an ungrateful hussy. Look at her. She's exhausted. And her clothes are hanging off of her. She worked herself into a size twelve!

"K, wake up." I gently prod her shoulder.

She blinks her eyes, but doesn't rub them, lest she smudge "her face."

"The doctor says I'm good to go, so you're off the hook. No more taxi driver."

I can't help but think she looks disappointed. "Oh, that's great. Yeah, great." She's not fully awake yet, so I hook my arm in hers and we wobble out to her car.

"K?" I steady her outside the driver's door.

"Yeah?" "I can't thank you enough for everything you've done for me. You're the best cousin a girl could ask for." I wrap her in a firm embrace and smile when I feel her arms tighten around me.

She pulls back and dabs under her eyes. "You're my best friend, June."

All the way home, I can't stop thinking about that. I've always defined Kendra as my cousin, which, obviously, she is, but it never occurred to me to call her a friend. But the more I think about who she is, and how she's always been there for me, the more I realize that she's been a best friend the whole time—I just never had a slot open for one.

Chapter Forty-Five

Nelson's haggling with the salesman over the used SUV that I'm buy-ing. He looks like he's enjoying himself, so I wander over to the car to check it out. It feels weird to sit behind a steering wheel again. Riding in a car hasn't bothered me since the accident, but the thought of driving again is freaking me out a little.

I still can't remember much about the morning I crashed. I've seen the police report, but the exit number means nothing to me. It's like there's a void in my mind about where I was going, about what I was planning to do, about the last thing Ally said to me—ever.

It's so hard to accept that she's gone. It's like I'm grieving her death all over again, ten years later.

Nelson keeps asking me what's wrong, but how can I explain it to him? He'll think I'm crazy. So, I put on a happy face and pretend that my heart isn't broken.

He's shaking hands with the guy and giving me the thumbs up. I guess that means I can drive my new car home. If I can just catch my breath.

I keep having these dreams about Ally. Sometimes we're at the frat party the night she died, and I watch Brad take her upstairs, and I try to stop them, but I can't move.

Other times, we're in my car and I see the truck, and I swerve and miss it. And we laugh about what a close call it was.

Mostly, though, I dream about us as kids. Playing in the fort behind her house, or curled up on the couch watching *The NeverEnding Story*.

Last night's dream was about the night we decided to run away. We were eight, and we wanted to go see a scary movie, but our moms wouldn't let us because it was rated R. We pulled the I'm-sleeping-at-her-house-she's-sleeping-at-mine ploy and we started walking to the mall. Now, we didn't exactly think it through, or we would have realized that by the time we got to the mall, the movie would be half over, they probably wouldn't even let us in, and we only had $3.82 between us.

We made it as far as the park. It was getting dark and we were tired from playing all afternoon, so we stopped and swung and made up our own version of how the movie went.

"Mr. Whiskers rises up from the grave and goes to haunt the dog that killed him."

"His tail is broken, so it just hangs there, swingin' in the breeze."

Ally rose up out of her swing, arms in the air. "And he flies over the city, claws extended, ready to pounce on anyone who looks at him funny."

We dissolved into a fit of laughter, making cat noises and pouncing on one another.

We stayed in the park until almost midnight, but I was never scared. Ally was brave enough for the both of us.

My whole life, she pressed me to do more, to try more. She's the one who pushed me to follow my dream and open the daycare.

With Ally gone, I feel like I've lost my confidence. I've lost part of who I am.

"Are you sure it's absolutely vital that I go?"

It's the night before Thanksgiving and Nelson and I are sharing a late dinner at a Cuban place. The only thing on my plate that looks familiar are the banana-looking things.

"Well, it might be hard to explain who your mom and Harry are without you there."

"We could call them and tell them it's been cancelled."

Nelson has the look on his face that says he's humoring me. I've become familiar with this look. "The Annual Brantley Family Thanksgiving Brunch has been a tradition for forty-three years. Besides, my mother sent your mother an embossed invitation."

Embossed? That seems so sophisticated. What if I don't know which fork to use? "Work's going to be so busy tomorrow." "Which is why Sarah's going to help out until we get done at the brunch. I'll have you back by two." He stabs a forkful of the stringy stuff that he claims is pork.

At least I can be assured food I'll recognize tomorrow. Like turkey, and yams. 'Cuz I can tell Nelson's not going to let me get out of this. Whether I like it or not.

We're standing at the entrance of what can only be described as a mansion. Nelson has tried to downplay his family's wealth, but the only house I've seen that's bigger than this one is the Biltmore Estate.

I wonder if this place has a bowling alley in the basement.

The massive door opens, and an honest-to-goodness butler waves us in. "Nelson, so wonderful to see you. Who are your guests? I shall announce them."

"Henry, this is Miss June Hinderson." He gestures behind us, "and this is her mother Helen, and her friend, Harry Walters." Nelson steps into the foyer.

I can't move. This is surreal. Surely there must be cameras somewhere. Do people actually live in houses like this, and have butlers who announce their guests?

Nelson steps back outside and wraps his arm around my waist, whispering near my ear. "It'll be fine, June. They are normal people, I assure you." He applies gentle pressure until I start moving toward the door.

I can hear my mother tittering to Harry behind us, but I'm less concerned about how she'll act than about meeting Nelson's parents. I'm just a struggling business owner who has to reuse plastic baggies. I don't know how to act in a place like this.

The foyer rises at least four stories, and a massive crystal chandelier fills the space above us. If that thing comes crashing down, a la *Phantom of the Opera*, we're toast.

My mother leans over to Harry, but fails to lower her voice. "I wonder how they clean that thing."

Okay, so I'm a little worried about how she'll act.

Henry takes our coats and I feel completely underdressed in my black velvet skirt and silk blouse. But this is the fanciest outfit I own. I'm not a fancy sort of girl.

A waiter comes by and offers us champagne. We're still in the foyer. But I'm not turning down alcohol. I grab a flute off the tray and drain it. My mother tilts her head to the side and purses her lips. By the time we enter the dining room, I've had two more glasses.

The table is set up buffet style and hundreds of people—literally—are milling about talking and eating finger foods. Good, at least I won't have to worry about using the wrong fork.

Searching up and down the table, I realize there isn't a turkey in sight. I also can't locate cranberry sauce, stuffing, or candied yams. What kind of Thanksgiving is this?

"Mm, June, you have to try this lobster." Nelson holds out a butter-soaked bite.

Sure enough, it's lobster. Which has never impressed me much. Give me a plate full of crab claws any day.

I'm too nervous to eat anyway. I pluck another glass off a tray passing by. I'm not too nervous to drink.

I spot my mom and Harry across the room. Mom is speaking to a woman who must be at least ninety, but is dressed to the nines in grey chiffon. Harry looks bored.

"June, I want you to meet my parents." Nelson swings me around, no warning or anything, just, bam! Parents.

I totter a bit, but I'm sure it's just residual vertigo from the head injury, certainly not the five—or is it six?—glasses of champagne I've had so far. "Mr. and Mrs. Brantley. It's so nice to make your adquaint, abquaint, a...to meet you." Who knew that was such a complicated word?

Nelson's dad pumps my hand up and down like he's trying to strike oil. "June, we've heard so many nice things about you."

Mrs. Brantley has a smile on her face that clearly says, "you aren't good enough for my son."

Nelson's doing this little twirly thing on my back, which feels nice, but it's making me sleepy. He's saying something to his parents about the daycare, or healthcare, or something. I can't exactly make it out. Which is weird, because I'm right here beside him.

Suddenly the room is doing a little twirly thing to my head and I'm no longer standing up. Before I know what's happening, Henry is carrying me up the stairs.

Why is my boyfriend's butler carrying me up the stairs?

So apparently you aren't supposed to mix alcohol with the little pink pills I've been taking the past month. I've become so accustomed to taking them, I forgot all about them. And the little picture of the wine glass with a slash through it on the side of the bottle.

My mother keeps insisting it has more to do with the ratio of champagne (seven, it turns out) to food (that one bite of lobster). She's mortified. Her word, not mine.

But Nelson assures me it's okay, that he explained to everyone that I'm still recovering from a head injury. I wonder how long I can milk this excuse.

I'm enjoying this comfy bed so much; I'd really like if they all just left me alone to my thousand thread count Egyptian cotton.

"Mom, please go downstairs, enjoy the party. I'll be fine, honest."

She hesitates, but I know it's for show. She can't wait to get back to the caviar and watercress salad. "Well, if you're sure…"

"I'll stay here with her, Mrs. H." Nelson sits on the bed beside me, but at a respectable distance.

That's all she needed. She happily scampers out the door.

Nelson walks to the door, says something to the butler, and then closes it softly. He comes back to the bed, but this time the distance isn't quite so respectful.

"You wouldn't take advantage of a girl who's hopped up on drugs and booze, would you?"

His eyes have this intense look in them and he's getting closer. "I'm hoping I don't have to take advantage."

I snuggle deeper into the covers as he looms over me. "It's hard to believe we're alone. Well, except for the two hundred guests downstairs."

"Don't forget the servants." He's nuzzling my neck, his breath coming in short, hot bursts.

"I cannot believe you have servants."

He's unbuttoning my silk blouse. "I don't have servants, my grandfather does. And he treats them very well, I can assure you."

I don't think I'm ready for Nelson to take my clothes off. Especially not at Thanksgiving brunch, in his grandfather's mansion. I squirm out from under him. "Nelson."

"Why are you over there?" His face is flushed and his tone is less playful.

I sit up against the upholstered headboard, redoing the buttons on my shirt. "I'm not ready for this."

"I'm sorry. You really aren't feeling well, are you?"

"That's not the point, Nelson. Even if I felt perfect, I wouldn't be ready for this."

He swings his legs off the bed, his back to me. "I don't understand, June."

I move across the expansive bed and sit behind him, arms circling his neck. "We've only been together a short time, and Kendra's been around for most of it. I don't feel like we've connected yet."

He turns around, unlocking my hands and letting them fall. "We were connected before. I picked up where we left off, June. I'm in love with you."

In love? With me? How? We haven't had a moment to ourselves. And before, well, I was connected to two men. "I'm sorry, Nelson. I had to start over. I'm trying to do it right this time."

A range of emotions flash through his eyes: disappointment, anger, resignation. He stands up and walks to the door. "I won't press you, June." Then he's gone.

The Egyptian cotton feels soft and cool against my skin. Which isn't helping right now, because I can't stop shaking.

I need to talk to Ally. She'd know what to do. I've never had a guy tell me he's in love with me before. Well, except for when Troy Handler told me during a make-out session in his dorm room, but I'm pretty sure he was just trying to get me to sleep with him. And when I didn't, his love seemed to fade rather quickly.

I always assumed that when it happened, I'd love the guy back. I mean, I do love Nelson, but I don't think I'm in love with Nelson. There's a difference, I think.

I spot his suit jacket at the foot of the bed and grab for it, trying to stave off the chill that has invaded me from the inside out. I'm sure the grandfather can afford to heat the mansion; this is just me.

Tucking my arms into the sleeves, I feel something hard. I reach my hand into the inside pocket, but quickly pull it back. No. It can't be. A month. One month. With Kendra. And a head trauma. He can't seriously be thinking about proposing.

Maybe I'm jumping to conclusions. I reach my hand back in, trying to convince myself that it's a pair of earrings, or maybe the first tooth he lost. Honestly, I'd rather see that than a ring.

The black velvet box feels heavy in my hands. Not so much its weight, but its meaning. I crack the lid open, but close my eyes tightly, terrified to look inside.

Suddenly I hear the door opening. "June."

I snap the lid closed and shove the box between my ass and the Egyptian cotton.

"I'm so sorry about before." Nelson comes to the bed and sits in front of me. "Can you forgive me?" He cups my face in his hands and looks so remorseful and he's so good to me and of course I forgive him.

I nod my head.

He kisses me then, slow and long. And it's quite pleasant, but the whole time I can feel the box jammed against my right butt cheek, taunting me. He's in love with you, June. Is that where you're going?

Pulling back, he smoothes the sleeve of his jacket. "That looks good on you."

"I was cold."

"You ready to go downstairs?"

Biting my bottom lip, I nod. "Can I have a few minutes to freshen up?"

"Of course. I'll be outside."

As soon as the door closes, I grab the box and shove it back into the pocket. Removing the jacket, I throw it to the end of the bed. I only saw a glimpse. But it blinded me.

Chapter Forty-Six

I need time. Time to figure out how I feel about Nelson before he pulls that ring out of his pocket. So, I may be avoiding him a little.

Well, not so much avoiding *him*, as avoiding quiet, romantic restaurants. Tonight, he wants to go to the new French place that opened near South Park. I picture candlelight and soft music. Not good.

"Why don't you let me cook for you tonight?" Did those words actually just leave my mouth? The closest I've come to cooking since Kendra left is dumping my spicy orange chicken onto a plate.

His face lights up. "That'd be great." He's probably excited to finally see the domestic side of me.

I'm not sure I have that side.

"Kendra, I need your help. I told Nelson I'd cook him dinner tonight."

Laughter bubbles from the other end of the line.

"I'm thinking about a pot roast. That's easy, right?"

She's laughing so hard; I can hear her start to hiccup.

"K, you aren't helping."

Attempting to control herself, Kendra breathes in deeply. "Sorry, I just...well, the image of you in an apron...Anyway, you can't do a pot roast. You would've needed to put it in the crock pot this mornin'. I take it you're doin' this after work?"

I glance up at the clock. It's after four now, and Sarah can't work late, she has another date with Austin. Maybe fixing them up wasn't the best idea for my social life. "Yeah, I probably won't be out of here until 7:30 and Nelson's coming over at eight."

"Sounds like you need a genie."

"Even if Ally were around, this isn't the sort of thing she'd help with. She didn't have magic powers, K."

"I know, I'm just sayin', a meal in half an hour? Even I can't do that."

I knew I was getting in over my head.

"Why doesn't Nelson just take you out?"

"Oh, he offered. But I can't take the chance."

"Take the chance? What on earth are you talkin' about, June?"

I wave my hand at Sarah to let her know I'm going outside. Once I'm out the door, I check to make sure Nelson is safely inside his building. "Well, I haven't had a chance to talk to you about Thanksgiving yet."

"Yeah, the big soiree that I wasn't invited to."

"Trust me. All you missed was me making a fool out of myself." I wander down the street a ways, but try to keep Nelson's door in my sights. Can't have him sneaking up on me during this conversation. "I saw a ring, K."

"I'm not following."

Sighing, I lean against the brick wall of the stationary store. "An engagement ring, Kendra. In Nelson's coat pocket."

K sucks in her breath.

"And he told me he loves me."

"June, that's awesome. Oh my gosh, I'm so excited. You're going to be a gazillionaire!"

That is so not the point. "He hasn't asked me yet, K, which is why I'm trying to avoid charming little French restaurants."

"Okay, I'm still not following."

"I'm not ready for him to ask me, because I'm not sure if I'm in love with him."

Kendra is speechless. This rarely happens.

"So, I promised I would cook tonight, but my chef skills are limited to Boyardee."

"Let me see if I understand this correctly. You break up with Luca because you think you are still in love with Nelson. Nelson comes back and the two of you are all lovey-dovey and you seem happy, but now he tells you that he loves you and buys you an engagement ring, but you aren't sure if you're in love with him or not."

Mostly accurate. "The box looked kind of old, so I'm thinking it may be a family heirloom."

"Even better. He gets his dead grandmother's ring to give to the woman he loves, but she can't make up her mind about whether or not she wants the great guy. June, I don't understand you. I'm practically in love with Nelson. How can you not be?"

Now I feel about two inches tall, and she still hasn't told me what to make for dinner. "So, I should order in and hide the containers?"

"Crippy!" Click.

She's typically much more helpful.

Well, I may not have cooked this meal, but I worked really hard to pick up the food, get it onto plates, dirty a few pots and pans and run the containers to the dumpster before Nelson arrives. This domestic stuff is hard work. I'm lighting the candles when he knocks. Oh crap, that's too romantic.

I snuff them out and pitch them under the sink before going to the door.

He's brought me roses. Which I suppose is super nice, but it just makes me more nervous. Couldn't roses be a prelude to popping the question?

I wish I'd had time to throw on a pair of sweats. No way he can propose to me if I'm wearing sweats.

"June, you seem stressed." Nelson lowers me onto the couch and kneels in front of me.

No kneeling! I jump up, nearly knocking him over. "No, I'm not stressed. What makes you think that? I just don't want our dinner to get cold, that's all."

He's looking at me like I'm crazy. Trust me; I'm familiar with the look.

"So, what are we having?" He sits in the chair across from me, trying to act like I haven't completely lost my mind.

Funny how I'm appearing crazier now that my dead best friend doesn't talk to me anymore. "Seafood alfredo. I'm afraid I didn't have time to do anything too fancy." I notice the Olive Garden bag on the kitchen floor. It must have fallen out of the cabinet when I threw the candles in. "Would you like some wine?" I step into the kitchen, kicking the bag out of view.

"Sure." Right now, I think he'd agree with anything I asked. Don't want to send the loon over the edge.

I pour the wine and then sit back down. I'm trying to breathe normally, but I can feel the flush in my cheeks. I've gotten myself quite worked up over this engagement thing. There are worse things than having a great guy propose, right? "Nelson, I can't lie to you."

He sets his fork back down and wipes his mouth with a napkin. "Okay."

"I didn't cook dinner. This is from Olive Garden."

Why is he smiling?

"Yeah, I figured. The breadsticks were a dead giveaway."

I glare at him over the table.

He covers my hand with his. "June, I don't care if you ever cook a meal for me. So that's not your thing. I love you, just like you are."

I rise from my chair and cross over to him. Sitting on his lap, I link my arms around his neck and lean my forehead against his. "I love you too, Nelson." How can I not?

Cupping my face in his hands, he kisses me first between the eyes, then on each cheek and finally settles on my lips. The kiss is tender and sweet and his hands remain on my back. When he pulls away, he smiles. "Shall we eat before it gets cold? Don't want all your hard work to go to waste."

As I walk back to my chair, he slaps me playfully on the bottom. "Hey now, Mister."

"Sorry. I'll try to control myself."

But I'm not sure I believe him, as he follows it with a wink.

Chapter Forty-Seven

The temperature is dropping and my daycare numbers are rising. I'm accepting applications for holiday help, and if I don't hire someone soon, I'm going to have to pay Sarah for overtime. Being this busy sure does get in the way of trying to have a social life.

But Sarah's closing tonight, and I'm letting Nelson take me to a special dinner. He won't tell me where we're going, only that I should dress up.

Things have been better with Nelson the past couple of weeks. I've managed to stop freaking out about where it's going and just enjoy the time I spend with him. But that time is limited due to long holiday hours. His and mine.

I realize that tonight could be "the night" and I honestly still don't know what I will say if it is. But Kendra keeps telling me to relax, so I'm trying to follow orders.

It's five-thirty and already getting dark outside. The streets of Belmont are lit up with festive holiday lights and wreaths circle the lamp posts. It's hard to maintain a pessimistic attitude with Christmas around the corner.

"Sarah, you got everything under control here?" I'm already gathering my hat and gloves, because I know she can handle it. I really got lucky when I hired her. I hope I can get that lucky with the next one.

She waves me off and wishes me a fun time. She has no idea that tonight might be the beginning of the rest of my life.

Nelson looks dapper in his sport coat and bowtie. I swear he was born in the wrong decade. But I think dapper is cute.

By the time we head into the city, darkness has fallen and I'm watching the traffic as we whiz down the highway. When I see the exit sign, my heart stills in my chest.

There's a flash of orange in my mind. It's morning. The windshield is fogged up. I see Ally in the seat beside me. "Isn't this the exit for that park you went to last weekend?"

I'm sure that's what she said, but what park? What had happened the week before?

I feel Nelson's hand on my thigh and I'm startled back to the present.

"Are you going home for Christmas?" Turning to my left, I try to blink him into focus. "Um, I'm not sure. Mom may come here this year."

"That'd be nice. Maybe both of you can join us at my parents' for dinner." "Yeah, maybe." I turn back to look out the window, but the exit is gone. And so is the memory.

"We have a reservation for Brantley." Nelson is shaking hands with the Maitre'd. I'm almost positive he slipped him some money.

"Your table will be ready in a few minutes, sir."

The restaurant is located in a high-rise in uptown, towering seventeen stories over the city. Definitely a special occasion kind of place. I'm feeling a little less relaxed.

"June, I'm going to run to the restroom. I'll be right back." Nelson turns down a short hallway to the left.

I'm lowering myself onto a settee when I see him. He's pulling on an overcoat, talking with a group of men. He's got his briefcase, so I assume it's a business dinner. When he turns around and sees me, I'm still hovering over the bench, stuck between sitting and standing.

His eyes lock on mine and as he walks toward me his expression is serious, unmoving. The other men exit the foyer, but Jesse stops in front of me.

"Junie." His voice is breathless, as if he's just completed a marathon, not a meal.

I can't stop staring into his hazel eyes. I reach my hand up to touch his cheek—to make sure he is real.

His hand covers mine and his eyes close as if he's memorizing the feel of my hand against his skin. Like I'm memorizing the way his face feels.

He's grown a beard—trim and neat—and the hair feels soft under my hand. He looks good with a beard. Almost like his face wasn't complete before.

"Jesse, you coming?" One of his associates has stuck his head back in the doorway.

His eyes open and he backs away from me, not letting go of my hand or my gaze.

Our fingertips touch as he steps out of my reach. Then he's gone.

"Hey, our table ready yet?" Nelson's back from the bathroom.

I continue to stare at the doorway, committing to memory exactly the way he looked. "No, not yet."

I'm trying to focus on Nelson, but I can't stop thinking about Jesse. It's clear to me now. That morning, that early dawn when I crashed, I was going to find him. I was going to sit in that park until he came running by. That was the plan that I was trying to keep Ally from figuring out. And by trying not to think about it, I had forgotten it.

Nelson's going on about Christmas sales and a special order of rare first editions, but it's Jesse I see across the table from me. I can't get his face out of my mind.

"June? Are you listening to me?"

I shake my head, and Nelson reappears. "Yes, I'm sorry. I guess I'm just tired from trying to get ready for Christmas. What were you saying?"

A flash of annoyance crosses his face, but is quickly replaced with concern. "You've been working a lot lately. You need to get more help."

"I'm trying, but the last few applicants I've had are hopeless. One guy couldn't even spell daycare."

The waitress clears our dishes and asks if we'd like dessert. Nelson tells her to bring us each a crème brulee. Then he pats his chest. As if he's checking to be sure something is there...

I don't even like crème brulee. And I know I can't marry Nelson.

I jump up from the table, grabbing my purse. "I'm not feeling so hot." I leave him looking dazed and fly out of the restaurant.

I don't wait for her to speak, or even start with hello. "Kendra, I finally remembered."

"Aren't you supposed to be at your fancy dinner with Nelson?"

"I sort of left."

"You sort of left?" Her voice squeaks over the line. "Before or after he proposed?"

I flag down a taxi and hop inside. Nelson reaches the door just as we speed away. I squeeze my eyes shut to block out the look of confusion and pain stretched across his fine features. "Before. I couldn't possibly let him ask."

"Wait, back up. What did you remember?"

"Where I was going the morning of the accident."

"Yeah..."

I lean back against the vinyl seat. "I was going to find Jesse."

Silence. Then, "Whoa."

"And then he was there."

"Jesse? At the restaurant?" She's following pretty well tonight.

"Yes. We had just arrived and Nelson was in the bathroom. And he...oh Kendra. His eyes, and the way he felt..."

"You *felt* him?"

I cover a laugh. "I felt his cheek. Get your mind out of the gutter, K."

"What did he say?"

"Nothing."

"He didn't say anything at all, but you felt his cheek?"

"Well, he did say 'Junie.' But nothing else." I close my eyes, trying to remember the way it sounded when he said my name. The name reserved for him. And Ally, but she's not around to use it anymore. A tear slips down my cheek.

The cab driver glances at me in the rearview mirror. "You okay back there, Miss?"

Wiping my cheek, I nod. "Yes, I'm fine. Thank you."

"June, focus." Kendra tries to draw my attention back to her. "What else happened? Did Nelson see Jesse?"

"No, I don't think so. But when I saw him touch his pocket, I knew he was going to do it, and I couldn't bear to disappoint him."

"So, what are you doing now?"

I look out the window at the skyline as we speed down the highway. "I'm going home. From there, I don't have a clue."

Lying on my bed, I stare up at the ceiling and try one last time. "Ally?" Nothing. "Are you really gone? Do I have to do this on my own?" Tears roll down my cheeks, soaking my pillow.

I'm alone, and I'm scared I'm going to screw up. And make the wrong decision—again.

I'm trying to picture her, but she's fading away. I'm trying to remember her laugh, but I can't hear it anymore.

But when I close my eyes, I do see someone. And I realize I'm not alone.

Dialing, I hold the phone to my ear—a lifeline. "Kendra?"

"Yeah, sweetie?"

"I don't want to screw this up again."

I can hear her sigh on the other end of the line. "Honey, you're not gonna screw it up. You're gonna do exactly what's best for you."

The tears are coming steady now. "She's really gone, K. I don't think she's ever coming back."

"And you'll be fine. It's hard to let her go, but it's time. You had an extra ten years with her, June. But you're grown up now, and she's a wonderful memory."

"She would know what I'm supposed to do."

"I think *you* know what you're supposed to do."

Well, if I did, I wouldn't be so upset, would I? "K..."

"Okay, then, what would Ally say?"

"She'd tell me to get over myself and just pick one." I can almost hear her again.

"But it isn't that simple, is it?" Now Kendra's being the reasonable one.

I wipe my face and sit up on the bed. "Nelson wants to marry me. And I do love him. But how much can I love him if I'm feeling this way about Jesse? And I don't even know if Jesse wants me back."

"So, you have a sure thing that you're so-so about and an unknown that you're sure about?"

"When I see Jesse, K...I can't deny what my heart does."

"So, what would Ally tell you?"

"She'd tell me to follow my heart. Life without passion isn't living at all..." Where is that music coming from? I head toward the living room and the sound gets louder. "Hey K, can you hold on? My neighbor's got the music up too loud." I raise my fist to the wall, but stop as I recognize the song—"Won't Go Home Without You"—and realize it's coming from outside.

Sliding open the glass door leading to my balcony, the song becomes clearer. The sky overhead is also clear, stars dotting the darkness. My eyes travel down, trying to locate the source of the music. What I see below stops me dead.

"June? What's going on?" Kendra must be screaming, because the phone is now lowered to my side and I can still hear her.

Raising it back to my ear, I don't take my eyes off the image below my balcony. "K, I'm gonna have to call you back."

"June! Wait! Don't hang—"

Standing on the grass below my apartment is Jesse, arms raised overhead, holding his phone in one hand and a speaker in the other, a la *Say Anything*. Well, the new millennium's version.

Damn. Why do I have to live on the second floor?

I drop the phone on the couch as I race out the door and down the steps, Midge at my heels. I fly down the first set of stairs, oblivious to the cold or my pink camouflage pajamas. As I round the corner to take the second flight, I pull up short. Midge is unable to halt her momentum and nearly flies down the second set of stairs, landing in a furry heap at Nelson's feet. "Midge!"

I race down the remaining stairs to where Nelson is crouched over my little dog, who looks up pathetically and gives a small yelp. Nelson reaches out to her and she manages to emit a low growl, but she can't complete the threat. Her eyes close and my heart clutches in my chest. Not my Midge. I scoop her into my arms and look up at Nelson, panic pounding in my head. Removing his coat, he tucks it around Midge's limp body and leads me to his car. Without a word, he speeds off toward the emergency vet.

Chapter Forty-Eight

The doctor says Midge is in shock from the fall. She's not the only one.

I'm huddled in a molded plastic chair in the lobby of the twenty-four hour emergency vet clinic, tears soaking my thermal pajama top. Nelson is on the phone in the corner, but I'm unconcerned with who he could be calling at eleven o'clock on a Friday night. The receptionist behind the desk keeps glancing over at me, a worried expression on her face. Maybe it's the mascara streaked down my cheeks, or the snot bubbling out of my nose, or the uncontrollable shaking. I don't really care. She should be focusing on my dog, not on her emotionally unstable owner.

They've assured me that Midge is going to be all right. They are warming her and giving her IV-fluids. She doesn't have any broken bones or even a concussion. So why can't I stop crying?

Nelson looks completely lost as to how to comfort me. He's offered to run to Starbucks, or a bar, or someplace that sells chocolate. He's tried to hold me, kiss me, plead with me to stop crying. He doesn't realize that he's part of the problem.

Tucking his phone in his pocket, he crosses the lobby and kneels in front of me. "June?"

Coherent speech, or even thought, is not a possibility right now. I drag my sleeve across my snot-filled nose and look into his eyes. If I could think clearly, I'd probably think about how sad it is that I'm going to have to tromp on this sweet man's heart.

"I just got off the phone with Kendra. She's on her way."

I don't deserve K as a friend, or even as a cousin. Sobs once again shake my body. Surely the vet has a tranquilizer he can give me.

Nelson moves to sit in the chair next to me. He appears to be staring at the "Spay or Neuter your pet" poster. "This isn't just about Midge, is it?"

My sobs cease as I suck in my breath.

"Why did you run out of the restaurant, June?"

Does he actually expect me to talk about this in my current state? I'm going to need a Valium, or a stiff drink, or maybe a strait jacket. A padded room sounds kind of nice right now.

"June! Breathe!" Nelson clamps his hands on my shoulders and shakes me.

My breath shoots out of my mouth, accompanied by the pecan-encrusted tilapia and scalloped potatoes I had for dinner. Nelson's countenance morphs from concern to horror. I have to break his heart, and now I've ruined his suit. Releasing my shoulders, he approaches the desk and confers with the receptionist. He disappears through the swinging door to the back and the petite woman behind the counter produces a mop. She keeps looking at me like I'm an alien or something. And she's crinkling her nose up in disgust. Come on lady, I'm sure you've seen a lot worse. This lobby has probably been covered in blood and diarrhea and barf. Animals emit some gross stuff. I know.

She pokes the mop at my bare feet. Seriously? You're going to mop my feet?

This night has certainly taken an unexpected detour. I started the evening in my new plum-colored cashmere sweater and tweed skirt, paired with fabulous suede boots, dining at one of the fanciest restaurants in town. Despite my revelation that the wrong man was getting ready to propose, it was an exceptionally nice meal (although I doubt I'll ever be able to eat fish again). Then my night got even better when the *right* guy showed up at my apartment in a grand gesture of his love and devotion to me. Well, I'm assuming that's what the gesture meant even though I never really got to find out what with Nelson showing up and Midge getting hurt and all.

Now I'm sitting in an emergency vet clinic, in my pink camouflage pajamas, snot streaked across my face and crusting on my sleeves, and the remains of my dinner spewed all over my bare feet.

It's a lot to process.

First, I'm happy that I'm not still wearing my new suede boots, considering I haven't even paid them off yet. Getting anything out of suede is a pain, but pecan-encrusted tilapia and scalloped potatoes? Ugh.

Second, Nelson was so sweet to chase after me and all. Even if he did totally screw up my reunion with Jesse, the man I think I love, and cause my poor little dog to vault off a flight of stairs. He did drive us to the vet clinic. And he didn't yell when I spewed all over his dapper suit.

Third, it seems like Midge is going to be okay. The vet said that like a hundred times, probably because I couldn't stop crying.

Fourth, Jesse showed up in a grand gesture. For those two minutes before Midge hurt herself, I was ecstatic. But I'm a little worried about the fact that I never made it around the building to tell him that I didn't want him to "Go Home Without" (Me). As soon as Midge gets out of here, and Nelson takes me back to my apartment, and I break up with him, and I figure out where Jesse lives, I am going to plead my undying (I think) love to him.

What number am I on? Anyway, Ally would be so excited to know that she was right all along, and Jesse is so perfect for me. Although she'd probably rub it in for like an eternity, so maybe it's better that she's not around. But I do miss her a ton.

Luckily (and finally, because my brain is hurting from this thinking overload), my super-supportive cousin/best friend Kendra is coming here from Raleigh right now to comfort me. Or commit me, whichever seems most appropriate when she gets here. I trust her judgment.

Nelson comes back into the lobby just as I've managed to wipe the remainder of the snot from my face and chunks of my dinner from my feet. He's wearing a pair of scrubs with superhero cats all over them. He doesn't even look mad. Why can't he at least be mad at me? I'd be mad at me.

"You look like you feel better." He's keeping his distance, which I don't really blame him for.

"Nice scrubs."

He smiles, his dimple appearing, and moves a little closer.

I back up. "Nelson..." This seemed so much easier before I actually had to do it. But having not spoken for the past hour has not exactly prepared me for having to come up with an eloquent and sensitive way to break up with this wonderful guy I care about.

"You know about the ring, don't you?" He pulls the black velvet box out of the front pocket of the scrub top and begins shifting it from one hand to the other.

The sight of that damn box nearly causes me to start hyperventilating again. I nod and the tears return. If I cry much more, the vet's going to have to give me fluids too.

Nelson sinks into a chair, oblivious to the fact that it hasn't been completely cleaned yet. "I'm guessing you don't want to marry me."

I fall to my knees in front of him, slipping a bit. I hope that's because of the mopping. "Nelson, I'm so sorry. I *want* to want to marry you." I clutch at his hands in a desperate attempt to make him understand, but when I touch the velvet of that box, I recoil in fear. "You are such a great guy, and so sweet. It's just..." What is it? What are the right words? "...my heart is torn."

"I think your heart is Jesse's." He raises his eyes to meet mine, but they hold no bitterness, just resignation.

"Ms. Hinderson?" The vet steps into the lobby, clipboard in hand. "Midge seems to be perking up. Would you like to see her now?"

I look from Nelson, to the vet, and back.

"Go. It's okay. Go see Midge."

With a final kiss on his cheek, I follow the vet through the swinging doors.

Chapter Forty-Nine

"Junie?"

I jerk up from my makeshift bed, exam paper stuck to my face. "Ally?"

Kendra's arm encircles my shoulders and she peels the paper from my cheek. "No, honey, it's just me."

"Oh, K, I'm so glad you're here." I turn into the comfort of her embrace and hold on for dear life. I don't know how long I've been asleep in this exam room, cradling Midge in my arms, but as I become fully awake, I'm reminded of the emotional tides of this night.

Kendra releases me and reaches out to stroke the fur back from Midge's eyes. "The doctor says she's okay, huh?"

"Yes, thank goodness."

"It's been quite a night from what I hear." She sinks into the chair opposite the bed, exhaustion written across her face. Considering it's two in the morning and she just drove here from Raleigh, she has every right to be exhausted.

I resume my post beside the table where Midge is resting, still attached to the IV. "I broke it off with Nelson."

"I heard."

"He's still here?"

K shakes her head, and stifles a yawn. "Not anymore. I sent him home." She blinks rapidly, and picks a piece of mascara out of the corner of her eye. Her perfectly-applied face can't make it this far into the night. Even her hair has deflated from its typical height and is falling gently around her shoulders. She looks real.

"It was awful." I feel the tears coming back on, so I raise a hand to my eye, but it's dry. I've finally run out.

"I think he knew, honey. He doesn't blame you."

Well, that's something.

Kendra rises from the chair and pulls Midge's chart off the door. "You think we can break this girl out of here and get some sleep?"

"Well, unlike you, I don't have any medical training, so I'll have to ask the vet." I flick the clipboard she's studying and try to hold back my smirk as I leave the room.

Her voice trails me out to the lobby. "Glad to know you haven't lost your ability to sass."

Because I'm a dog-care professional (ha!), they release Midge into my care and Kendra drives us home. On the way, I fill her in on Jesse's display and my (lack of a) plan to find him and profess my love.

"Can't you just call him at work? Or better yet, show up there?"

Apparently, fatigue has made my cousin stupid. "Kendra, it's Friday night—well, Saturday, technically. That would require me to wait until Monday."

Her eyes move from the flashing red light to my face and back again. "And obviously, that isn't acceptable."

"Obviously." If I'm not mistaken, she's laughing at me.

Kendra clears her throat and crosses the intersection. "Okay, so you don't know where his new house is, and he's not listed, and his cell number is out of service."

"And he probably thinks I rejected him tonight."

"That is unfortunate." Pulling into a parking space in front of my building, K turns the car off and looks at me. "Don't worry, Junie. We'll figure it out—after we get some sleep." That's twice. She's never called me Junie before tonight. I'm too tired to figure out what—if anything—it means.

I'm dressed before the sun signals morning. Remembering the failure of my last early-morning excursion, I scribble a note to Kendra letting her know where I'm headed. I check on Midge, who's sleeping soundly in her crate, before I slip out the door.

The air is bitter cold, and my breath comes in short puffs of frozen vapor. I zip my jacket up to my chin, wrap a scarf around my head and pull on the purple glitter gloves I swiped from Kendra's coat.

I'm not operating on much sleep, but my mind is clear and my purpose determined. I scrape the frost from my windshield and patiently wait for the defrosters to clear the fog away *before* I start driving.

When I pull off the exit leading to the greenway, I see a flash of orange and for a moment I'm disoriented. Ally is beside me in the car, only it's my old car, and is that a truck up ahead? I pull onto the shoulder and put the SUV into park. Closing my eyes tightly, I draw my breath in in even measures.

I'm in the Element. It's December. Ally is gone.

When I open my eyes, I see a sign indicating a gas station 0.2 miles to the left and a campground 0.4 miles to the right. No truck. No orange cones. No Ally.

Maybe I should have had Kendra drive me.

I make it to the greenway with no further incidence, and pull the car into an empty parking area. This odd snap of pre-Christmas winter seems to be keeping even the most sadistic, um, dedicated, runners away.

But I'm on a mission, so I situate my face in the blast of heat emanating from the vent in an effort to prepare myself for the cold awaiting me outside. My clear thinking doesn't extend this far, because this only causes the difference in temperature to be that much more shocking and I think my eyebrows just crusted over with actual icicles.

It's hard to believe in global warming when it's this cold in my southern town in mid-December.

Mission.

I head down the path, toward the bench where I saw Jesse—how long ago was it now—a month? Two? I see the events of the last six months as through a haze. Granted, I was either crying, or doped up on pain meds, or suffering from a head injury for a good chunk of that time, but I'm clear on one thing this frigid December morning—it's too freaking cold to be out here waiting on a man who is probably smart enough to not go running in this weather. Okay, two things. I love Jesse. If I could feel my hands right now, I'm certain I would remember what it was like to touch his face last night. Was that just last night? It seems an eternity ago.

By the time I reach the bench—at least I think it's *the* bench, they all look the same really—my legs are numb. I fall onto the bench, attempting to curl myself into a ball to block the wind from touching the exposed skin on my face. Hunched over like this, it will be hard to see anyone running by.

I'm beginning to doubt this plan.

Mission.

Frostbite.

Jesse.

Loss of my fingers.

Okay, it was a valiant effort. I hiked three miles—okay, I know it wasn't the same bench, because I didn't make it past mile marker one—in the freezing cold and waited for like an hour—round trip, I think I was out of the car a total of seventeen minutes. I mean, there's a difference between commitment and lunacy, right? Actually, I don't think I'm comfortable with the answer to that question.

Shivering, I turn the car around and head back home. Maybe after Kendra wakes up, we can start canvassing the neighborhoods around the park. In the car. With the heat on.

Chapter Fifty

Turns out there's something close to 300,000 single-family homes in Charlotte. Kendra doesn't think it will be a wise use of time (or gas) to start randomly driving around.

"Love, Kendra. L-O-V-E. Love."

She flips a chocolate chip pancake in the air. "Stupidity, June. S-T-U-P—"

"Thanks for the vote of support, Cuz." I stab my fork in the pancake as it slams back onto the griddle. Chocolate might be the only thing that will comfort me right now.

"I'm just sayin'..." K shoots me a look her future children will learn to hate. Smugness, mixed with a hint of I'm-humoring-you. She pours batter onto the griddle in a perfectly round puddle. "It's only two days. And it'll give you some much needed time to clear your head. Last night was pretty emotional. You need to process it all."

I roll the pancake up, dip the end in powdered sugar and gnaw off a huge bite. It's more than I can comfortably chew, but I need the time to develop my argument against her obnoxious logic.

"Jesse's obviously in love with you too, Junie. That won't change between now and Mon—"

"Junie!" My arm flails out, pancake pointing at K in an accusatory manner, as I try to hurry through my chewing. I swallow the majority of the bite, only gagging briefly. "You've been calling me Junie. That's like three times."

Kendra turns off the burner and sinks onto a nearby stool. Are those tears glistening in her eyes?

"I mean, I'm not mad, it's just different." If she starts crying, then I'm gonna start crying, and honestly, there's been enough of that. "I was just wondering why you started calling me that all of a sudden." I perch on the stool beside her and pat her knee.

She turns to look at me, eyes searching my face, probably wondering why I didn't put any make-up on to go running after my man. "You don't remember, do you?"

"Remember what?"

"I'm the one who gave you that nickname."

"No, Ally did." I can picture us as little kids, swinging from the monkey bars, Ally singing my name. *Junie, lives on the moonie, singing a tunie, like a loonie, she's my Junie.*

K massages her temples. "Think hard. Did she start calling you Junie before or after she went to the state fair with us?"

We rode the Ferris wheel, and ate cotton candy, and saw the state's fattest pig, and... "You were cheering for me—when I was doing the ring toss—and Ally said, 'What did you call her?' And you said, 'Junie. She's my cousin. I can call her whatever I want.'"

"Ally called you Junie from then on. And during my next visit to Asheville, you told me to stop calling you that, because it was Ally's special name, and she was your best friend."

"Gosh, I was so mean. Why didn't you give up on me altogether?"

She lays her hand over mine and rubs her thumb across my knuckles. "You were six. And you're my cousin." The tears, which had been threatening escape, finally broke free and fell from K's rosy cheeks to her flannel pajama top.

Wrapping my arms tightly around this woman who has spent her whole life loving rotten, spoiled me, I blink through my own tears, trying to replay my memories. Thinking back to the time before I met Ally. Before I so completely gave her my life. Every scene in my head includes Kendra. Every moment special enough to be saved, she was there. And she's here now. Always has been.

"Get off the couch." Kendra is standing before me, hands on hips, hair reaching for the popcorn ceiling.

"Do you want to lay here? 'Cuz I can just go to my bedroom." I swing my feet to the floor, no energy to fight for my spot on the sofa.

K rolls her eyes at me and shakes her head. "No, I don't want the couch. We're goin' out."

"You changed your mind? We're going to look for Jesse?" This I can get on board with.

Her sigh sounds forceful as she grabs my hand and pulls me to my feet. "No. We are not goin' to look for Jesse. We are goin' to pamper ourselves and forget all about Jesse and Nelson and emotional trauma."

I'm not sure how I'm supposed to not think about Jesse, because that's pretty much all I've been thinking about since my early-morning rendezvous with the cold, but pampering sounds nice. "Like a spa?"

"Yes, like a spa. Come on." As K drags me to her car, I realize how nice it is to have a friend do things with, and you know, talk to in public without people thinking I'm crazy.

"Kendra?" I force myself to turn from the window, because the thought of seeing that exit sign is too much to bear.

She keeps her hands on the wheel and her attention focused on the heavy Christmas-shopping traffic. "Yeah?"

"I'm sorry I've been such a rotten friend to you, well, all of my life."

Her right hand leaves the two o'clock position and lands on my left knee. "You have been no such thing."

She's lying. And I appreciate the effort. "I love ya, K."

"Love ya, too, Junie." She turns her head briefly to offer me a smile.

We spend the rest of the afternoon treating each other to massages, pedicures and even something called a deep algal exfoliation. Kendra says it's my Christmas gift. Her gift is me not telling her I'm thinking about Jesse.

Chapter Fifty-One

At church the next morning, I remain in the back, kneeling near the prayer altar, alternately apologizing for my hit-or-miss attendance and begging for God to send Jesse back to me. I realize that He probably doesn't appreciate 911 prayers, but Kendra assures me that He'll take what he can get.

"Sometimes I think the Lord pushes us into difficult situations so we *will* turn to Him." She's navigating the car into the parking lot of the diner where we're having lunch.

I look at my cousin in disbelief. "You think God wanted me to date two guys at once, fall for both of them, break up with both of them, date one again, realize I was in love with the other one, and end up alone? Just so I'd pray more?"

K hunches her shoulders. "He works in mysterious ways." Placing the car in park, she turns to face me. "And you aren't going to end up alone."

I decide it's better not to argue.

She steps out of the car and glances across the parking lot. "What's the deal with men and fast cars?"

Following Kendra's gaze, I see a couple guys standing near a Porsche, having an excited discussion. The taller of the two men reaches out to close the car door and turns in our direction. "Oh crap." I duck down behind Kendra's car, but I fear it's too late.

"June, what's gotten into you?" I hear her suck in her breath and then she's crouched down beside me. "Isn't that Luca?"

"Yes. And I think he saw me."

She peeks around the bumper of the neighboring car. "Yeah, I think so."

"June? Is that you?" Luca's voice is followed by the appearance of his loafered feet. Loafers. This all started with loafers.

My brain is struggling to come up with some plausible excuse for my behavior when Kendra shrieks and stands erect.

"Here it is! June, I found it. You can get up now." She reaches a hand down and pulls me upright. "Luca. Well, what'd ya know? Funny to run into you here. We were just looking for my contact. Crazy thing just flew right out of my eye, but I got it now, huh June?" She's rambling, but at least it's drawing the attention away from me.

"Hi Luca." I guess if I had to run into a guy from my recent past, Luca is a better option than, say, Nelson.

"Hi June." He looks a little stunned. I'm not sure if it's running into me, or if it's Kendra. She does tend to overwhelm people.

A silence, long and uncomfortable, stretches between us. I can see Kendra out of the corner of my eye, and she's dying to break it, but seems to realize that it's not her place.

Luca appears to snap out of his stupor. "How have you been?"

"Fine." What an answer. Could anything be further from the truth?

"And Nelson?"

It's obvious he's probing, but is there any simple way to answer that?

Kendra sticks her foot right in it before I can form an appropriate response. "Things didn't work out with Nelson."

Way to give the guy false hope, K.

Luca's shoulders relax and his reserved smile breaks into a more natural one. "Really? I mean, that's too bad."

I glare at Kendra. "Hey, K, can you go on in and get us a table?"

"I guess." She seems reluctant to leave, obviously wanting to stick around, either to witness another tragedy or possibly to comfort Luca after I break the news to him that there's another guy in line ahead of him. But she turns and heads toward the diner.

"Luca—"

"Wait, June. Just let me say something." His hand is warm on my arm and his eyes are boring into mine. "I know you said you weren't over this Nelson fellow, but since things didn't work out... I mean, it's weird that we would run into each other here, right? Like it's fate or something. I haven't been able to get you out of my head, June."

Lord, did you get my prayers mixed up? I said Jesse. Not Luca. Is this my punishment for spotty church attendance? Having to break up with all these great guys over and over again? "Luca, I'm sorry if Kendra gave you the wrong idea, but there's somebody else."

"But she said it didn't work out with Nelson."

"Because there's someone else."

The poor guy looks terribly confused, and maybe a little angry. "You mean you met someone in the last month, while you were seeing Nelson?"

Okay, so from his perspective I'm not coming off really well. I kind of sound like a slut. "It's a little more complicated than that."

"Wow, I didn't think you were that kind of girl." He's backing away from me like he might catch something if he's too close.

"Oh Luca, this isn't coming out right." How do I word this so I don't come off looking like a promiscuous tramp? "See, I was dating this other guy, Jesse, a few months back." Maybe if I just leave out the part about dating Nelson at the same time...

"You were dating me a few months back." Now he definitely looks angry.

Do I really need to defend myself to this guy? This guy who did nothing wrong? "It was before I met you, Luca. I was dating Nelson and Jesse at the same time, which is what made it so complicated. I broke up with both of them because I couldn't choose between them. Then I met you—and I wanted to move on—but I still cared for them.

"Then Nelson showed back up and I decided to give it another shot. That's why I had to break things off with you." Luca is now leaning against Kendra's car looking as if he needs it to support him. But I have to finish this. "I was with Nelson for a while, but I couldn't get Jesse out of my head, so I ended it with Nelson. I think I'm in love with Jesse." I sound like a nutcase. And I'm not even talking about my dead best friend.

"You think? You think you're in love with Jesse? Well, I feel sorry for the poor guy." With that, Luca turns on his Italian loafers and marches back to his Porsche.

I'm still standing there when Kendra comes looking for me. Apparently, the shock has melted the soles of my shoes to the pavement.

"Junie? You okay?" She waves a hand in front of my face, but I can't seem to speak, or move.

What if Luca's right? What if I find Jesse, profess my love, and then change my mind a month later? What if I hurt another guy I care about, again? It's so clear now. I only care about my own feelings. I am completely self-centered. I go around, willy-nilly, with no regard to anyone else's feelings.

That is absolutely not who you are.

Ally? I flail around wildly, searching for her, feet still rooted to the spot.

"Junie? You're scaring me." Kendra is reaching for me, but I push her away, straining to find Ally.

You were just confused. You aren't now.

Correction. I am completely confused. I can hear you, but I can't see you.

Did you really think I would leave you?

"Ally, if you came back to screw with Junie's mind, I'm gonna kill you." Kendra is standing in the middle of the parking lot pumping her fist in the air.

It's hard to hold the laughter in. But I fear that if I let it out, that fist will be redirected at me. "Sorry K. I guess I'm acting a little nutty, as usual."

Her brow forms a perfect V, but she lowers her fist and smoothes her skirt. "She's not back, is she?"

"No. She's not here." Not a complete lie.

"What got into you?"

I hook my arm in hers and head toward the diner. "Something that Luca said got me thinking is all."

I felt less crazy when I could actually see Ally. Her voice randomly popping into my head at odd moments is freaking me out.

The other problem is that I don't have any control over it. I got those three sentences in the parking lot, and one quick one during lunch, but whenever I try to initiate a conversation with Ally, I'm met with silence.

I guess this is how it is for most people with dead best friends.

I throw out the I'm-selfish theory over lunch with Kendra. Mind you, this is when Ally chooses to pop into my head again.

"Honestly, June, I've never known you to take dating anyone lightly. I think you're making too much of this." Kendra cuts into her country-fried steak, stirring a bite around in the gravy.

Ever since the confrontation in the parking lot, my stomach has been feeling a bit uneasy. I look away from the mystery meat covered in chunky sauce. "I could never forgive myself if I hurt Jesse again." Nibbling on a piece of dry toast, I attempt to hold back the dam of emotions threatening to erupt.

Kendra's fork clatters onto the plate. "Honey, when it comes to matters of the heart, there's always a risk of someone gettin' hurt. You can't worry y'self over every little thing that could happen."

Besides, I have insider information, and I know for a fact that you love Jesse.

My toast falls to the ground. Ally's regained the ability to surprise me.

"June? You okay? You're lookin' a little green around the gills." Kendra starts to rise from the table, but I wave my hands to indicate that I'm okay.

I raise the water glass to my lips, mostly to buy time. Ally? What do you mean by that? How can you know for sure? Nothing. Ally?

"I think we need to get you home, Junie. I'll bet you caught somethin' bein' out in that blasted cold yesterday morning." K waves to a waitress for the bill and pops a few more bites of her gray mush into her mouth.

Why am I still so hung up on the dead friend when I have a perfectly good living one right here in front of me?

Chapter Fifty-Two

After nearly seventeen hours of Kendra-imposed bed rest, I've feeling extremely well-rested and a little stir-crazy. But what would a day be like for me if I wasn't feeling some sort of crazy?

K's gone to open the daycare until Sarah arrives around lunchtime.

I've been dressed and ready for over an hour, but I can't seem to make it to the front door. I wish I could get back the urgency of Friday night, and Saturday morning, before I started doubting my feelings for Jesse. If only men had a return policy like Nordstroms. Refund anytime, no questions asked.

But I've tried this one on, and couldn't find a thing wrong with it. I just had too many at the time.

What am I so worried about?

The directions to Jesse's office are pulled up on my phone and ready to direct me to my future. I shouldn't have any trouble finding my way, if I can just get out the front door.

Maybe I should change my clothes. These pants are a bit wrinkled and there's dog hair on my sweater.

Just go already. This man has seen you in your pajamas.

She has a point.

I make it out the door.

And down the stairs.

And into my car.

Which won't start.

You have got to be kidding me.

I twist the key again. Nothing.

I quickly locate the problem. After arriving home from our spa day on Saturday, I neglected to turn the lights off. Apparently, a battery can't run for a day and a half.

Is this some sort of sign?

A sign that you're a doofus.

Can I be expecting to hear voices for the rest of my life? I just want to prepare myself. And maybe pick out a nice mental institution.

Three hours later, I'm slouched on the couch with Midge curled up in my lap.

Kendra bursts through the door, bringing a blast of cold air. "How'd it go? Was it amazing? Is he comin' for dinner?"

I move my still-sedate terrier to the adjoining cushion and rise from the couch. "I need your keys."

"Sure, but why aren't you answering my questions?"

"I'll call you from the car."

She looks as if I've just told her Mary Kay no longer carries Precious Pink eyeshadow. But I don't have time to comfort her, or wax poetic about my car woes. I need to get on the road.

Before I'm out of the parking lot, my cell phone chirps. And they say Southerners are slow.

"My car wouldn't start, Kendra. The battery's dead. I must've knocked on thirty doors and not a soul was home. Unless you count old Ms. Meyers, who hasn't left her apartment since the Reagan administration; but without a car and some jumper cables, she wasn't much good."

I can hear her pop a bubble over the phone. "That sucks, Junie. I figured you were gone and back. And I must say I was a little perturbed that you hadn't called yet to update me."

"Next time I play meet the neighbors, I'll be sure to give you a call."

"You don't have to get sassy with me. Just go get the guy."

I glance down at the speedometer, which is hovering around 70 mph. The fastest I've driven since the accident. Amazing what motivation can do. "That's my plan, K."

In my rush to leave the apartment, I cleared the address to Jesse's office out of my phone and my signal isn't strong enough to reload it. Because why would a major metropolitan area need reliable cell service? So, I'm winging it. In uptown Charlotte this can be disastrous at any time of the year; five days before Christmas it's a joke.

This is my third pass down East Trade Street, but I keep managing to miss the turn. Finally, there's an opening in the traffic to my left and I'm able to turn the correct way on the one-way street. Proceeding slowly, much to the chagrin of the sedan behind me, I strain to see the numbers on the buildings. A discreet sign heralds Jesse's company. Apparently, they don't want to be found too badly, or they'd have a bigger sign, or maybe neon arrows.

I pull into the garage beneath the building and just as I'm searching for a parking space, Jesse emerges from the elevator.

I slam the car into park and jump out. "Jesse!"

Two rows of cars separate us and my cry reverberates off the concrete walls and back to me. He walks determinedly to his car, appearing to not hear.

"Jesse!" Now I'm running between cars, raising my voice, and drawing the attention of a nearby parking attendant. The man's hand is raised as if to garner my attention, but I duck around another car and catch up to Jesse just as he reaches his. Out of breath, I choke out his name once more.

"June Bug? What on earth are you doin' here?" He throws his briefcase into the passenger seat and leans against the open door.

The attendant has caught up with me and looks none too happy. "Ma'am, you can't leave your car in the middle of the throughway."

I look between the two men, gasping for breath, trying to determine the most immediate threat/need. Jesse wins. "Jesse, I've got to talk to you about the other night."

"Ma'am…" From the look on this guy's face, I'm guessing he's a police academy dropout and he's been waiting for the moment to bring somebody down. This is his moment.

"She'll be moving the car now, Merv. She's leaving." Jesse folds his long body into the driver seat and grabs the door handle. "It's okay, June. I saw you leaving with Nelson. You made your choice." The door slams and he starts the car.

Merv? No way am I letting a guy named Merv take me down. And—wait—what did he say? He saw me leave with Nelson? "Nooooooo!" I slam my body against the side of the car, arms outstretched in a futile attempt to stop it from backing up.

The window hums down and Jesse looks at me with a mixture of frustration and amusement on his face. "Junie, I'm backing up now. You might want to step back."

"Aha! You still love me!" I peel myself off the car and try to establish a dignified pose.

"You got that from 'I'm backing up?'"

Merv inserts himself between the car and me. "Lady, I'm not kidding around." He pats his oversized flashlight. "Don't make me use this."

What? Is he gonna blind me into moving my car? I push past him and crouch at Jesse's window. "You called me Junie."

Jesse looks straight ahead and I can see his features contorting.

"I didn't choose Nelson."

He turns back to me, moisture evident in his eyes. "I saw you leave with him."

I reach through the open window and grasp his hand, squeezing it like I'm holding on for dear life. "Midge got hurt. Nelson drove us to the vet. But I was on my way to you when it happened. The song, it was—"

"Midge? Is she okay?" His hand turns in mine, our fingers entwining.

"Yeah, she's fine." I feel a smile spreading across my face, right up until I hear Merv talking into his walkie-talkie about a tow truck. "Jesse, can you please wait right here?"

He looks up into my face, as if studying my sincerity, or my soul, I'm not sure, then nods.

I don't let go of his hand until the car settles into park. Merv looks triumphant as I head to move my car, but when his back is turned, I let the air out of one of the tires on his golf cart. Has the man never been in love before?

Chapter Fifty-Three

It's Christmas morning. Wrapping paper lays strewn about and Midge thinks the scraps are her gifts. She's shredding it piece by piece. Obviously, she's recovered from her trauma.

I carry two mugs of steaming cocoa in from the kitchen and hand one to Jesse. Then I settle into the crook of his arm and tuck my feet underneath me.

We've spent the week catching up—picking up from where we'd left off. Exactly what I hadn't been able to do with Nelson.

I kept the boarding numbers small at work so we'd be able to spend most of the day together. We've already been to the daycare this morning and walked everyone. The dogs adore Jesse.

Last night I told Jesse about the accident that took Ally from me—well, actually, both of them—and he doesn't think I'm crazy.

Now, sipping my hot chocolate, nestled against this man I love, things couldn't be more perfect. Well, maybe if Midge hadn't just pooped behind the tree.

"Tell me more about Ally."

I haven't heard the voice in my head since she called me a doofus. I wonder if that's the last I'll ever hear from her. Great parting words, huh? "You really want to know?"

He tucks my hair behind my ear and kisses the tip of it. "Absolutely. She was important enough that you kept her around for over twenty years. Sounds like a pretty special friend to me."

You don't know the half of it.

"Besides, she's the one who told you to go out with me, right?" His hazel eyes are crinkled in the way I've grown to love. "Must be a smart lady."

I can't believe she was right again.

The End

www.ingramcontent.com/pod-product-compliance
Lightning Source LLC
Chambersburg PA
CBHW021045310726
48969CB00006B/1817